Flowers of
Darkness

The Salem Novels

The Disinherited (1974)

The Colours of War (1977)

The Sweet Second Summer of Kitty Malone (1979)

Flowers of Darkness (1981)

Matt Cohen

Flowers of
Darkness

Quarry Press

The publisher gratefully acknowledges the assistance of The Canada Council, the Ontario Arts Council, the Department of Communications, and the Ontario Publishing Centre.

Canadian Cataloguing in Publication Data

Cohen, Matt, 1942—
    Flowers of Darkness

(Canadian literature classics)
Publ. originally: Toronto : McClelland &
    Stewart, 1981.
ISBN 1-550-82-072-9

    I. Title. II. Series.

PS8555.04F65 1993   C813'.54   C93-090077-4
PR9199.3.C64F65 1993

Cover photograph by Joan Finnigan.
Series design by Keith Abraham.
Typesetting by Quarry Press, Inc.
Printed and bound in Canada by Webcom, Toronto, Ontario.
Published by Quarry Press, Inc., P.O. Box 1061, Kingston, Ontario K7L 4Y5.

"Anyone can be good in the country."

— Oscar Wilde

One

At noon Therese served him a salad of lettuce, hardboiled eggs, and olives. Afterwards he hurried back to work, saying that an accountant was coming. The truth was that after one of Therese's diet meals, George Mandowski, owner and proprietor of Mandowski's General Store, needed one of the cellophane-wrapped pastries that he kept in the glove compartment of his Chrysler.

This time it had been a chocolate confection with round swirls of icing on the top: a two–humped camel filled with golden running caramel. He bit into it and the sweet liquid flooded into his mouth, obliterating the dry, sour taste of the salad. For a moment he was swamped by that first rush of sugar; then without thinking, he finished the rest. His lips, his teeth, the roof of his mouth were slippery and glazed. Contented, he licked them clean.

Feeling lazy and torpid, his mouth still buzzing, Mandowski took a slow route back to Salem, zig-zagging around the concession roads so that eventually he was led past the old Beckwith farm and the stone church across the road.

It was a warm day, the sun a strong and unseasonable yellow. It travelled across the February sky like a hot breath, giving the big car such a welcome and lazy warmth that Mandowski was able to cruise along with his window partly open.

And through that unusual and unseasonable gap he heard what he otherwise would have missed: a scream from the church.

He stopped the car and got out. The ancient widow, Katherine Beckwith Malone, still lived on the farm, but the church was no longer in use, hadn't been for over twenty years. He was wondering if some strange mission had carried her into the church when he heard a second scream; only it wasn't a scream, it was more like a cry of triumph.

"Teenagers," George Mandowski said to himself, "they shouldn't be bringing their dirt into the church." And he stepped forward to peer in the window.

That was when he saw him, kneeling, the black beard like a curse in the darkness. Kneeling opposite, her nakedness pressed against him, was Nellie Tillson, the check-out girl who worked the cash register in Mandowski's own grocery store. Nellie Tillson's skin was goosebumped in the cold, her ivory back arched and frozen as a statue. Mandowski could see the beginning curve of her breasts, which were crushed flat against Finch's open shirt. His hands gripped round the sweet curve of her haunches, holding her tight against him. Mandowski's hands themselves suddenly filled with warmth, as if they too surrounded Nellie Tillson; his tongue and lips began to tremble. There was another cry from Nellie Tillson and her back arched farther. Mandowski forced himself to turn from the window as Nellie Tillson's breasts came away from Finch's shirt and her straining face rose towards the ceiling of the church.

When he got back to his store, the assistant manager told him that Nellie had a dentist appointment and would be away until three o'clock. At three o'clock exactly Mandowski was in front of the store, talking to the driver of the bread truck. As the truck pulled away, Finch's car arrived. Finch was wearing his dark suit, his smile a pale white slash in the cloudy February afternoon. Oh Finch, Mandowski thought, Finch you bastard, this time you've gone too far.

Nellie stepped out of the car wearing not even galoshes but only leather loafers with white socks. One of them was blood-stained at the ankle, and Mandowski couldn't stop himself from saying, as they stood in front of the store watching Finch drive away: "You must have cut your foot."

"My foot? Oh no, I don't think so."

"Look at your sock."

She glanced down, and then suddenly she blushed: a deep crimson red that reminded Mandowski of his shame when Therese gasped beneath him. A weight dropped from his belly to his groin. And for a moment his eyes stayed fixed on her private face, the face he had glimpsed in the church. Then he pushed past her, through the door and up the back stairs to his office.

At five thirty the store had been closed for half an hour. To help himself through the afternoon he had started on a bottle of Coca-Cola; when it was halfway empty he had refilled the bottle with rum.

Leaning back in his chair Mandowski turned to look at the horizon where the sun had recently set. He was not much of a drinker and that alone made him almost a freak in this small town. What was even more unusual was that his father had been a foreigner; after escaping the invading German armies he had fled Poland, arriving in Salem with a butcher's cleaver so sharp and heavy that bones splintered at its first touch.

Bone slivers: Mandowski looked down at his own large body and imagined it shrinking under his father's knife. He shook his head, thinking that he must be getting drunk.

His mouth was filled with the mysterious goodness of rum: he had had just enough to make himself mellow but not angry, contemplative but not bitter, and looking at the electric blue-tinged red of the sky he licked the corners of his lips, then switched off his desk lamp.

The pink February light filled his office and turned it into a giant rum-smelling candy. And the sugary suggestion, the sweet rush of colour, made Mandowski remember once again what he had seen that afternoon.

The greatest virtues were forgiveness and compassion; Therese said that. She was always crying over someone else's misfortunes. Therese, Mandowski thought, had a gentle heart. Now he felt himself beginning to unlock. Love and anger: in the magic winter light of his office they were gathered like opposing armies threatening to explode in the pink humming air.

Nellie Tillson: she too could explode in this pink winter twilight.

Nellie Tillson: Mandowski said the name, said it again slowly, possessing each syllable as it rested in his mouth.

Nellie Tillson: Mandowski said the name and then, sharpened by the rum, he saw the image: a pale-skinned blonde girl with breasts like polished marble. Mandowski realized that his teeth were clamped together so tightly that his jaws hurt.

Nellie Tillson, yes, there was no doubt that Nellie Tillson looked good enough to eat. Jailbait, they used to call it.

Before Mandowski's father died, sick with some mysterious ailment of the heart that turned his hair white in two weeks and stained his cheeks a bitter autumn red, he had summoned his son to the living room of his house. Dressed in his best suit, prepared to be lifted straight from his horsehair-stuffed chair into the elaborate oak and silver coffin he had ordered for himself, he begged his son to leave Salem and start a life somewhere else. In his wide-palmed hand he extended a cheque for ten thousand dollars: his parting gift.

Mandowski refused. "It's my town."

"Georgie — your life — "

"I'll live it here." And then he had laughed because finally, after all these years, he had managed to sound like one of the movies he saw every afternoon. "I'll live it here," he said again, drawling, his thumbs in his belt loops; and he looked expectantly at his father, waiting for him to recognize the triumph.

But of course he didn't. His English was sparse and comical — all the words he knew were Polish, and Polish words had had their funeral long ago. Sometimes at night Mandowski's parents whispered them to each other, guarding them like obscenities from their child's ears. And now the child, Mandowski, was the man. But once he had been a baby, fleeing the war in his parents' arms, and then he too had spoken the forbidden language.

He wondered where the memory was in him, how deep it had been pushed. Sometimes he could feel a word trying to surface in him: a knocking against a hollow door. And sometimes he imagined that all the ignored memories had banded together to become his own hidden demon, raging with hunger and frustration.

To contain a demon you didn't know — that wasn't so bad, Mandowski thought. Not like the other townsmen who were stamped of one cloth only and could barely see past their own noses. Not, for example, like Finch, who was the minister of the crazy Protestant church up the road. Sometimes it seemed his whole life had been passed with Finch as the enemy, Finch as the embodiment of everything he could never be. Finch who had been a rough and arrogant boy now roamed the whole county like a wild randy stallion; Finch with his demagogue's tongue and his eye for the ladies; Finch with his fists like rocks that Mandowski had felt more than once hammering into his ribs and belly — if there was anyone to be forgiven it was surely not Finch. Even if Finch were strung up by his heels and tarred, Therese would surely not weep for *him*.

The thought of Finch and Nellie Tillson pushed Mandowski out of his chair, turned him towards the window. The sun had disappeared completely; only a faint rim of pink remained on the horizon. The sky was dangerously clear. The warm spell was over now: outside, he knew, the February air would be growing cold and hollow. By midnight the thermometer would touch at thirty below, and there it would stay until morning. In the glass he could see the reflection of his round face, his straight hair combed straight back. He had small eyes, set close together: pig eyes, Finch used to call him in school.

Mandowski reached for the bottle, which was empty, and his mind moved inevitably from Finch to Nellie Tillson. She was seventeen years old and had been working the cash desk for two months. Therese had teased him when he hired her because surely Nellie Tillson was tempting fate: with her delicate, flower-petal complexion and her quick bright smile she was a burst of summer in the midst of the Salem winter.

Nellie Tillson made him wish he didn't weigh two hundred and seventy pounds. He was so swollen that Therese sometimes groaned under his weight, and when she did he would blush a bright red in the dark and promise himself that this would be the week his diet began.

The office was almost completely dark now; the feelings that had flowed so violently a few minutes ago were now freezing in the night air. Mandowski realized that he was hungry, that it was past the usual hour for his dinner.

Nellie Tillson was waiting for him. "She's got a head on her shoulders," Mandowski had said to Therese, trying to justify his hiring her, "she's learning fast." She had thick blonde hair that was the bursting golden colour of ripe corn, and even the weak fluorescent light was enough to make it glow.

As always, when he came downstairs to perform the Thursday night counting of the money, he beckoned Nellie to the meat counter at the back of the store, so she wouldn't have to shuffle through the bills in front of every curious eye.

"I'm late," Mandowski said.

Nellie shrugged.

"Is your father waiting for you?"

"He can't tonight. He got stuck in Kingston with his car."

Mandowski looked at her uncertainly. That afternoon, her instant reaction had told him that she must have seen him looking in the church window, but now she was meek and calm. She was wearing her coat open over a tight sweater and Mandowski wondered what it must be like for her to know that she was perfectly constructed, that every man's eyes wanted to stare her sweater away.

"I'll drive you home if you like. It's on the way."

"I can walk."

"I'll drive you, Nellie."

"Thank you, Mr. Mandowski. I didn't want to ask."

He had turned to the checking of the money but the sudden change in her voice when she said 'I didn't want to ask' had reminded him that she was only a child, awkward and needing. Jailbait.

"One thousand four hundred and eighty-two dollars, and twenty-two cents."

"That's what I got."

He put the rolls of bills and coins in the brown canvas bag, then turned to go. Somehow Nellie hadn't seen him coming. They collided and his arm was suddenly pressed into the soft warmth of her breast. The tension that had held him all afternoon in his office now clawed deep into the pit of his stomach.

"Oh God, Nellie." He stopped, shocked, unable to believe the words had actually escaped. Her breast still rested against him and he could feel her heart beating.

"What's wrong, Mr. Mandowski?" Her voice dutiful and concerned.

"Nothing's wrong. I just remembered that I promised to bring home a loaf of white bread."

He forced himself to step back; he was holding his arm in front of himself as if it had been broken. "Could you take a loaf from the shelf for me?" Mandowski finally said. "We'd better get going."

He was just about to leave the store when the telephone rang. "General Store."

"George, I'm so glad I caught you. It's Maureen Finch speaking. My husband forgot to bring home the groceries this afternoon and I was wondering if on the way home you could . . ."

Even over the rural lines Maureen Finch's voice was full and throaty. Some days its rich sound allowed Mandowski to remember he had once been young; today it made him see once more what he had been trying all afternoon to forget.

Outside there was a raw, bitter wind and the cold was immediate and sharp, biting into his cheeks the moment he stepped away from the building. Mandowski pulled his coat close to his neck and, carrying the carton of Finch's groceries, walked quickly to the sleek black Chrysler in the parking lot. Therese teased him about wanting to own such a big car, but he wasn't going to spend his days squeezing himself into one of those foreign tin things.

The big engine started at the first turn of the key. Mandowski let it warm for a few seconds and then eased out of his space and drove the two blocks to the bank. There he climbed out and put the canvas bag into the after hours box. The bag rattled down the chute, then clunked to a stop. There was a dead silence. As always Mandowski thought of how long and impossibly twisted an arm it would take to steal the money back.

By the time they were out of town the big car was warm and heat was blowing through the interior. Mandowski drove slowly past the sparsely scattered bungalows on the outskirts of Salem, watching for black ice on the roads.

The needle was touching forty on the wide green illuminated dash. Nellie was sitting primly beside him, in her section of the seat but not right at the edge. He wondered how Finch had found his way to her perfect naked body, if it had started with the innocent offer of a ride. Jailbait, he could put Finch in jail. He wondered what Maureen Finch would think of that.

They were past the bungalows now and into the farmland. Like many others in the area, Nellie's father owned a small farm, which he worked at night after putting in his daytime shift at the plant. Sometimes, on a Sunday, Mandowski would talk to one of these men at the Catholic Church. Not during the summer, of course, when there was hay to be taken in, nor during the fall when there was wood to be cut and fields to be ploughed for spring planting; but on the occasional winter Sunday such a man might accompany his wife to church and doze through the service in his unaccustomed suit.

But Mandowski had never seen Nellie Tillson's father at the Catholic church. He was a Protestant and like all the Protestants in Salem submitted to Finch's rantings.

"Here," Nellie Tillson said. "You can let me off at the corner."

"I'll take you to the house."

"The corner would be fine, Mr. Mandowski."

He slowed the big car, taking care not to fishtail on any sudden slippery patch. He didn't want to be found dead in a ditch, his neighbours joking about his size while they pried him out of the car. The headlights, with their high beams, showed a long yellow-white tunnel of road with snow at the sides and fence posts and page-wire marching through it.

She was leaning towards him, looking at him, and he wondered what she was waiting for.

"Thank you, Mr. Mandowski."

"It's on the way."

She put her hand on his arm and bent to him, kissing him on the side of the cheek. For a moment her lips stayed still, so moist and alive that his whole face wanted to melt into her mouth.

"Good night, Mr. Mandowski."

Two

*A*nnabelle Jamieson had spent the last summer of her university years having her face photographed. Glossy black hair framed her narrow features: high cheekbones, a fine straight nose, ironical sensitive lips. "You make," the photographer had said, "the perfect lady."

Her lips were fuller now. First they had learned to kiss the photographer. And then, a few years later, Isaac — a crazy married drunk with whom she spent two disastrous months. That was before she had found Allen, the lawyer who was to pour oil on the troubled surface of her life.

Annabelle Jamieson still had the face of a model, still lived with her lawyer husband, and her life had become orderly and calm. Her black hair was longer than when the photographer first noticed it, and men found her beautiful instead of merely pretty and awkward; but there was still a curious hesitation in her movements, a whippet-like tension that went across her shoulders into her arms and neck. Perhaps this was merely the result of the days she spent moulding raw clay into vases and dinnerware. Or perhaps it was something deeper, the physical force that made her a tomboy as a child and then take, as a challenge, the karate course her university offered to women. She was small, the instructor had said, but not too small, as it turned out, to throw him one night across the mats and into the cinder-brick wall of the gymnasium.

But it was her eyes that were truly striking. Almost too large for her face, they were a deep and luminous brown, shaped into delicate almond ovals, bracketed by full black lashes.

"They make people trust you," the photographer had said.

"They make your face look thin," her mother had said. "You'll be glad for it when you're older." At least they can see, Annabelle had always consoled herself; and through the window of her studio Annabelle looked first at the snow-packed street, and then over to the white-painted church spire that reached up into the cold sky.

There was no place in Salem from which this spire, the spire of the Church of the New Age, was not visible; on this particular February afternoon it reminded Annabelle Jamieson to look at her watch, as she had been doing every few minutes for the past hour. The gold watch was a souvenir of Isaac, of her youth, of her whole unformed and turbulent life before she had met Allen.

Two o'clock exactly.

Nervous, and feeling foolish for being nervous, Annabelle went into her living room where she had already laid out the white sable fur coat that Allen had given her to encourage her through the winter. Through her front window she could see Donna Wilson's house and the cleanly scraped steps that led down to her sidewalk.

"It would just be for tea," Donna had said. "I thought you would want to meet him. It's time you started meeting the people here. We're not so bad, really."

Annabelle put on her coat and then, having no further excuse for delay, stepped out her front door.

The afternoon sun was so bright on the snow that the glare made her briefly dizzy. With a gloved hand she reached up and pushed the hair away from her face: it was that gesture that had first caught the photographer's attention. Now, ten years later, it exposed her skin to the reflected warmth of the winter sun. She took a deep breath of cold air, then another. The whole winter had gone by without her taking a single long walk; and yet they had moved to Salem full of talk about the outdoors and nature.

Nature: Allen was crazy about nature; he seemed to think it was some mysterious balm that would heal all their wounds. In the fall, even before they had moved, he had taken to driving out into the countryside and parking the car on the edge of some hill so they could watch the sun setting over the fields.

"That's something," Allen would say. "Look at the way those colours rise up from the trees. It's just like a picture."

Annabelle had crossed the street and was just lifting the knocker of the Wilsons' door when Donna opened it.

"Now," Donna said. "Here you are."

Annabelle stood for a moment on the plastic carpet protector, then leaned over and took off her boots. On the living-room coffee table Donna Wilson had already set out trays of cookies and the tea service.

"We might as well sit down," Donna said. "He'll be a few minutes late." Her streaked blonde hair was coiffed into a bowl shape around her head; her eyes were china blue and her round doll's face was perfectly smooth and unlined. She had put on, Annabelle noticed, the same navy dress she always wore to church.

They walked into the living room and sat on the couch in front of the tea things. The couch, like the two armchairs, was upholstered in a cloth of yellow and brown checks.

"We'll stay here when he comes," Donna said. "He can sit in the chair with the ashtray beside it. Sometimes he smokes a pipe."

Donna's voice was tiny and high-pitched and Annabelle, at the thought of their having to conspire to invite a minister to tea, wanted to giggle.

"Now remember," Donna said, "he's married."

It was Donna Wilson who had first told Annabelle about Finch and his lady-killing reputation.

"Oh come on," Annabelle had said, "he's a minister."

She began to wonder what scheme Donna might be concocting. Donna, after all, had lived in Salem her whole life. And Annabelle, looking over at Donna, knees closed primly just inches from her own, wondered if to Donna she was just a city woman out of her element, an alien and a fool who would never be able to survive in Salem.

"Finch is married," Donna said again, "so don't get any ideas."

Irritated, Annabelle looked out the window. There, re-assuringly, was her own house, shining like a stone postcard in the brilliant winter light. In a few hours Allen would be home, she and he would be inside the windows that now reflected the white glare of the snow.

"I'm married, too," Annabelle said, feeling better.

"You are, but . . ." Donna's toy voice sounded brittle.

"But what?"

"Well," said Donna, and now she edged closer on the couch, her knees touching Annabelle's, "it's just not the same before you have children, at least it wasn't for me."

Annabelle looked down at one of the plates of cookies, wrapped in clear stretch plastic

"Finch?"

"No," Donna said. "It wasn't Finch. That would be stupid." This spoken in a calculating tone that Annabelle had not heard when Donna, her voice full of mischief had suggested they invite the Reverend Finch for tea one afternoon.

Now Donna's voice softened and she laughed; once more Annabelle felt included in her little game.

"Annabelle, don't play around with Finch. You never know what he's going to do — him or that bitch Maureen."

"Don't worry," Annabelle said. "I wouldn't play around with Finch. Not Finch or anyone." And then, ashamed of the closed and prudish tone of her own voice, she reached out to touch Donna's hand. And couldn't help, at that moment, remembering the way Allen's face got when it was angry: the skin pink with suppressed rage, white patches appearing on his forehead and cheeks as if his blood was actually evaporating in its fury.

Annabelle's fingers were still resting on the back of Donna's hand when the door knocker sounded: two sharp cracks.

Annabelle's stomach clenched the way used to when she was going to do something stupid, before she met Allen. Donna grabbed at her wrist and looked so frightened that Annabelle bit the inside of her cheek.

"You get it," Donna whispered in a hoarse voice that filled the whole room and set them both laughing.

Annabelle jerked to her feet, knocking her shins against the coffee table. She looked desperately at Donna, who was holding her hand over her mouth, then walked quickly to the door. In the hall there was a mirror and she couldn't help seeing herself: black hair, pearly white blouse cut by the dark maroon V of her jacket. One last time she hesitated, looked back at Donna who was struggling to pat down her skirt, and then, afraid she would start laughing again, pulled open the door.

"Reverend Finch."

"Mrs. Jamieson." Close up he was even bigger than he had seemed in the pulpit. His face was wide, his cavernous eyes gleamed, his black beard was a mask growing down into his black coat.

"I have been looking forward to meeting you, Mrs. Jamieson." His deep voice buzzed through her, his hand wrapped around hers.

Annabelle stepped back but Finch retained his grip on her hand, was refusing to step into the house and behave like a normal person. Instead he was staring at her fixedly, as if she was supposed to first acknowledge that this meeting was something more than a visit between a minister and two of the ladies of his parish. Finch's huge eyes were black and liquid, and they were fastened to her own, pressing against her.

"My pleasure, Reverend Finch," Annabelle said. The muscles across her back were tight and sore, and regretting this already, she wished she were home. Finch wasn't attractive at all, he was only overpowering. Even the skin of his palm, finally releasing hers, was thick and insensitive.

While Donna came to take Finch's coat, Annabelle went back into the living room and stood by the couch. Schoolgirl pranks: even in a small town like Salem, she should have known better than to try a trick like this.

Finch too was wearing his church suit; up close the black cloth fitted him poorly, bagged at his waist and wrinkled across the back, and the collar of his white shirt curled at its tips with repeated washings. Without his coat he looked less forbidding, and when he smiled Annabelle saw that his teeth, which were very white and even, had small gaps between.

"We thought," Annabelle started, but then couldn't remember what they had thought, or had decided to pretend.

"I am honoured," Finch stated gravely. His voice, as at the door, was deep and funereal, his preaching voice, and Annabelle wondered if this was the way he talked all the time. Finch reached into his pocket and a small black Bible appeared in his hand. Donna hadn't said anything about Bible readings.

"My wife and I are always happy to meet new members of the congregation."

His voice, his eyes, the way he moved: all dark and liquid. A small-town Lothario, Annabelle thought, what a ridiculous man. He had even invoked his wife, Maureen Finch, the beautiful ghostly cripple who sat like a rock through Finch's entire sermon. And now Finch, amazingly graceful for his size, was gliding towards Annabelle, towards the couch, and she was suddenly aware of his smell: warmed by the Wilson's, central heating, Finch's clothes had released a sour sharp odour of animals and barns.

Annabelle stepped back, turned towards Donna, then realized that Donna had left the room. At the same moment Donna re-entered, carrying a steaming teapot which she placed on the table with the cookies. Then she moved back to the yellow and brown checked armchair, the one that was to have been Finch's, and sat down.

Finch continued in Annabelle's direction. She lowered her eyes and edged into the farthest corner of the couch. She was starting to feel angry with Donna for arranging this bizarre situation, angry at Finch for his overbearing manners. As she settled into the plaid cushion she could feel the couch sagging farther, Finch's weight suggestively following her own.

Finally he began speaking to Donna. When Annabelle turned to look at him she could see the path his razor had made. A trail of dried soap remained high on one cheekbone; where the moustache should have been was shaven clean, exposing Finch's upper lip, which was sensuous and full.

The beard itself was thick and wiry, a country of its own. Above and below it had been trimmed; the shaven skin was dark with hairs struggling to sprout forth. Only the skin beneath his eyes was different: an oasis, soft and moist, almost girlish.

Finch was sitting so close that Annabelle, despite herself, imagined reaching out to touch him, putting her fingertips to those soft and vulnerable islands, stroking closed the eyes that now focused on Donna with total concentration.

"Could you pour the tea?" Donna asked Annabelle. And as Annabelle leaned forward she felt suddenly exposed, as if Finch, unobserved, might lunge and throw himself on top of her.

She filled the three cups, all the while aware of Finch's eyes burning into her neck.

"Milk or sugar?"

He was staring at her, absorbed; and his expression remained so puzzled that Annabelle, thinking her city words must be unintelligible to him, said them again: "Milk or sugar?"

Annabelle was looking at Finch, her mouth still open, waiting for him to respond; and as her face began to twitch Annabelle saw that Finch too was struggling. His black eyes opened blankly into hers, his mouth trembled as though to overcome a stammer.

"Regular," Finch finally said. When he spoke his voice was normal, deep and smooth, the engine of an expensive car. "I take it regular."

"Milk and sugar," Donna interceded. "He means milk and sugar." Her high voice cut across the room and to Annabelle it seemed that each sentence was so long in being arrived at, and so strangely said, that they might have been playing an unsuccessful comedy, reciting lines from a script that needed to be revised.

Annabelle tipped milk from the silver pitcher into the tea. It swirled white clouds until the surface of the tea was a dark beige colour. Then she measured out two teaspoons of sugar, heaping, stirring them in slowly and trying to avoid the click of the silver spoon against Donna Wilson's best china.

"And so," Finch suddenly demanded, "what do you think of our peaceful town, Mrs. Jamieson?"

His eyes had mercifully left hers.

"It's very nice," Annabelle said. "A beautiful town."

The first time she had seen it had been the previous fall,

driving with Allen along the edge of the lake, winding among the pines and the golden autumn maples: and then suddenly the stone buildings were upon them, a burst of settlement in the midst of nowhere.

"We sometimes forget," Finch said, as though he had been reading her mind, "what is around us." His eyes swivelled to hers again and Annabelle felt her stomach close in on itself like a fist. Finch was so big; when he turned, his knee seemed to search hers out, and she kept having to push herself deeper into the corner.

Finch's eyes were locked into hers. Annabelle tried to remember the sentences that had been spoken: did she owe him a line? She could feel the seconds passing.

"You're holding your breath," Finch said.

Annabelle felt her face turn scarlet as she exhaled.

"I used to hold my breath," Finch said. "When I was nervous."

"I'm not nervous —"

"The best thing is to breathe deep," Finch continued, "make yourself breathe deep by pushing out your stomach as you take in the air. Make room for the air in your chest and your belly."

Finch unbuttoned his jacket and illustrated his own advice, pushing his stomach out until his shirt bulged like a great pale melon.

"Try it," Finch said.

Annabelle could smell the tobacco on his breath, the odour of manure rising from his shoes. She glanced over at Donna, but Donna, one hand patting her sprayed blonde hair, was only leaning forward and waiting.

"Try it," Finch said again.

She tried to inhale, but the breath stopped at her chest. She tried again, pushing her belly out the way she had learned at karate class.

"That's better," Finch approved. "Do it again." And then, as Annabelle breathed in, this time feeling the oxygen reaching down to the bottoms of her lungs, she saw Finch's hand reaching towards her.

Slow to react, she kept breathing.

Finch's hand, the rough palm open, settled like a huge moth upon her stomach.

Annabelle's fist shot out, the old reaction bursting out of her, knuckles twisting as they smashed into Finch's unmoving chest.

Finch's eyes opened wider: pain, surprise, a flicker that might have been laughter.

"Is that what they teach you in the city?" he asked.

Annabelle, on her feet, didn't answer. She took Donna's cup of tea across the room, then seated herself in the other armchair. Finch was still. In one hand, he held his small black Bible. It lay, the perfect alibi, in the crease of his palm.

"Have a cookie," Annabelle finally said. "Mrs. Wilson is famous for her cookies."

Her fingers were bruised and her shoulder felt as though she had pulled a muscle. She looked out the window, for the comforting sight of her own familiar house. On her belly, burnt right through her modest suit, was the imprint of Finch's hand. Finch, the nerve: Donna hadn't warned her about his nerve.

Now Finch was holding the Bible forward and looking at them, back and forth. What can he say? Annabelle wondered, what can he say now?

"God bless you," Finch began. "God bless you."

Three

*T*he warm break ended and was followed by a series of blizzards and storms. By the beginning of March the weather had settled again, cold and implacable.

The streets of Salem were scraped down to the bare pavement, and the ridges of snow along the gutters rose to the height of a man. Snow, too, had collected around the bases of the trees and along the branches that arched over the stone houses of the village.

Only the Church of the New Age looked different: its steps were wide and clean, its doors and window frames were a dazzling white, and its spire rose high above the other buildings in the town, above the tallest branch of the tallest tree, so that from every home its tip was visible, sharp and clear in the still air.

Outside town the alternation of warm weather followed by severe cold had left the fields and pastures covered with large patches of ice worn shiny by drifting snow and constant winds. There were even trees with crusts of ice on the south sides of their trunks. This ice caught the morning sun, threw its complicated light back into the sky: the yellow March Sabbath turned black and silver by the frozen bark and snow.

Reflected in this light, the ghostly transparent colour of a moon, was the face of Maureen Finch. It was a face that had spent its whole life absorbing the stares of the surrounding township:

creamy white skin, now gone slightly soft along the jawline; brilliant green eyes that had, when they were young, burned with what Maureen's father had said was the entire insane energy of Ireland, now, as she approached her fortieth year, were sometimes bright as ever but more often smoky and clouded; and most remarkable of all the hair, a red flag of temper and sin, a luxurious coppery mass that held in it her whole body's movement and growth.

In church and in her increasingly rare expeditions to the town, that hair, which the publisher of the town's newspaper had once described as being like a drunken symphony composed by a man whose own lips were purpled by a two-week binge of drinking nineteenth-century port, was worn in a tight coiled roll. But now it was unpinned and hanging below her shoulders; as she brushed it out Maureen Finch listened to its dry electric crackle, turning her head to avoid the sparks that sometimes jumped to the tender lobes of her ears.

She was sitting this morning, as she did every morning, in her wicker wheelchair. After swinging into it from the bed she had wheeled it up to her dressing table, a fine cherry piece adorned with brass-handled drawers and a swinging three-panelled mirror. Once the table had been her grandmother's, and there was a London name on the brass plate beneath the mirror, but the table had been bought in New York, not in England. "When your grandmother came to Canada," her mother used to say, "they weren't bringing their furniture with them."

But they had brought the silver brushes, which were laid out on the shining surface of the table. With each wedding the brushes were passed on and rebristled, but it was the name of her great-grandmother that was etched into the silver on the back, etched in a flourishing hand that had almost worn away with the years: Maureen O'Connell. Her grandmother had been Maureen too, and then the name had skipped a generation to herself.

The silver brushes and the luxurious copper-tinted hair went together. Maureen, sitting opposite the mirror and gradually working free the tangles of the last twenty-four hours, tugged until her scalp hummed with the flow of blood. This ritual brushing of the hair was her first memory: herself as a young and even paler child combing out this unwieldy inheritance under her mother's careful eye.

Nowadays the brushing often made her eyes fill up with tears, because the arthritis that had crippled her knees and hips had also invaded her wrists and hands: so the humming Maureen Finch felt in her scalp was accompanied by a throbbing pain; today it was from her right wrist, and part way through the brushing she had to stop.

She could hear the girls, in the kitchen below, eating breakfast with their father. There was the occasional spoken sentence, but mostly the sounds were of cutlery against china, chairs scuffing on the wood floor as the girls wriggled around. Her own breakfast was on a tray set on the roll-top desk from which she ran the house. Built into the desk were dozens of crannies where she kept everything from the farm's tax receipts to the love letters Finch had sent her right up to the week they got married. There was also a thin-necked, old-fashioned telephone. This she used for ordering groceries from Mandowski's store in Salem and for organizing the parish business.

Hanging on her wall was a rogue's gallery of her ancestors and the houses they had lived in. Featuring the worst rogues of all was a single wedding picture. That picture had been taken in front of the old Reverend Finch's house in Kingston: Maureen in white between the father and the son. For one crazy moment as the photographer instructed them to hold the pose and smile she had felt like some early Catholic martyr — doomed to marry them both.

In that picture her hair had been pushed back to show her face. Finch was thinner then, but already wearing his beard. Now he looked more like his father than the young man he had been.

She finished massaging her wrist and picked up the brush once again. This past year her knuckles and fingers had begun to swell and sometimes she believed she could *see*, through the skin, the tiny ridges of coral forming on the joints.

She heard Finch's voice rise, telling Valerie and Clare to hurry for church. Next he banged the kettle on the stove: he always did that when it boiled, to keep the scales off the inside he claimed, and then he walked over to the counter. Soon the heavy footsteps had moved out of the kitchen and into the hallway.

"I'm going out to warm up the car. Do you want some tea?" he called up the stairs.

"No thanks."

She set the silver brush on the dressing table and looked at the reflection of her own eyes in the mirror. It was strange that people so loved to see themselves.

She could hear the breath of Finch's waiting: a sharp intake of exasperation, a slow and guilty release. His heels made a small sound as they turned on the floor and he walked quickly to the door. From her window she watched Finch as he crossed the pocked snow of their front yard to the car in the driveway.

When they had first lived here, he had always looked back as he walked. But then the fights had begun and there was the first time he had actually hit her: his open palm making her ears ring and sending her spinning across the kitchen where her head thunked into the corner of the cupboard. She'd fallen to the floor, then looked up to see Finch standing in the doorway, his hand still extended, his face a rubbery red. She staggered to her feet, bleeding from one temple, unsure whether she wanted to fight or console him. But he had just turned and walked out the door, not looking back, not then or ever since. Bitch, he had said then, bitch, coughing the word out like the name of a disease, a new and mortal sin.

Born a Catholic, born to sin. She'd been born Maureen Newell, born a Catholic girl in a brick house five miles away. Her mother's name had been Clare O'Connell and her father's Michael Newell. They had been born Catholics too, but not here, not in this sudden rocky cusp that had first nurtured them and then suddenly started to suck them dry; they had been born in Ireland, in mud houses without glass in the windows, and they had come to Canada with their parents and they had watched their parents sweat until they were old enough to sweat themselves. And then they had met and they had married and suddenly there was Maureen Newell the flaming young beauty of the third concession whose grandfather's farm was the best in the county. He had raised in its centre a red brick house with not only glass windows, but some windows made of coloured glass so that when she was a girl and standing near the coloured panes the light came through just like in a church.

Once there had even been a story that Maureen Finch liked to tell herself, the story of how Maureen Newell the Catholic girl had married the Reverend Gordon Finch, the Protestant minister. It was quite a story, she used to say to herself before her daughters were born, a real old-fashioned story of love and passion that ran through her mind like a popular song. A favourite song from the time before things had gone bad and she was still inventing the wonderful world that she would give to her children.

Now it was the first Sunday in March. Outside the air was a bitter crackling cold, but the coal furnace of the church had been on for twenty-four hours, and even those who sat scattered in the back rows had taken off their heavy coats.

As always Maureen Finch was placed at the very front: she was in the folding wheelchair that was kept for her at the church, and beside her in the family pew were her two daughters. They were singing hymns, and their strong voices enthusiastically rang out the words. They liked singing, Valerie and Clare; they liked singing and school and going to visit other families, even working in the garden: they liked anything that took them out of the house.

To keep them company, Maureen sang along. Once she'd had a powerful contralto and had even sung solos in the Catholic church. Here, in the Protestant Church of the New Age, she sang with voice subdued, slurring the words she could never quite get used to.

Born to sin, her father had said. She could feel the eyes of the congregation focused on the back of her head. Finch was a lady-killer, oh yes, everyone knew that. Gordon Finch, the Protestant minister of the Church of the New Age, certainly had an eye for the ladies. Two eyes.

Finch had a wide confident face, and up there in the pulpit, with his black hair and black moustacheless beard, his deep lady-killing eyes, his muscular arms and shoulders bulging right out of his suit, he didn't look like a man to be worried by a few whispers.

Not Gordon Finch, preaching son of preaching Bob Finch, the carpenter from Kingston.

"Rock of Ages," they were singing, and Maureen Newell Finch looked down at her hands. She was used to them: the sight of the arthritis growing into the bones wasn't going to make her cry, even in church.

Finch, the lady-killer: well he had killed her and what could anyone think of that? God in His heaven must have long ago given up on His one-time Christmas angel, His once meek Maureen Newell. He must have looked down on His angelic Maureen and the two daughters she had failed to baptise into the faith, and He must have lost count of her sins. Might better save His eyes for falling sparrows.

It was quite a story, she thought, the story of herself and Finch, but it was not exactly the kind of story they taught in Sunday school. Love and passion, yes: but after that the story had gone downhill and by the time Valerie and Clare were old enough to hear it, it was no longer worth telling.

She was cold, he should have known better.

She was twenty-two, amazingly old for an unmarried woman, and he was already twenty-five and living on his uncle's farm. Every day he contrived to walk down the dirt road where Maureen galloped her horse.

She was a beauty, then, a true beauty with fiery red hair that streamed out behind her when she rode at the reckless gallop that was the only speed she knew. Her features were fine and carefully moulded with a few faint freckles over the bridge of her snub nose, her green eyes that were brighter than the sky and her skin so white and dear that he was at first afraid to touch her, afraid that his own dirty and calloused fingers wouldn't even be able to feel the buttery smoothness of her.

They said that the reason she was unmarried was that she

didn't like men — and maybe that had been the truth. But it had also been the truth that she had been taking care of her mother, who was sick, while her father worked out. And she liked Gordon Finch well enough.

She would gallop up to him on the road that first spring, half-standing in the stirrups, urging on the roan gelding she always rode, and Finch would lose himself listening to the chaotic thunder of the hooves, and watching apple blossoms fall like snow at the sound of her approach. Then she would rear the horse up in the air, its front legs pawing wildly; but Finch had been celibate a whole year in a strange Virginia town and his eyes stayed fastened on the tanned bare triangle of her throat.

"You walk a lot?"

"Every day."

"I like to ride."

That had been their first conversation. He already had the beard then; it was grown in the Virginia seminary after the fashion of one of his teachers. But it made him self-conscious, and he was always reaching up to touch his face.

Some days she wore a knotted red scarf around her neck and as she walked with him she would untie the scarf and wave it in her hand as she walked. Once she stopped to adjust her boot and handed him the scarf to hold for her. With Maureen Newell's red scarf wrapped round his fist tightly enough to make his knuckles ache, he wanted her so much he could hardly breathe.

"You get asthma?" Maureen asked.

"Must be," Finch said.

"My mother gets asthma," Maureen said. "It's the spring that brings it on, all the pollen."

Apple blossoms, flowering dogwood, lilac: as they walked, the countryside rolled with life exploding and mating. Even the air thickened with the sweet smells of flowers and the hysterical joys of mating birds.

"He's called Sean," Maureen said.

"Who?"

"My horse. He's called Sean after one of the great Irish war chieftains."

It was tall, Finch noted, but its legs were narrow and the

ankles, each with its white sock, were slender and fine. As they walked it followed docilely, the end of its bridle hooked carelessly into Maureen's belt.

"You're a Catholic, then."

"Of course. And your father is the minister at the New Church."

"Just on Sundays," Finch said. "The rest of the week he's a carpenter."

"And don't you carpenter with him?"

With her teasing voice, her creamy white skin and her beautiful mane of red hair, Maureen Newell was considered something special. When she started riding around in her pants that flared at the thighs and tucked into shiny knee-high boots, people began to say that she had her nose in the air, which wasn't surprising since she had spent several years at a private school in Toronto. There were rumours, too, that she had stayed an extra year to have a baby fathered by one of the priests there, but when she came back to take care of her mother there was no sign of baby or priest: just a young woman already past the age of marrying, a woman so ripe the whole township was waiting to see which way she would fall.

"I don't have the hands for working with wood," Finch finally said. "They say it takes something of the artist, so I help my uncle at the farm instead."

"You've got a beard," Maureen said.

"What?" Finch, startled, took his hand away from his chin.

"You've got a beard, I thought artists had beards." She looked at him, at his bewildered expression, and she laughed. The sound of her laughter was like the day breaking apart. His chest was so tight that trying to laugh with her only made him gasp, and he had to hit his breastbone to free his breath.

At the farm, that night, Finch ate silently.

"I was out looking for you today," his uncle said. Benjamin was his name. He was wide, like his brother Bob Finch, and had the same strong arms, but his face was gentle and round; it seemed that his years with cattle had softened him into their image.

"I was at the back," Finch said, "walking the fence."

"You were walking the fence yesterday."

"I got lost," Finch said.

"Mary? Did you hear that? The boy says he got lost." Benjamin wiped his face on his sleeve and pushed away the plate that had been heaped with pork hocks and boiled potatoes. In the centre of the table was a loaf of white bread, each slice generously buttered, and a wide, round pan filled with a fresh apple pie.

"If you got lost," Benjamin said, "and if you crossed the back concession, you might come out at the Newell place. Do you remember them, Mary? They're Catholics, I think."

Mary, who was at the other end of the kitchen, shouted back to Benjamin. They always shouted at each other, and when he was younger Finch had always thought this was a sign of their great love. Then he had found out that Mary was quite deaf and, as her only revenge, always outyelled her husband.

"Catholics," Mary called out. "That's right, they're Catholics. The girl went to one of those Catholic schools in Toronto, you know. They say terrible things about her."

"Not here they don't." Benjamin boomed. "I think she's a fine girl, a fine girl."

"A fine girl," Mary echoed back.

Finch began to push away from the table but Benjamin reached out for him. "We were just teasing you, boy."

"I was going to muck out the horse stable."

"Don't you want some apple pie?"

"What are you men talking about?"

"Apple pie," Benjamin shouted.

"What happened about the Newell girl?"

"We were teasing him," Benjamin shouted. "We've stopped now."

Mary, who was shorter than Benjamin and twice as wide, finally reappeared at the table with a quart of ice cream. "We were just teasing you," she said to Finch.

On Sundays his father, the Reverend Robert "Bob" Finch, the carpenter from Kingston, would preach at the Church of the

New Age in Salem. The Reverend was taller than Benjamin, but he too was wide and muscular, with arms thick from a lifetime of saws and hammers. He had dark, deep-set eyes; and his hair, which waved at the front and was combed straight back, was coal black with a streak of white at one temple. When they did the radio program about him, they said, referring to that streak, that the carpenter from Kingston looked as though he had been touched by God Himself; they said also that he had a voice that could find his congregation's heart the way a wolf runs down a sheep.

Standing up in the pulpit of the old stone church Bob Finch would glower down at the Protestants of Salem: two hundred souls in the fall and winter, townspeople and surrounding farmers, and in his pulpit he was such an imposing, even awesome figure that in the spring and summer visitors to the church would almost double its population.

"Do you think the Lord meant for you to sit on your arse when His work needs doing?" he would roar. Benjamin may have shouted because his wife was deaf but the carpenter from Kingston roared because his red-faced, knock-kneed listeners needed to feel the fear of the Lord right down to the soles of their sinful wandering feet. *"Do you think?"* he would roar. And his right arm would come down onto the lectern with a mighty crash as if Jove's tongue itself was lashing them. *"Do you think?"* *Whap* came the arm. *Whap, whap,* WHAP and the flat of his calloused hand descended with such force that the old stone church was practically split in two.

Visitors would stare, transfixed. Children would shrink into their parents' arms. But the regulars stayed smug and unmoved in their seats. To Bob Finch's shouts, to his storming about the pulpit, to his great right arm crashing down on them as if they were a collective child with its pants down — to all this they were inured. But when the roar subsided, when he leaned forward in the pulpit, pushed back at his thick hair so you could see his palm lingering on the white streak, when he lowered his voice down to a hoarse, threatening whisper and his eyes started to glisten with the fear of hell, then even the old regulars who scoffed, outside the church, at the powers of the Reverend, even the secret unbelievers, slid to the edges of their seats and gripped the wooden pews in front of them until their hands ached. Then, in the huge gravelly cavern of Bob Finch's voice, as it rattled around the stone church, were described the perils and terrors of the kingdom below. With his voice literally creeping into their ears he told them of the pits of biting snakes that awaited the covetous; the leprous diseases that invaded the hands and arms of thieves; the snapping turtles that hung from the genitalia of fornicators; the rabid bats that attacked the tongues of gossips until they swelled up like mushrooms and split open their skulls. When the Reverend spoke of hell the whole stone church became a huge collective skull itself, his voice running through their unprotected minds like grassfire, their eyes transfixed with his; and there was no one whose dreams did not finally mix with Bob Finch's words, rooting themselves in those Sundays when he let lie his big right arm and told instead about the world below.

After the sermon and the shaking of hands, there was dinner back at the farm. Finch would drive back to the farm with his father, first making the ritual stop at the cemetery to visit his mother's grave.

"God bless your mother," Bob Finch would say. In fine weather he would drop to his knees in the grass in front of the grave, briefly bow his head and mumble a prayer. Before he went away Finch was so habituated to this he never thought about it, but when he came back from the seminary and watched his father kneel in the spring grass he was astonished. By this time Bob Finch's clothes were getting a little baggy in the shoulders and tight around the belly, and though he still stood as tall and frightening as ever in the pulpit, the white streak over the right temple had grown and spread, so now it was as though a whole handful of white paint had been drawn through his hair.

"He looks winter-killed," Finch said to Maureen. "Since I came back he's not the same."

"He's the same," Maureen told him. "You're the one who's changed."

When she said these things to him, things about himself, he

would twist inside with pleasure and surprise. Of course there had been girls before he went to the seminary, but none of them had been like Maureen, none of them could talk the way she did, every word so polished and considered she might have been reading it out of a book. Not only could she read his own heart and mind, but she could also explain the actions of others. Beneath what was to Finch the roiled surface of human relations, Maureen saw only a clear and simple truth, the beautiful map of what each person was doing to every other person.

"Your father wants to destroy you," she told Finch. "That's why he acts the way he does. He wants to destroy you with half his being and with the other half he wants you to be more than his match, so that when he dies he can be sure you're strong enough to survive."

Finch had always sensed the contrary moods of his father, the alternation between destructive rag and encouragement. But he never could have captured it in words, put it into a few simple sentences he could carry around in his head. It was true, he now knew, what people said about women having special knowledge: the secret underside of life was utterly visible to Maureen.

Sometimes, as they walked the back roads with Sean following docilely behind, her words killed the desire in him. Then it came back in a renewed and stronger rush, and he would be clapping his fist to his breastbone.

"You ever seen a doctor about that?"

"Nothing a doctor can do."

She stopped, put her hand to his chest. "Now breathe deep."

His heart was so startled it jumped right to her palm.

"What was that?"

There had been the whole week of meeting, of walking down the road and talking, but he still hadn't touched her. Without thinking he reached for her shoulders. She stood motionless as he raised his hands and traced the edges of her ears, searched out the soft skin beneath the fall of silky hair. She was smiling, her mouth parted, and in the moisture of her lips he could see tiny reflections of the sun. He wanted to lean towards her and lick the golden suns away.

But she was so still so absolutely still.

He dropped his hands and they started to walk. His legs could hardly move through the thick clouds of his tension. She held his arm and the heat of her fingers branded his skin.

"Gordon, I've gotten so used to our meetings."

Her hair was coppery with the sun, and the day was so warm that he could see the beads of sweat forming on the thin white skin of her forehead. Even the small valley at the base of her throat was growing moist.

He turned to her and reached for her again, this time holding her at the waist.

She looked at him; obedient, passive.

He could feel the heat of her running through his hands.

"Gordon," she said.

He waited, but there was nothing else.

And then finally, unable to contain himself any longer, he tightened his grip and swung her up in the air. As he staggered to keep his balance, he held her above him with his hands squeezing into her waist; reeling, he turned her round and round until her long hair fell down over his face and he was surrounded by her excited breathing. Then he slipped and fell into the grassy ditch. Maureen, screaming, fell on top of him. Into his chest and groin crashed the sweet warm weight of her. She smelled like wild strawberries and he met her with his lips; needing to drink her down, sweat, bones, clothes and all.

And when his mouth was finally filled with her, and they were lying at peace in the ditch, joined skin to skin to half-torn clothes to grass to sun; when they were finally lying in the ditch he could feel the cold earth in his back again and the sun on his face. It was spring, spring turning into summer, and he was lying happy with one hand filled with the soft white breast of Maureen Newell, Catholic, and the other shading his eyes against the blue sky.

She liked to tell the story from both sides, his and hers, needing to know every detail: how it was to be inside his skin and feel the earth shaking to Sean's gallop; how the spring had smelled to him that year. She felt again the sudden breezes that whipped through the valleys of flowering trees, the rising fragrance as their own bodies baked together in the sun, the need finally to take the chance, break apart the glass cage of fear and sin that had encased her for twenty-two years.

Maureen Newell, Catholic: yes, she had known what sin was.

"A mortal sin," the priest said when she confessed. "That was a mortal sin."

A silence.

And then he had added: "And you say it was with a minister of the Protestant faith?"

"Yes, father."

"May God forgive you, my child."

She had almost laughed. Right in the midst of the most terrifying confession she had ever imagined. At the depths of her own fear that she had gone too far, placed herself beyond any redemption, the priest's jealousy of Finch had made her giggle and she had bitten her palm, started snuffling.

"I wanted him," Maureen said. And then the calm broke and the pretend tears turned into real ones; she was crying, crying, and as she cried she dug her fists into her eyes, hating her tears and everything in her that they represented: the craziness, the temper, worst of all the wilfulness that had pushed her through the convent school in Toronto in one long, screaming push, made her alternate between being the favourite of the teaching nuns and spending her Saturdays doing penance on the stone floor of the church, scrubbing until by the end of high school her knuckles were as calloused as her knees.

Humility.

Yes, humility was what she lacked, Maureen Newell who was the great-granddaughter of Maureen O'Connell and looked her spitting image they said — and they meant spitting. Even the sight of her own mother's gradually freezing bones didn't make her fear for herself, not in those days. It only made her ride farther, faster, mount Sean and send him galloping headlong through the fields, her knees squeezing him tight until her insides shook with pleasure.

"You went to Loretto Convent School?" the priest asked.

"Yes," Maureen said. This wasn't her old priest, the one from the church in Salem. She never could have told him, so she had driven to Kingston the day after Finch had thrown her up in the air and caught her, broken her open in a moment so brief and pleasurable she had hardly had time to go dizzy and lose herself in the smells of the daisies and columbine when it was over and she was sitting half-clothed, Finch's hand covering her breast as if it had suddenly grown there.

"You didn't have the calling to be a nun?" the priest asked.

"No," Maureen said. "Not quite." She was still crying, kneeling in the dark booth, and she could smell the priest's breath; it was stale and old.

"Not quite?" the voice raised. The booth was filling with his sour curiosity, but the tone of his voice was growing sharper, as if finally the whole irrefutable disaster of her sin was waking him up.

"Not at all," Maureen said quietly. "Not at all, really."

A new silence. Maureen found her mind slipping away from Finch, away from that whole delicately wound week of needing, and back to what had been before: the flat black street of her own duty.

"I was going to teach," she finally said. "I trained to teach and took a year in nursing too, but then my brother left the farm and my mother got sick."

"You were needed," the priest supplied.

"Yes."

"And you are needed still?"

She had never been in a booth for so long. Her eyes had grown accustomed to the light, but it now seemed as if they had used up both the light and the oxygen, and as well as the priest's breath she could smell the fear and fatigue of her own body.

"She's not so bad," Maureen said. "Not so bad as she was."

As the priest kept asking his questions, the sound of his voice began to blur and blacken, to become not merely a voice but the walls of the church, the weight of all men's voices: shutting out all light, closing her in, pressing her down and into the stone.

She shrank against the wall of the booth, unable to cry, unable to respond.

"What happens to sinners?" the priest insisted.

"I don't know . . ."

"When they die, girl."

"They go to hell," Maureen had finally whispered.

"Hell," the priest rasped. *"Hell."* And his rank breath swept through the booth like a warning wind from below. "If you sin, you go to hell. Do you want to go to hell? Do you? Do you?"

Maureen Newell, Catholic. Born to sin, her father said. There was nothing worth telling in that.

Now it was her husband, Gordon Finch, who stood at the head of the congregation. Mounted in the pulpit, huge arms outstretched, eyes slowly surveying his parishioners.

Maureen watched Finch's face.

Saw his eyes stop: once, twice, three times.

Sometimes she believed that each time his eyes stopped, they had settled on one of his mistresses.

Now his eyes came to her own and, as always, glided by without pausing.

"God bless you," Finch said. His strong voice filled the old stone church; his arms were still raised, no one moved. He was smiling, his white teeth and glowing eyes shining over them all in a mysterious benediction. "God bless you," Finch said again. "May God bless you this coming week."

His arms dropped, he bowed ever so slightly as if after a performance and then he descended from the pulpit to Maureen's chair.

She stiffened, knowing what was coming.

Finch passed her by, giving her that same evasive look, this time decorated with a smile, and then, from behind, took the handles of the chair and pushed it to the back of the church. There he twisted it around to face the centre aisle — a sudden turn on one wheel that never failed to make her stomach flutter — and let his hand fall to her shoulder.

Despite everything, the weight of his hand through her dress was so familiar that she needed it, welcomed it; and thus reinforced Maureen Finch put a smile on her own face, ready to say a word to each of the congregation as they left the church. Stories, yes: Maureen Finch knew that her own story would have passed through every mouth in Salem; but she wasn't going to back down, no, not now.

Nellie Tillson's turn came near the end and she was, Maureen noticed, looking particularly beautiful, even radiant. Her blue eyes were like bright foreign gems, her pale skin glowed from the inside, and her golden hair was so clean and fine that the light from the stained glass windows wanted to catch in it.

"Mrs. Finch," Nellie said. At one time she had been Maureen's pupil, then she had graduated to being a teacher in the Sunday school.

"Hello, Nellie." As Maureen looked up at the girl she felt Finch's hand tighten on her shoulder; and at the same time Nellie's lower lip trembled and her face turned to Finch. Maureen, watching this, felt a familiar panic.

Nellie was still staring at Finch. Maureen saw a vein in Nellie's neck begin to pulse; heart-throb, lady-killer — the words raced into Maureen's mind — she wanted to shout them out, to scream out to the whole church that Nellie Tillson, standing in front of her husband, her husband the minister, was having such a huge heart-throb of desire that she was going to strangle.

And then Maureen felt her own heart throbbing, her temples pounding and for a moment she succumbed, closing her eyes.

"You must be Mrs. Finch." This new voice spoke her name carefully as birds' eggs laid on a silver plate.

"My name is Annabelle Jamieson. My husband and I — we've been to church before — but we haven't really been introduced to you."

Maureen, listening to these careful city words, looked up to see a nervous, well-groomed woman about ten years younger than her.

"I'm pleased to meet you, Mrs. Jamieson. Welcome to Salem." Maureen extended her hand, then she felt the city fingers meet her skin, lie narrow and cool in her palm. Afraid, Maureen thought and, still angry at Nellie Tillson, she squeezed. The fingers squeezed back, skinny and tense. Later, going over that first encounter, Maureen could recall only a few details of the woman's looks: brown oval eyes, dark hair, pale lips and a narrow and delicate jaw. A city face to go with the city voice.

Instead of paying more attention to Annabelle Jamieson, Maureen Finch had turned away and looked to the door of the church: there stood Nellie Tillson, shrugging her arms into her coat as if she expected to be crucified, her gold-crowned silhouette framed in the bright winter light.

Four

Annabelle Jamieson did not forget Maureen Finch. Her first impression had been of Maureen's ramrod-stiff neck, unmoving in the church as she stared at Finch. Old bedroom eyes, Donna had called him; and when his eyes had gaped and shone the bonds between Finch and his rapt audience were so strong that his body seemed to swell with their attention, and the whole congregation stretched and rolled like dozing cats taunting the sun.

Maureen Finch was the exception. Through his most impassioned words, she sat unmoving. Her white neck and brilliant red hair were held up like a silent protest against her husband's passion.

Only on the day she decided to introduce herself had Annabelle gotten a proper view of Maureen. She was sitting at the door of the church, and the face that had been hidden was turned towards her. But even the ivory skin of the neck had not prepared Annabelle for the face itself; it was the deep, beautiful white of a flower grown in darkness. The eyes were emerald green, the hair a bright, coppery red. My rival's face, Annabelle had thought, the words coming so forcefully into her mind she thought she must have spoken them aloud.

The face stayed fixed in Annabelle's mind. Fascinated, she would find herself sketching it again and again: it was, Annabelle thought, the face of a victim — a victim of her own strange beauty, of her wandering husband, of the illness that had forced her to watch passively. The lines of Maureen Finch became so familiar that Annabelle would find herself drawing them without thinking, and one morning late in March, she was pencilling in the shadows beneath Maureen Finch's eyes, drinking her first cup of coffee of the morning, when the telephone rang.

She took a sip of her coffee, which was no longer at the boiling heat she preferred, and looked indecisively towards the hall. Since she and Allen had moved from Ottawa to Salem, her mother's phone calls had not lessened. But this was the day her mother had finally agreed to pay their new house a visit, and Annabelle was afraid that on the other end of the line would be some new and extravagant excuse.

By the fourth ring Annabelle was walking rapidly towards the telephone, coffee in hand. She was wearing an old pair of paint-stained blue jeans and as she hurried some of the coffee spilled, creating a warm island against her left knee. She stopped, pressed her hand against the denim to make sure her leg wouldn't burn, and then, when the phone didn't stop, finally lunged for the receiver. The line sounded blank, as if whoever had called was just hanging up.

"Hello?" She was already putting down the receiver when the reply came.

"Mrs. Jamieson?"

"Yes, speaking."

"This is Reverend Finch, Mrs. Jamieson"

The voice reached into her, a long, preaching finger that probed right through to her heart; which stopped then speeded over the next few beats, bouncing like a car on one of the local washboard roads. In the silence she could smell Finch again, feel him twisting towards her on the couch.

"Yes, Mr. Finch, what can I do for you?"

"The ladies are having a tea next Tuesday at the church, Mrs. Jamieson, to discuss ways of raising money for the orphans of Thailand." His tone was more organized, more impersonal than it had been at Donna Wilson's.

"Thank you, Mr. Finch, but I'm busy next Tuesday. I'm afraid I have to go into town that day." After the long silence the lie sounded rehearsed, and as she said the words she could almost see Finch, brows knit together, judging them.

"Is it your art, Mrs. Jamieson?"

For a moment she thought he had said *heart;* and was silent again, growing slowly furious with the persistence of this small-town Lothario. Then she realized that Finch was only inquiring after her pottery.

"No, Mr. Finch, it's not my art."

"Then perhaps you could go another day, Mrs. Jamieson. The orphans of Thailand deserve our help."

"Thank you, Mr. Finch, but I have a doctor's appointment."

"I don't mean to pry, Mrs. Jamieson." Even his own voice sounded unconvinced.

"Thank you for calling, Mr. Finch."

"I hope you're not trying to discourage me, Mrs Jamieson."

"No," she said. The word was small but she said it quickly, without thinking; and as soon as it was spoken she knew she had given Finch the encouragement he wanted.

"Goodbye, Mrs. Jamieson. God bless." Then the line went dead.

Annabelle walked into the kitchen where she dumped out the cold coffee and plugged in the kettle once more. Then she opened the refrigerator. It was empty. There was no juice, nothing at all. Still on the stove was the frying pan in which she had cooked Allen's breakfast, and the smell seemed suddenly pungent and sour.

She slammed shut the refrigerator door and spooned instant coffee into her cup. She was shaking, she noted, there was no doubt that her hands were shaking; even the spoon jumped as she held it, scattering dark grains on the carefully polished table. *Is it your art?*

Through her front window she could see the house across the street. The door of that house now opened and Donna Wilson emerged, snow shovel in hand, and began scraping the ice off her steps.

"Not Finch," Donna had said. "That would be stupid."

Since the meeting at her house, almost a month ago, Annabelle hadn't spoken with Finch until this morning. Yet, in addition to going once more to church, she had seen him twice in the grocery store; but after waving to him across the aisles she had hurried out.

"Finch," Annabelle said. The word was like a stone in her mouth. She sipped at the coffee, but though it scalded her lips, the stone wouldn't dissolve. "Finch," Annabelle said again. "What could I want with Finch?" Her neck and shoulders were tense, and she wished she had some way to explode. She was just remembering that that was how she had been before she met Allen, temperamental and explosive, when she realized the insides of her thighs were sore, the way they got when she wanted to make love.

Annabelle walked back into her studio and looked at the clay waiting to be worked. It was hard to imagine where Finch might be calling from: his own house where Maureen Finch could listen in? A telephone booth in Salem or in Kingston? The house of another parishioner?

And she wondered, too, what Finch would think of her own home, the pine antiques that had been carefully stripped, the studio where she spent her days.

Other visitors were always impressed by the wooden wheel, the shiny steel of the kiln, and most of all by the smell and softness of the clay. It must be rewarding, they would say, to work with earth itself. But as far as Annabelle was concerned, clay was not earth. Earth was the repository, the garbage heap, even that wonderful stuff that knew how to grow grass and flowers. Unpredictable, earth was like the photographer who had taken his pictures, made his jokes, left forever on an airplane.

Clay was the opposite to the contradictory nature of earth. Pure and predictable, it was of one consistency and fitted itself to the hand. Surely Finch would appreciate that.

The Bible said that God made Adam out of clay, in His own image. Finch would appreciate that too, the idea of God shaping a man to His own perfection. And perhaps Finch even thought that his own tall and muscular frame was the perfect replica, God's body in the flesh sent to walk the earth and harvest the love and admiration of grateful female parishioners.

Annabelle sipped at her coffee. She had often pictured God creating Adam: God, a big, muscular middle-aged man with a curling grey beard, a living, moving Michelangelo sculpture, standing naked by a pond with a mound of fresh clay at His feet.

Taking the clay in His large hands, looking curiously at His own image in the still mirror of the water, then pressing it between His palms, trying to shape it to the image.

Finding it difficult — even God might need practice — He might then have the great inspiration of actually moulding it to Himself. Excitedly leaning down and scooping water from the pond, splashing it all over His white marble skin, then slowly and awkwardly putting together Adam by shaping each bit, by pressing it first to His own rolling muscles, His own perfect bones.

And when she imagined Him, wet and shining in heaven's glorious sun, covered with bits of clay that clung to Him, inspecting the replica He had made of Himself and comparing it to the image in the shining water, Annabelle always thought that this must have been the first art class.

Not bad, God must have decided, a few places that need patching and a few places that might not wear too well but then He had seen that Adam's mouth had an opening and, being curious, God had stepped up to this open mouth and sent His breath shooting through it.

Not bad for a beginner, but He might have done better if He'd taken His time and practised for a couple of years.

Practice was what God had needed, Annabelle thought, and it was what she too could use. For she was not accustomed to living in small towns, and these past few months in Salem her life had become an endurance test. Yet it had been her desperate inspiration to leave the scandal behind and move to a small town where Allen could start a new business. Where he could be trusted and grow close to the people in the community while she took advantage of the slower rhythm of life to spend more time on her pottery.

In the mornings she made sketches of people from the town. These evolved into little clay figurines with arms and legs she could roll between her fingers, and then assemble against backgrounds that would eventually fit together to form a gigantic mosaic.

This mosaic would, she explained wryly to her husband, be made up of panels that would depict "the human condition, the agony and the ecstacy, the glorious, suffering, wonderful ordeal and history of mankind, etcetera."

Allen had not exactly appreciated this explanation, which was meant to be ironic and unspeakably subtle. All week Annabelle had been embroidering upon it, practicing up to deliver it to her mother. Her mother always demanded explanations, and a nice fancy speech, nothing too long, would come in handy: her mother had an ear for fancy words between women.

But after Finch called, Annabelle's mind would not stay on the impending visit of her mother. Finch: how had he gotten this power over her? He had started off being a game, a game she wanted to look at but not to play, and now it was no longer amusing. But Finch wouldn't let her go; instead he was haunting her like a tin-pot shaman.

On Annabelle's work table was a moist mound of clay, covered with a damp cloth. This was the clay she used for her figurines and now, frightened, she decided to make a figure of Finch; that would be a good addition to the fancy explanation for her mother. She could say that she made figures of the townspeople and then put them in her electric kiln, just to see if they could stand the heat.

She took a handful of clay and threw it down against the table. She would do the whole family: Finch, Maureen, the two daughters. Finch she would show in the pulpit; the two daughters would be singing, their hands clasped together; Maureen would be in her wheelchair, watching.

In the church, as she had bent to introduce herself to Maureen, she had felt Finch turn towards her. The acrid smell of the barn had been replaced by aftershave, and sweat from the force of his preaching.

"Pleased to meet you," Maureen Finch had said. Her voice icy, her nails painted blood red, as if they had already torn apart not only Finch but whole battlefields of pretenders.

Walking home, boots squeaking in the cold snow, Allen had said that Finch and his wife made a handsome couple.

Her mother arrived six hours early. When the door bell rang Annabelle was still in her studio; she was sketching Maureen Finch's face, turned up towards the preaching Finch. As she walked to the front door she tried to brush clean the jeans she had intended to change before her mother's arrival.

"Annabelle, oh, I'm sorry, you're such a mess — I must be early."

Annabelle laughed, then hugged her mother who felt all angles and bones.

She took her mother's suitcase and then showed her around the house. Every room had to be seen and inspected in detail.

"This must be where your father stayed at Christmas."

"I'm sorry," Annabelle apologized. "I was going to vacuum it this afternoon." Annabelle had set the suitcase in the doorway, but neither woman entered the room.

"How nice," continued Mrs. MacLeod. "I haven't shared a bed with your father in a long time." Her eyebrows raised and her forehead wrinkled. This was the position her face always took after a telling remark, and Annabelle, as always, was silent after being told. Her mother's comments about her father were as mysterious to Annabelle as had been their separation. This had taken place six months after Annabelle, their only child, had left home.

"It's the European way," her mother had explained. "I've taken care of you both for twenty years, now I want to live a life of my own." She always called what she wanted "the European way." She had even been to Europe, but that hadn't stopped her. After she came back she started claiming that her grandfather had been a French aristocrat. The European way included all sorts of bizarre rules: for example, she loved to receive extravagant presents on her birthday; she never cooked for Annabelle and Allen, they always met in restaurants; although she was separated from her husband it was the European way to meet with him once or even twice a week for shared social events or simply for dinner.

Now Annabelle felt her mother's hand on her arm. She stepped forward and hugged her mother again: not the way she had at the door, careful not to disturb the expertly applied makeup or the perfectly tailored clothes, but unreservedly. With her eyes squinched tight she wrapped her arms around her mother as if she were a little girl again, as if her mother's flesh were still solid and able to shelter her from the world, from houses that weren't worth living in, from men who weren't worth having.

"Are you happy here, Annabelle, are you really happy? You could come home, you know, it wouldn't be a crime to visit your mother."

At the word *crime*, Annabelle stepped back. Her mother, in her European way, never mentioned directly what Allen had done. Only suggested that Annabelle come to visit, even said once that the two of them could live together, mother and daughter, the way they did in France.

"I'd better change," Annabelle said. "I can't go out like this." Then she stood for a moment, holding her mother at arms' length: black-haired, with sharp features, the years had turned her mother into a slightly smaller and sparrow-like version of her previous self. The only real change was that the skin around her eyes was pitted, as if from tears uncried.

"You're looking good," Annabelle pronounced. "You're looking just perfect."

Allen's office was in an old stone building on one of Salem's two downtown streets. At the southern end of these two streets, rising over and surveying the town and its inhabitants, was the Church of the New Age. In earlier eras it had been called Presbyterian and then Methodist, but the name changes were only incidental, like new coats of paint. What stayed constant was the church's meaning, because it was placed at the edge of the stores as if to say: corruption — this far and no farther.

At the other end of the town, facing the farm and bushland to the north, was the town's other main institution. This building had neither spire nor stone, but was a low, sprawling log structure, since covered by clapboard. It was the town's hotel and tavern. Its name also changed, sometimes by the generation and sometimes by the year, but its meaning too was constant: a fortress of comfort that stood between civilization and the terrifying wilderness.

Between the poles of tavern and church Salem's inhabitants swayed or sometimes staggered.

"You know," Finch had told Annabelle as he was leaving Donna's house, "there is a saying that in this town a man's life is taken up with the trip from one end to the other. If you get my meaning."

"I get it, Mr. Finch."

"And I'll tell you another thing, Mrs. Jamieson, if you don't mind me speaking in symbols, but God chooses very few to swim against the current."

Beside Allen's office, in an attached stone building that was taller and had a large window facing the street, was the town's printing establishment and the home of the *Salem Weekly News*. The proprietor was stepping out just as Annabelle and her mother were coming to Allen's door.

"Good morning, Mrs. Jamieson." He was a short and stocky man with powerful shoulders and a thick red beard.

"Good morning, Mr.—" Annabelle mumbled, and promised herself for the tenth time to ask Allen the man's name. And how did he, whoever he was, know hers?

The door to Allen's suite had stencilled onto it,

ALLEN JAMIESON B.Sc., M.A., L L. B.

and was opened to the hall. The anteroom was empty; his secretary, who only worked in the mornings, had already gone for the day, and the door to Allen's own office was also open. Allen was reclining in his swivel chair, dictating into a microphone. He waved at Annabelle and her mother as they entered, mumbled a few legal phrases and final postscripts before switching off the machine and standing up.

He took his jacket from the back of his chair and tucked his shirt into his pants. He wasn't a big man, Annabelle thought, but he was growing wider. He had thick blonde hair and a ruddy complexion to match. In high school he had been a football player but now he was growing into an early and prosperous middle age, high-toned and sleek, layers of fat marbled through the muscle.

As Annabelle watched, Allen stepped forward and kissed Mrs. MacLeod on the cheek.

"Is it cold out?"

"There's a wind," Annabelle said. Then, looking down at herself: "But the coat is warm, I hardly feel it."

Allen laughed and turned to Annabelle's mother. "She's like the princess and the pea," he said. "One bit of frost in the air and she turns blue all over."

"What a town," Mrs. MacLeod exclaimed. "What an enormously beautiful town. It's like something out of, something out of . . . ." She looked across the restaurant table to Allen for help. "It's like something out of Europe."

Annabelle saw the waiter approaching with their second carafe of oversweet Ontario wine.

"Of course it's newer. It still has a certain raw charm."

"Raw charm," Annabelle whispered to herself. Her mother's eyes seemed to be growing into the soft, liquid colour of green-black olives.

"The streets are so peaceful," Annabelle's mother continued. "And the trees, they must be splendid in the summer."

Annabelle tried, without success, to imagine Salem in the summer. In the fall, the towering maples with their delicate golden leaves had made huge arched canopies over all the streets, golden bridal pathways that led from house to house and down to the small lake. Now the lake attracted only the cold winds that whipped across it and the snowmobilers who tirelessly crisscrossed its frozen surface.

"And the people," Annabelle's mother said. Annabelle gazed out the window of the hotel and saw a car emptying itself of men in red and black plaid bush jackets. Unshaven, tuques pulled low over their foreheads, they headed towards the tavern. "Don't you wonder what people like that *do* all day?"

"They drink," Annabelle said.

"I think," Annabelle's mother insisted, her voice firm but not so loud as to be overheard by their waiter, a large and friendly teenager with a cut over one eye, "I think that people in a place like this live with such *integrity.*"

She looked at Annabelle and then at Allen with her liquid eyes so widely opened that only a member of the family could know that what she was expressing was scorn not sincerity.

"It must be so fascinating," said Mrs. MacLeod, "to carry on the practice of law in a place like this."

Annabelle watched as her mother now focused on Allen, waiting for his response. She was so crazy, her mother, so insistently two-edged. On the one hand she made it clear to Annabelle, but only by glances, shrugs and her silly little innuendoes, that she had absolute contempt for Allen and what he did, but actually, as Annabelle knew, she was totally taken by Allen's bland charm, by his willingness to listen attentively and flatter her at every turn.

"Some men are fools," Annabelle's mother often said. It didn't need to be added that women were *never* fools. Women were intelligent, shrewd, in control at all times. Men were babies but women were adults.

"I'm only a real-estate lawyer," Allen finally replied.

"A lawyer," Mrs. MacLeod had crowed when Annabelle told her that she was getting married. "How terribly original of you to marry a *lawyer.*"

"You don't have to meet him."

"But don't be foolish, Annabelle; you always take everything the wrong way. And besides, better a lawyer than a schoolteacher."

Annabelle's father, Henry MacLeod, had been a schoolteacher. A big, dour man with sloping shoulders and a pot belly, he was now retired and consulted part time for the school board. When his wife had insisted they separate he had agreed, though not without resisting, and had moved to a bachelor apartment in a downtown building.

"A real-estate lawyer," Annabelle's mother now said. "You know, sometimes I think that a man's property is more dear to him than his wife." Allen laughed and then Mrs. MacLeod continued, "If he can tell the difference, that is. But of course you two hold your house in common, don't you?"

The waiter was standing above them, pouring their coffee from an old, dented silver pitcher. He had already told them that the cut on his forehead had been received in a hockey game, when one of his friends had brought a stick down on his skull.

Annabelle looked across the table at her mother. Her mother's face, like her own, could be mean some days, generous others. But it seldom looked full of love and Annabelle wondered, suddenly, if her own face ever looked full of love.

"Coffee?" her mother asked. "Annabelle, the waiter wants to know if you want more coffee."

The coffee was black, a dark brown-black lake that was contained in the wide-mouthed mug. Slowly Annabelle tipped the mug back and forth: the lake tried to stay level, its surface sliding up and down the smooth bank of glazed clay.

They were sitting in the living room: Annabelle and her mother. Though winter had maintained its grip, these March days were growing longer and pushing back the borders of the night. Filling the room was the golden glow of the late afternoon sun, making it look, Annabelle thought, like a painting covered by a thousand years of varnish, transforming her mother into a delicate figurine swimming behind the surface. Each of her slow movements was perfectly graceful, perfectly controlled; even her eyes had been muted by the sun: always dark and opalescent, they now had the dark closed smoothness of a statue.

Annabelle watched her mother's hands as she stirred sugar into her coffee — her little finger was poked so high into the air that Louis XLV must have woken up in heaven.

The dark lake of coffee rippled.

"Are you trying to get pregnant again?',

In this hollow light her mother's voice was like an echo.

"I guess so."

"You're not stopping it."

"No," Annabelle said.

Mrs. MacLeod sighed loudly, almost a groan. In the hospital Annabelle had woken up to that sigh, the morning after the miscarriage. She had thought it was her own breath being expelled, her mixed disappointment and relief finally coming out. But then she had seen her mother, dressed in the blue suit she had worn to the wedding, sitting with her hands twisted around a lace handkerchief, her cheeks wet.

"It's all right," Annabelle had said, as if it was she who was supposed to do the consoling. Just as it was she, the night before, who had been the one to order the taxi while Allen sat and gaped at the blood on her nightgown.

Since that time almost a whole year had gone by. "It was a disappointment," her mother had said, trying to be tactful as if it were some moral deficiency of Annabelle's that had torn at the insides of her womb, spit out a future that wouldn't be allowed to live. And Allen, useless when it happened and depressed after: his wide, ex-football player's body had slumped into itself for weeks.

"You aren't having any trouble?" Mrs. MacLeod asked.

"Trouble?"

"Trouble getting pregnant."

The sun had set behind the Wilson's house. Words floated, one at a time, across the darkening room. In her mother's tone Annabelle could now hear the "men are fools" voice that was reserved for them alone, the voice that connected them flesh-to-flesh into one being surrounded by a world where others existed only as watery shadows. Annabelle wondered what her mother would have thought of the tea party across the street.

"No," said Annabelle, "there won't be any trouble." She looked down at the surface of her coffee. It was now absolutely opaque. When she talked with her mother this way her voice changed too, becoming part of the conspiracy.

"And I suppose Allen is getting along?"

"He's busy," Annabelle said. "That's what he likes."

"He's clever," Mrs. MacLeod said. "We are always amazed by clever men." She reached up and snapped on the first lamp of the evening. It threw a soft yellow light around her, making the whole room focus on her face, the knowing shape of her mouth, her now wide-open eyes and raised eyebrows. Annabelle began to think about preparing supper. The conversation always ended with Allen, because after Allen's name was mentioned, there was nothing else that could be said.

Clever. Annabelle knew exactly what her mother meant by clever; when she said something in her telling way you could always hear the knife twisting in the background. *Clever:* sales-men who got you to buy a new miraculous vacuum cleaner, politicians who promised the earth and delivered themselves, lawyers who got caught using government money to sell land to themselves were clever.

The next morning, when she woke up, Annabelle realized that she had forgotten to buy grapefruit, her mother's favourite breakfast food. Dressing quickly she slipped out of the house and walked, almost ran, the two blocks to Mandowski's General Store. A blonde girl she had seen at church was at the cash, still rubbing the sleep out of her eyes as she rang Annabelle's purchases through the checkout counter.

Annabelle went out the door, still breathless from her rush through the cold air, and was distractedly clutching her bag of grapefruit with one gloveless hand and turning up her fur collar with the other when she felt a hand circling her arm strongly, above the elbow.

And then she was looking up at him.

In the bright sun his eyes were a glittering black. His thick brows and dark moustacheless beard were tinged with frost.

"Mrs. Jamieson." Even through the fur coat his tightly gripping hand hurt her arm.

The reflex that had burst out at Donna Wilson's was asleep this morning: in a dreamy way she remembered that she could still stamp on his instep, bring a knee up between his legs. The image floated by: Finch, doubled over, still clinging to her sleeve.

"Mrs. Jamieson, how nice to see you." His voice sounded not distant, as it had over the phone, but soft and personal. Then Annabelle realized that she was standing so close to him that their coats were touching.

"Mr. Finch, I'm sorry. I should look where I'm going."

"My pleasure, Mrs. Jamieson." He released her arm and stepped back. Her flesh felt bruised right down to the bone.

"It's good to see you out, Mrs. Jamieson. Is your breathing better today?"

"My breathing is excellent, Mr. Finch. Your advice was exactly what I needed."

"You have a sweet tongue, Mrs. Jamieson, even on the telephone."

There was no trace of a smile on his face. That was the thing about Finch, you were never quite sure if he was a moron or a wit. His voice was curiously deep, almost hypnotic; she could feel herself being drawn to him, wanting the pressure of his body against her own.

"You're too kind, Mr. Finch." For a moment she thought she might suddenly break down, just take the one step towards him, let his strong arms circle around her, close her off from everything else.

Now she saw he was nodding goodbye and starting on his way. She started to follow him; his back was already turned. She thought of calling out his name. *Finch.* Annabelle shook her head and began to walk slowly in the opposite direction.

Finch: what did she want with him? Annabelle walked past the church, towards the southern edge of the town, and she found herself standing in front of Salem's newest business, a used-car lot with acres of shining cars surrounding a neon-lit building. Maybe, she thought, she should just get it over with, go somewhere with Finch and do it in the back seat of a car. She shivered with disgust. He would probably spend the whole time preaching to her about the orphans of Thailand.

Or maybe she should forget about Finch and buy a new car. Allen, miraculously, was making money. She could buy a new car and then, if spring ever came, she could drive around the countryside, get to know some of Allen's famous nature.

She realized suddenly that the air had warmed up, that she had been walking for fifteen minutes with her coat open.

When she got home her mother and Allen were sitting at the kitchen table, drinking coffee and chatting, hardly aware she had been gone.

Five

A mist rose from the ground to meet the water that was trickling down the grooves of the barn's tin roof, and with his shoulder leaning into the familiar cedar, Finch breathed the deep sweet odour of cattle and spring rain.

After a winter of dazzling snow and ice the weather had suddenly changed, releasing the frost in a great rush. Now the ground was secret and enclosing at night, loosing green and swampy smells into the cold air, then turning warmer in the day, colouring seductively if there was sun, brightening even to the rain.

From the back door of his barn, Finch could let his eyes rest on the surrounding crest of hills, and the still leafless trees that rose like old broken fingers from the horizon.

But today he was curiously unsettled, unable to find comfort even in this serene vista of his own land. Even more hopeless was the view in the other direction. In fact the front doors of the barn were kept permanently latched because what they saw was civilization: the hydro poles with their black ropy lines, the small frame house where Finch lived with his wife and two children. In that house his mornings began, first making the girls' breakfasts, then washing the dishes while the girls put on their outdoor clothes and went down to the road to wait for the yellow schoolbus.

With the children safely on their way to school he would reach for the coveralls hanging by the kitchen door. Then he would go upstairs and stand in the doorway of Maureen's room.

"You need anything?"

"No, thank you."

"I could bring you some tea."

Some days he would avoid the confrontation by calling from the bottom of the stairs, others he would go right to her and look at her calmly, as though there was nothing to be hidden.

On the way to the barn he always reached for his pipe and tobacco. He knew, as he walked, that Maureen was sitting in the wicker wheelchair in her room, and that her eyes were following his progress, shooting out their hatred to his back.

On this first day of April Finch was well insulated from such unpleasant thoughts.

The long interior of the barn stood between himself and the locked front doors, between himself and the hydro pole that fed both barn and house, the house where his wife would now breathe easy in his absence, the driveway that was rutted with the tracks of his own car and those of strangers, and the road itself.

That road was where the world began. It was a nuisance — because of what it brought towards him — but it was also the most necessary blessing — an escape route that could carry him away when his mind started to strain with the task of locking each person and feeling into its assigned room.

Finch, feeling restless still, stood at the back door of his newly cleaned barn, listening to the sound of cows grinding at their hay. To protect his eyes and his pipe from the rain he was wearing a wide-brimmed hat, and as he set out walking up the hill from the barn he tried to keep to the drier ground, stepping from rock to rock when he could.

At the crest of the hill he paused and looked out at the valley ahead: there was a sloping field that gave way to a maple bush, and in the midst of the trees was a narrow, rocky river that now overflowed with spring run-off.

So much snow and water had drained through the ground that the valley seemed to lie in front of him like an enormous and exhausted woman whom God Himself had come down and taken in a month-long frenzy of passion and rain; and in this slow drizzle Finch could see that the earth was woozily trying to resurrect itself, to ready itself for the wild explosion of roots shooting out from the hearts of millions of buried seeds.

In the winter the field at the top of the hill had been white with snow and ice. Now its ploughed furrows were long black canals, filled with water. If it kept raining like this, the seeds would rot and the field would lie dark and sullen the whole summer long. Every spring Finch worried this way, but every spring the field finally dried out; in a few weeks Finch would worry instead that the thick and flowery crop was growing too well, that the palsied engine of his old tractor would collapse under the strain of the harvest.

The fence Finch stood by had two layers. The first was composed of grey fieldstones, round and spotted with moss and lichen. The second was cedar rails, themselves looking ancient and scarred by weather and cows, hooves. But in fact Finch himself had built it, splitting and wiring together the rails with the aid of a parishioner grateful for his help with a cow in labour.

Most mornings, Finch would climb this fence and make his way across the field to the treed valley and the river. But today, as he stood and searched for a course round the edge of that field that would avoid his ploughing, the restlessness that had plagued him at the barn began to surface again. His coveralls were soaked through and a warm turbulent wind had started from the south.

There were still several hours before the schoolbus returned, and Finch turning and started walking back towards the road. His concentration was broken and his mind already captured by that whole complex swirl of thoughts and sensations that started up whenever he was in the car.

The highway that led south from Salem to Kingston had been a wagon trail when the farms around it existed only in the imagination of a surveyor. Now the trail was paved, and there was a point where the pavement curved suddenly and rose so that Finch's car was brought out of a small valley, to a height that looked over the city of Kingston.

This was the place where his father, driving in an uncertain old Model A with the dusty blue beauty of his own shabby suit, used to say to the young Gordon Finch: "There, look at that, the city." And when Bob Finch pointed out the city to his son, there was always a note of satisfaction in his voice, as though to say: "*There*, damn it boy, I've invented this city for you. It may be small but, damn it, I pulled it out of my mind while we were driving here, while the best you could do was lean against the door and keep from throwing up."

And so Finch, reaching this same place in the now widened and improved road, felt obscurely proud when he saw the city. Even its northward growth from the rim of the lake gave him a sense of something accomplished.

Today his arrival at the height of land coincided with a slowing of the rain. All morning the sun had managed only a luminous shimmer of light through the clouds; now it was a white, veiled disk threatening to break free.

Like a bride, Finch thought, and then wondered how it was that the sun, which showed itself naked every day, could be a bride. And the answer came to him right away: the answer was that the sun's innocence was so striking, so total, that the more naked it was, the less the eye could bear to regard it. That's good, Finch thought, and then wondered how his congregation would react if he explained this to them. Most likely they would not understand, unless their marriages, like his own, led to thinking about brides whose skin bedazzled the eyes.

In his own youth he had been sickly and thin and *his* skin was pale from staying up half the night reading the Bible and praying. At that time he even prayed when he drank, even, as Stanley Kincaid once teased him, drank in order to pray.

Now, at forty-two, Finch felt that he was just entering a long and well-earned prime. His shoulders were wide and his face, ringed by a dark, thick beard, was deeply tanned. His hands were swollen from working with animals, and when he brought his fist down on the pulpit's lectern, with the whole weight of his big body behind it, the lectern shook and the pulpit vibrated and the whole church echoed with the noise of his tempered fist slamming into the wood because he wasn't just a man anymore, he was God's messenger and God's wrath should shake a church, even a stone one.

As for his own anger, he wasn't sure what it could or couldn't shake. Not his wife Maureen, that was certain.

By the time Finch had driven through the outskirts of Kingston and reached his father's house, the sky had broken open, and black-faced clouds were rushing northward. It was almost twenty years since his mother had died. But it was only six months since his father had been killed, run over by a drunken driver as he crossed a downtown street, and the house still stood empty with a real-estate sign on the lawn.

Finch got out of the car and walked to the house. He unlocked the front door, scooped the mail from the floor and threw it on the dining-room table, then went upstairs to the bathroom. There he stripped off his coveralls and his shirt and shaved his upper lip with his father's razor. When he was finished he stood for a moment in front of the mirror, rubbing his throat where it itched, and inspecting the line of his beard over his jaws and chin.

He had a long, square-jawed face, and the beard gave it a strict and righteous aspect. But his teacher, whom he had copied, had approved. "You look older," he had said. "Up in Canada you'll need it. It takes a mature man to carry God's truth in a place like that."

Exactly what his teacher had meant by "like that" Gordon Finch had never asked. But he had agreed anyway, having already learned from his father that the force of God's word was precisely equal to the force of the body that proclaimed it.

Finch put on his shirt, then went downstairs and took a beer from the refrigerator.

This he drank while he walked round the house, checking that the doors were locked, the windows unbroken. He even went down to the basement to see if there was still fuel oil in the tank. In the six months since his father's death there had been not a single offer for this house. Covered with insulbrick and set on a cinderblock foundation, it was worth little more than the lot it was spoiling. And if it ever did sell, Bob Finch had directed that the money go to the Kingston Kiwanis Christmas

Club. "Might as well make a few people happy," said Bob Finch, "rather than have you waste it."

Finch, thinking of the funeral that still wasn't paid for, went to the living room and sat in an armchair for a few minutes. Restless, he had never been so restless. It was months since he had brought a woman to this house. A strange mourning — making illicit love in his father's bed — and for a few seconds he wondered what it would be like to have Nellie Tillson here, to still her trembling lips with his tongue.

He got to his feet and tapped his pipe into the fireplace. Nellie Tillson, no, she had been too young: he would have to wait a long time before he repeated himself with her.

He stretched. Nervous energy crackled through his bones like dry electricity. Nellie Tillson was only a girl: now he needed a woman, a stranger's hands to discover him, a stranger's body to release him. To his mind's eye came the face of Annabelle Jamieson. She was surely a stranger, a city woman like the tourists who wore coloured handkerchiefs around their hair in summer and shopped in the General Store wearing shorts and no brassieres. Annabelle Jamieson: he remembered her fist shooting into his breastbone — for days there had been a tiny twinge, small as her white, baby-sized knuckles, when he bent to throw a bale of hay.

Maureen had said she wanted him once. Maureen with her in-heat whisper had said that she could contain his explosions; but every time he needed her, every time he finally touched her, the nervous sweat would snap to the surface of her white skin. Her voice in heat, but her body frozen in the convent.

Finch was standing in the kitchen, putting the empty beer bottle in the highest of the several cartons stacked neatly beside the table, when he remembered the mail.

Aside from the usual bills there was only one real letter, and it was addressed to the Reverend Robert "Bob" Finch. This was neatly handwritten in a pen that used real ink. Every week there were a couple of these letters to his father. They were usually from former parishioners in the various old-age homes scattered around Kingston. At first Finch, feeling guilty and sentimental, would go to visit them, to bring in person the sad news of his father's death.

But most often the reaction to his news was querulous and angry. So now Finch usually wrote to say that the Reverend Robert Finch had passed away and that most mourners were donating five dollars to the Heart Fund. Finch walked to the front hall and put on one of his father's windbreakers. Then, still holding the envelope, which was by now crumpled from having been pushed through the sleeve, Finch inspected it once again and tore it open. What struck him at once was the handwriting; the words were written firmly, but with more strength than skill and looked like a fleet of ships, masts jostling for position.

Dear Reverend Bob,

I don't suppose you think of me but maybe you remember an old man who tried to contribute to your education. Now I am a bit down on my luck, though I have nothing to kick about, and I have to ask you to pay back the ten dollars I once loaned you at the Royal Hotel. I won't remind you what it was for, except to say that you did it upstairs, and I won't ask for interest even though that money went a lot further then than now. Don't be afraid to come and see me. I'm not sick and I'm not interested in any handouts, just what's coming to me.

> Your friend (in crime)
> Mike Taggart

Finch found him in a boarding house in downtown Kingston. At one time the house, which was three storeys of brick with two turrets and some elaborate, though decaying terrace work, would have been the residence of a British army officer. Now it was carved up into rooms and apartments.

Finch walked up the narrow stairs, which smelled of dried food and disinfectant. Taggart's room was at the back of the second storey. It was large and airy, with a glassed-in porch that was almost entirely surrounded by a huge dying elm.

When he knocked on the door he thought at first he had made a mistake, because the tiny figure sitting in the captain's chair looked like a child. But then the head turned and Finch saw walking towards him an old man dressed in perfectly ironed grey flannels, shined black patent leather shoes, a tailored shirt that was two shades of brown.

"Mike Taggart is the name." The hand he extended to Finch was supple and strong.

"Gordon Finch, Bob Finch's son." He looked down at Taggart, whose face was still upturned, waiting. He couldn't be five feet tall and Finch, who was used to children, had to restrain himself from patting his head. "My father was killed a few months ago, so I was the one who got your letter."

"I know," Taggart said. He withdrew his hand and sat back down in the captain's chair. "I wrote the letter because I thought it might get you to come here." From the breast pocket of his striped shirt he took out a leather case. Inside was a pair of horn-rimmed glasses, which he now put on. They made his eyes look like coins that had been buried too long.

"Well," Finch said. "I brought you the money." He reached for his wallet, then withdrew a ten-dollar bill. Taggart accepted the bill and, after inspecting it, folded it and put it in his leather case.

"Thanks," Taggart said. "But the truth is, I asked you here about something else." His voice had a rasping edge; he still had not invited Finch to sit down and Finch, standing, felt like an intruding giant. He backed away from Taggart, trying to find a comfortable distance.

"That girl down the Fifth Line is my niece," Taggart said. "You know who I mean?"

"Several families on the Fifth Line belong to our church," Finch said. "I don't teach the Sunday school anymore. My wife takes one class but mostly it's Mrs. Wilson now. I don't know all the names of the girls. I'm sorry."

"You're smooth, Finch but you're not going to wriggle off this one. The girl says she's pregnant and I don't think it happened in no Sunday school, do you?"

"I don't know what you're talking about," Finch said.

Taggart picked up a package of cigarettes. "Mind if I smoke?"

Finch shook his head.

"Some people ask before they light up," Taggart said. He took a cigarette, carefully rolled it between his fingers to test it for freshness, then inserted it in his mouth. "You look just like your father, and he was a randy bugger too. But he paid for what he got; even if he had to borrow the money, he paid." Taggart struck a match and took the first few puffs.

"It's Wednesday today, isn't it?" Taggart asked.

April Fool's Day, Finch thought.

"Well, boy, either you deliver ten thousand dollars to me at this address one week from today, or I'm going to have her slap a paternity suit on you."

"You're crazy."

"George Mandowski, the manager of the grocery store, saw you," Taggart said. "Your car was parked outside the old church opposite the Beckwith place."

"I'm interested in old churches," Finch said. "It's a natural thing." Mandowski, he should have known it would be him.

"He didn't recognize your car so he got out to make sure everything was all right. He walked across the yard and he looked in the window. It was you and the girl. You might have been down on your knees but you weren't saying no prayers."

"You're crazy."

"You said that," Taggart said. He casually held up one hand as Finch stepped towards him. "And before you get any ideas, I'd better tell you Mr. Mandowski has already been to visit my lawyer and has sworn out everything I just told you."

"Mandowski is the nosiest old woman in the county," Finch said. "His word isn't worth a forkful of sheepshit."

"Now, now," said Taggart. "Don't get agitated. It's a natural thing. It could happen to any man."

"It didn't happen to me," Finch said. He remembered Nellie Tillson clutching him to her, insisting, her cry of pain as he pierced into her.

For the first time Taggart grinned. Finch saw his teeth, which were false and perfect. "Your dad and I," Taggart said, "we used to go here and we used to go there. But he always paid before he played. Otherwise, it's them goddamn carrying charges that get you in the end."

"My father was a married man and a minister of God," Finch said, "and so am I."

"A week from today."

"God forgive you," Finch said. "I will pray for your soul." He walked out of the room and shouldered his way down the narrow staircase.

Mandowski's General Store was, like most of the other businesses of Salem, on that street which ran between the hotel and the Church of the New Age. In proximity it was closer to the hotel but otherwise it was considered neutral by the town, food being neither salvation nor sin.

George Mandowski had been the only foreigner in a school that hardly knew what a foreigner was, and after Finch himself had spent a year in Virginia, he had felt sorry for how Mandowski must have suffered. Not now though; as he walked into the store he only wished, thinking of Mandowski as a schoolboy, that he had hit him harder when he had the chance.

As he strode through the aisles Finch smiled at the noon-time shoppers. He was so angry that he could hardly see their faces. Then, two at a time, he mounted the back stairs that led to Mandowski's office. The way was familiar enough. Mandowski, although he was a Catholic, contributed to all the churches in Salem with equal and tax-deductible largesse.

At the landing Finch took a deep breath, trying to calm himself, then walked into Mandowski's office and slammed the pebble-glass door behind him. As always he noticed that beyond Mandowski and visible through the window rose the spire of his own church.

"Reverend Finch," Mandowski said. He stood behind his desk, and held out his hand.

Finch ignored the hand and sat down in the chair opposite.

Mandowski, still smiling and pleasant, also sat down.

"You've got a problem," Finch said. Every year Mandowski's face grew redder and softer. Today, it looked like blood pudding.

"A problem?"

"Either Mike Taggart is telling stories about you, or you are the stupidest fool in Salem township." Finch, hearing the threat in his own voice, tried again to be calm.

Mandowski smiled, but it wasn't the smile he gave when he was about to write a cheque. It was a weak smile, a curious, weak-but-strong smile, the one he used to give in the school-yard when he knew he was about to absorb another beating for his strange accent.

"You want a drink?" Mandowski asked. "Or I can have one of the girls get you a coffee?"

"You have a drink." Finch said. "You're going to need one." He wondered how Mandowski had thought he would get away with this.

Mandowski smiled. "I had to give it up," he said. "The doctor told me." All traces of his accent were long gone, and Mandowski spoke like any other prosperous pillar of the community. But although he was the same age as Finch, he appeared beyond physical activity. His arms were white and soft, and his chin and neck had come together to form a fleshy cushion that hung down from his jaws and was ended only by the collar of his shirt.

"You should get more exercise," Finch said, trying to keep the distaste out of his voice. Then the attempt at restraint broke; and Finch was leaning forward in the oak chair, his shoulders bulging out of his father's windbreaker. There was the small chain-like sound of a seam ripping; for the first time he realized that he was bigger than his father had been. "Don't ever let them put it to you," his father had said to Finch when he took over the parish. The nervous tension that had been running through Finch all day now sparked in his bones, ready to be released. He knew what his father would do in a situation like this.

"So," Finch said, keeping his voice soft, "you finally got the Tillson girl into trouble."

"No," Mandowski said, "I didn't do that."

"She's been working here all winter. It's awful nice of you to drive her home from work every night."

"Her father drives her home."

"Every night?"

"Sometimes my wife."

"I've been to see Mike Taggart."

"Uh-huh," Mandowski said.

"You did it, Mandowski, you've been wanting to get into that girl's pants for years and everyone knows it. You hired her so you could look down her dress. Then when she threatened to tell on you, you put her up to this."

Mandowski reached across his desk for a cigarette. It seemed very small in his large hands. He put it in his mouth. Finch slapped at Mandowski, breaking the cigarette and leaving the stub between Mandowski's lips. Mandowski pushed back from his desk and spat into the wastepaper basket. He stood up. His face and neck were flaming, and his hands clasped together. "She's a good girl, Finch, and she deserves what's coming to her."

"She doesn't deserve you, Mandowski."

"Just because you're a minister of that ten-cent church doesn't mean you can get away with your filth —"

Finch shot out of the chair, swinging across the desk. Mandowski was caught on the point of the chin and knocked backwards into the wall.

Finch, watching Mandowski struggle to get up, was suddenly reminded of the last time he had hit him, of the time he had caught Mandowski behind the school and pounded him into the clapboard wall, one blow after the other until Mandowski rolled up into a ball and covered his head with his hands. He never cried, Finch remembered, that was the thing about him: no matter how hard you hit he never cried.

"I don't insult your church," Finch said. "Kindly keep your mouth shut about mine."

Mandowski was now leaning against the window, breathing heavily and rubbing his jaw.

"About that affidavit," Finch began. His temples were pounding with the desire to fight. He wanted to be a child again, he wanted to be young so he could hit Mandowski until his arms were too sore to lift. If he did that now he would kill him.

"Get out."

"Maybe you'd think it over."

"Get out," Mandowski said, "before I call the police."

Finch stepped around the desk. Then he yanked Mandowski forward by the tie and pushed him down into his chair.

"All right," Mandowski said. He picked up the telephone.

Finch watched Mandowski's large white hands as he dialled the first two numbers. Then Finch grabbed the telephone from Mandowski and tore the cord out of the wall.

"You bastard," Mandowski said. His voice, so nervous that it squealed, was almost comical. Finch saw Mandowski open the top desk drawer; suddenly there was a revolver in his hand. "How I'd like to shoot you." Mandowski's voice trembled again. Finch hesitated.

He had never faced a gun before and now his eyes were filled with the sight of it, with the shining blue barrel and its gaping mouth, with Mandowski's pudgy hand with its pudding fingers that were squeezing themselves into a fist around the trigger. There was a deafening explosion. Finch swayed for a moment, unsure where he had been hit. He wanted to cough, his fist swung up to his breastbone, trying to knock the acrid smoke from his lungs. Then he turned and saw a large and jagged hole in the wall.

There was a rush of footsteps on the stairs and Mandowski's office door was pushed open.

"It's all right," Mandowski said. "I was just showing the Reverend my new toy."

Nellie Tillson looked back and forth between the two men. Finch watched her eyes widen, watched the way fear slowly gripped and contorted her features, forced her lips apart and her mouth open.

An ugly blue egg was rising on Mandowski's chin where Finch had hit him. A carton of papers had been overturned. White powder was slowly draining from the edges of the broken plaster, and Mandowski's hand hung at his side, the gun loose in his fingers.

"Good day, Reverend," Mandowski said.

Six

*K*neeling in her backyard, Annabelle Jamieson plunged her fingers into the cold earth. Officially she was supposed to be working. In her studio was a half-finished design for a new dinnerware pattern, but the afternoon sun had been too warm to resist and she had decided to walk to the store. There she had met Donna Wilson. And as they stood talking, she had chosen two flats of pansies for planting along the back of the house.

"They'll freeze," Donna Wilson warned. "You should leave them in the boxes and bring them in at night."

Now the sky had clouded over, and the first drops of rain were beginning to fall.

Annabelle watched the purple and yellow petals yielding to the wind, the stalks bending and the silky white undersides of the flowers flashing like cheerleaders' panties. She was using a soup spoon to dig out the earth, a silver wedding spoon that was now bent and twisted.

Methodically she pressed the roots into the ground, patted the moist soil protectively around the stems. Even though she was wearing a sweater she could see goosebumps on her wrists; and as she was finishing with the last plant she noticed that it wasn't just rain that was falling, there were little icy particles slamming into the stone wall of the house.

When she raised her eyes she saw a faint flash of lightning. Instantly Annabelle was on her feet, running for the house. When the first thunder came she shivered, but rushed outside again, her arms full of newspapers.

As the wind sprang up Annabelle spread the papers over the flowers, trying to shelter them from the hail.

There was a second flash of lightning. This one was much brighter, illuminating the dark sky and disappearing in a jagged line behind the steeple of the church. When the thunder came it seemed to explode upward from the ground, jolting the whole lawn as if it intended to search her out and knock her over.

Annabelle looked round the garden, then saw a pile of sticks from a dismantled trellis. As the wind grew stronger she carried them to the flower bed, laid them as weights to keep the newspapers in place. She was just wondering if the flowers would be crushed anyway when the lightning started again.

Inside her studio Annabelle closed the windows and switched on the lights. On her work table was the unfinished pattern. Her carefully designed sets of dinnerware had provided the down payment for this house, and sometimes Annabelle, thinking about Ottawa's diplomats eating from their smoothly glazed surfaces, wondered if their food tasted different because the plates from which they were eating had bought Allen's freedom.

Or perhaps they didn't think of such things. Rich diplomats had the problems of the world to consider: the difficulty of getting a good dry cleaner, their chances of being taken hostage. Allen was only one unimportant real-estate lawyer caught in one small attempt to bribe a civil servant, possibly even a civil servant who owned a set of her dinnerware. Allen had been caught but no charges were laid. Just a minor adjustment was necessary: he had paid the rest of his partnership debt; his name had been taken off the letterhead; and he had left the firm and the city. He had been lucky. Some people, people without money, had to go to jail when they were caught.

The wind was howling loudly now, and sleet rattled like bullets against the glass. Annabelle was sure the windows were going to break and she moved away from her table towards the middle of the room. As she did there was a new flash of lightning. This time the sky was a bright, malevolent yellow, a cat's eye, and the lightning zigzagged through it like a giant, throbbing vein.

She was still looking at this after-image when the thunder

followed — a single giant clap that shook the walls of the house.

On the mantel of the fireplace was an antique ship's clock that she and Allen had bought at an auction. It said seven o'clock. Allen was working late, but she knew he would have started home with the beginning of the storm.

The lightning was dancing above the church. As if, Annabelle thought, it was pointing at Finch: Finch, as demonic as the lightning. Finch, standing in his pulpit, his arms spread wide, needing only a cape to be a giant Dracula ready to ravish the entire congregation.

Her arms were folded across her chest, her hands cupping her breasts to protect them from the storm. The lightning flashed but she was oblivious. In her mind was first Maureen's white neck, stiff and rigid, and then Finch's face, leaning towards her on the street.

Old bedroom eyes, Donna Wilson called him.

Annabelle turned and walked out of her studio.

In her kitchen she was surrounded by things she had made: watercolours on the wall, dishes, mugs and bakeware, even the pine table, which she had not exactly made but had found and stripped down, sanded and varnished until the creased surface of the wood shone like old leather.

With its small window and warm, dark colours the kitchen was the one room that could shut out a storm. Storms, the slow-changing seasons of a small town: until Allen was forced out of his firm, leaving Ottawa never would have occurred to Annabelle. But when the crises had come — first her miscarriage, then Allen's disaster — she had been the one to realize that decisions were necessary. And she had been the one to say how sensible a small town would be; meaning of course, that it would be a sensible place for Allen to hide from the rumours that needed time to exhaust themselves.

But Salem itself had been Allen's inspiration.

One fall day they had spent the whole afternoon driving in the warm yellow-red haze of autumn leaves, the sun baking them through the windows of the car. "Look at this," Allen had said when, following a random road around a lake, they had suddenly chanced on Salem.

"It's just a town."

"It's like the village I grew up in," Allen said. "Only it hasn't changed." He opened the door. "Come on, let's get out and walk."

They had parked beside the hotel. There was a dirt road leading down to the lake. It was lined with huge, arching maple trees whose dying leaves were a luminous yellow-gold in the sun. Reluctantly, she had climbed out of the car. And then, stretching, inhaled the cool air. After the heat of the car it was suddenly fresh and pungent.

"Let's go this way," Annabelle said.

The water was absolutely still, a blue glass coma in the sun. They strolled along the shore and then turned into the town again, up another side road. That was when they saw the house. It was exactly the house she had dreamed of as a child: a solid stone house, not too big, with its front door in the centre, the porch roof held up by two fake Greek stone columns, large windows on either side. The lawn was clean and raked, the woodwork and eavestroughing were freshly painted white, there was a FOR SALE sign planted in the grass beside the flagstone walk.

They moved in on Hallowe'en. All afternoon and then into the evening they carried furniture and cardboard boxes from the moving van they'd rented. They bought a pumpkin, carved it with Allen's boy-scout knife, and set it in the window. The two children from across the street came and they gave them apples and bologna sandwiches. At midnight the sky clouded over and it began to snow, the first of the season, and while they did the final unloading, they were sheeted in white flakes.

That had been almost six months ago. Her money had provided the down payment for the house; and although the town had been Allen's discovery, it had been her decision.

She was standing in the centre of her living room, convinced that at any moment the glass would shatter inwards at her face, when Allen, soaking wet, burst in the door.

"Are you all right?"

"I'm fine. Don't come too close, the glass is going to break."
She still had her arms crossed and her fingers gripped her sides.

"I'll get you a drink."

"Thank you," Annabelle said, not moving. There was another burst of lightning and thunder and she dug her nails in deeper. After a bad storm there were sometimes little rows of red half-moons dug into the flesh between her armpits and her breasts where the nails had broken the skin.

"You didn't have to come home," she said later, "I would've been all right." She was on her second scotch and they were sitting in the living room, on the couch farthest from the window. The storm had moved away and their conversation was punctuated only by brief echoes of thunder and barely visible winks in the sky.

"It doesn't matter. You did just fine."

"It does matter, but let's forget it. How did things go at the office today?"

"All right. The Reverend Mr. Finch dropped in to see me."

"He did?" Annabelle found herself trying to mask her voice.

"He wants us to come to his church on Sunday. What is it, the Church of the New Testament or something?"

"The Church of the New Age," Annabelle supplied. "We've been there several times."

"That's it. Your family belonged to some crazy church, didn't they?"

"They were Free Methodists," said Annabelle, "and they weren't crazy, just very boring. In fact I was just thinking about the minister today; he was very sweet."

"What were you thinking about him?"

"I was remembering his funeral."

"You must have really liked him."

"You'd make a good lawyer." She shifted farther away from Allen on the couch. They never really fought, just sparred. She couldn't have stayed with someone who liked fighting. Some of their married friends in Ottawa had loved to fight, staged enormous dramas, which ended in their screaming at each other, saying unforgivable things that the women would confide to Annabelle the following day.

"He said he'd already met you. He's a real admirer of yours."

"I went with Donna to his women's group. We had tea and discussed various charitable projects. Then he went round and asked people if they had any problems. It was ludicrous, a sort of small-town group therapy." Annabelle looked at Allen, wondering if this would be enough. She felt a sudden nervous tremor, as if she had already deceived him with Finch. But she hadn't even lied yet, she had only omitted the detail that the meeting had been in Donna's living room and that she and Donna had been the whole group. Afterwards Donna had said she wasn't going to tell Charlie, because he didn't like Finch. Not that it mattered if he found out. "So I said I wasn't going to tell him my real problems, but that sometimes I had trouble breathing."

"That's a good one," Allen said.

"He told me to push out my stomach when I breathed in, that it would let in more air."

Allen laughed. "That's a good one," he said again. "I wouldn't have thought the Reverend would have a sense of humour." He stood up, holding his empty glass. "Anyway, I'm too drunk to eat. Let's go to bed."

As they were climbing the stairs, Allen added that he had agreed to bring Annabelle to church the following Sunday, just to give it another try.

"Do you mind?"

"Church? Of course not."

Before Allen, there had been others. "The usual," she had said to Donna Wilson, but she had no idea what the usual was. After she had graduated from university she had insisted on moving away from her parents to her own apartment. There had been college boys, the initial encounter with the photographer, then the uncontrolled affair with Isaac. At the time she had thought it was love; later she had decided it was just craziness. The day she met Isaac had been the day her mother told her she was leaving her father: in the European way.

Isaac was not in the European way. He was, as it turned out, in the family way: a wife and three children.

She had met Issac in a jewellery store — his — in downtown Ottawa. She had gone there to buy herself a ring, on a whim, because all her friends were getting married. Isaac was a tall gaunt-faced man with black woolly hair that had gone grey at the temples, and he had an arched Semitic nose that made him look proud, even vain. He looked more like a soldier than a businessman and as he tried different rings on her fingers she noticed that his own were long and strong, with tiny tufts of black hair.

Within a couple of weeks, it had turned out that her consolation was to be not a ring but Isaac himself. It would have been perfect except for one detail: her mother, who had warned her against everything else, had forgotten to tell her about married men.

Like an alarm, Isaac went off every midnight. "I have to go home," he would mutter. For a while, Annabelle acquiesced, grateful for what she had. But one night as she sat on the bed, she noticed small blue islands had formed on the insides of her thighs — bruises from their lovemaking.

"Don't you love me?"

"Of course I love you." This was the first time the word had been mentioned, love. Annabelle watched Isaac's face as he said it: he had dark bow lips that kissed her hungrily but seldom spoke. These nights of intimacy had not changed her first impression of him: a warrior, Isaac had a long sinewy body that twisted and grappled with such intensity that Annabelle thought he must be reliving old biblical wars.

"Why can't you stay?"

She watched him back away, suddenly weak: "I don't want to hurt her feelings."

"Hurt her feelings? Isaac, how do you know where to draw the line? Does she say it's okay if you see me until midnight, but if you sleep over, then that's bad?"

"I don't know." He reached for the bedside table, where he kept his perpetual glass of whiskey.

Annabelle's hair, undone the way Isaac liked it, lay curled on her shoulders, and she was conscious, as she turned towards him, of its silky drag across her skin.

Silky smooth for Isaac, washed and double-shampooed so that it would bring pleasure to *his* skin.

Annabelle stood up. In one hand she clutched the corner of a pillow. She stepped towards Isaac, who backed away.

"You don't know," Annabelle said. It was as though she had been possessed by a stranger. Angry, so enraged she could feel her face burning and her whole naked body tremble, she advanced on Isaac and screamed, "You don't know." Then with all her strength she swung the pillow into Isaac's face, hitting him so hard that his head twisted and knocked into the wall with a soft *plunk*.

"Isaac, you bastard."

His bow lips were pressed tight, his stone face still except for a nervous rippling of the skin beside one brown eye. Isaac's mouth opened to speak and Annabelle stepped back, covering her nakedness with the pillow.

"I love you," Isaac said, his voice tight.

"You love your wife, your comfortable life, your shop that brings in pretty young women."

"I love you, Annabelle. I love you most of all."

"If you love me," Annabelle said, "then the next time you come, you can stay all night."

"You know I can't."

"Then don't come."

"But I love you." Isaac had begun to cry. Now he fell to his knees, weeping, and crawled towards her, his long arms reaching out. Then he was covering her legs with kisses, kissing her feet, kissing her shins, weeping and kissing her thighs while Annabelle at first melted, relented, and then finally started pushing him away. But Isaac was too strong for her; he only kept crying and trying to seduce with his kisses while she weakly pushed and beat his jacketed shoulders with her fists. Finally she slid her fingers into his curly black hair and, pulling it as hard as she could, screamed, *"Isaac!"*

Isaac, clutching his scalp, fell to the floor. Annabelle bent down, picked up Isaac's glass of whiskey; as he struggled to his feet she threw it in his face. "Drink this, you pig!" she shrieked. Then collapsed on the bed, crying uncontrollably. But in the midst of her tears she had the idea that the photographer, were he to see this scene, would burst out laughing.

"Annabelle, Annabelle."

The bed sagged with his weight and Isaac's jacketed arm scratched at her back. Annabelle pulled the sheet over her head. The comic possibilities of Isaac had never before occurred to her.

"Annabelle."

"Leave, Isaac. Go away, disappear, eat a pig on Sabbath."

The bed bounced as he stood up.

"Annabelle, you can't talk to me like that."

"Get out, Isaac."

"Maybe we could see a movie on Monday."

She sat up and opened her eyes. "What?"

"Goodbye," Isaac said. "I'll see you Monday." Through his whiskey-soaked shirt Annabelle could see the dark shadow of his chest. His face was normal again: the strong nose and wide brown eyes, the pursed bow lips. She wondered what it would take to force his mind, for one second, to focus on something outside of itself.

When he was gone she went back to the bedroom and got dressed.

The ache that had been so sweet and loving when Isaac was there to satisfy it was now an unpleasant stranger. She walked around the apartment, switching off all the lights, and then she put on a record. In the dark with the sounds of jazz piano filtering through the rooms, she lay down on her couch. Soon she was caught up by the melody and, half-hypnotized, she looked contentedly out at the play of the streetlights off the new green leaves of the basswood tree that grew outside her window.

On her left wrist was a gift from Isaac, an expensive gold watch with a matching strap and a Swiss brand name she had never heard of. Even when she had swung the pillow into his face she must have been wearing it, and thinking of that she heard again the contrite *plunk* of Isaac's black woolly hair being driven into the plaster of her bedroom wall. According to the illuminated watch dial, it was now twenty-six minutes after twelve. Despite her tantrums Isaac had left, as always, exactly at midnight.

Now, almost calm in the darkness, Annabelle took off the

watch and rested it in her palm. It was miraculously light, miraculously small, and yet inside, chorus of tiny gears was performing a wonderful metal ballet.

"It glows in the dark," she had said to Isaac.

"It glows just a little."

"I thought that watches that glow in the dark gave you cancer."

"This one just gives you a little cancer."

She balanced the watch in her fingers. If in one decisive gesture she could just let her arm swing back, could just fling the watch against the wall, it would shatter and she would be rid of Isaac. Now, before it hurt too much.

Suddenly remorseful she thought of Isaac standing by the door, his gold tie-pin glinting in the hall light, irresistible Isaac with his gaunt, shadowed cheeks and his desperate needs. She set the watch on the bookcase. "Poor Isaac," she whispered. Then she went to the bathroom and ran a bath. Once in the warm water, she propped her feet up at the end, and set the hot tap to drip in new water at exactly the same rate as the overflow drain let it out. In one hand she had a paperback novel, in the other Isaac's bottle of whiskey. Occasionally, when the taste was too offensive, she held the neck to the dripping tap. The best comedians, she remembered, always kept the stage to themselves.

Annabelle woke up with a start, fear pumping through her so strongly she thought she must be having some sort of attack. In the night she had twisted away from Allen and now she was almost clinging to the edge of the bed. As she stood up she felt, in her stomach, a tugging sensation. That was how her miscarriage had started, a light and innocent tug at her insides, a small hand caressing the inner wall of her womb, experimentally pulling itself free.

She bent over, pushed in her stomach with her hand as if to preserve the mythical child. Then she remembered it was only a week since her last period; there was no one to save.

Through the window she could see the spire rising from the stone church. A narrow triangle, it perfectly pierced the few stars bright enough to be visible against the moon.

Annabelle walked out of the bedroom into the hall. There she had once more the strange sensation of fibres tearing free from the walls of her insides, and she stopped, rigid with fear, her hand pressed to her belly.

In Ottawa it had started the same way. One night, when she was three months pregnant, she had woken up to go to the bathroom.

Everything had been perfectly normal; the morning sickness was over and her body was adjusting to this new and growing presence that had just started to make her belly round, a little pot, a balloon at that point where it had just stopped resisting.

That night she had taken the first few steps from the bed to the bathroom and then, through the webs of sleep felt the sensation that had haunted her the whole night, the feeling of small fingers tearing free.

She had tried to convince herself that this strange feeling was only another of those unusual feelings that happened with a first pregnancy, the gradual chorus of physical events that had started to blend into the sounds of an orchestra tuning up for a grand performance.

But as she took the last few steps to the bathroom, panic flared through her; and when she sat down on the toilet her whole insides caved way, the bubble inside her exploding, blood like flames on the insides of her thighs.

Now Annabelle switched on the bathroom light and got herself a glass of water. Her face in the mirror was flushed with sleep; her eyes were moist and glistening. Thirty-two years old was young enough; the doctor had said there was plenty of time to get pregnant again.

Annabelle stepped back, trying to see herself as Finch did. There had been a time, after all, when men had pursued her for her looks. But would Finch care about such things? Would he send her flowers, as Allen had, with a card saying that he had dreamed about her eyes until he couldn't sleep? Would he chase her home and throw her in a snowbank, die of shame if she didn't return his love, burst into tears if he couldn't kiss her on the first date?

Finch: she had known as soon as Allen mentioned his name that it was time to start lying.

Finch, Annabelle thought: whatever Finch saw couldn't be found in a bathroom mirror, couldn't be figured out by knowing Allen. Allen, who spoke into a dictaphone, was not a preparation for Finch who shouted and ranted at his congregation. And Allen, who was clever and had secrets, was going to be no warning for Finch who was bold and violent. Finch had tried to kill Mandowski in his office at the store; Donna Wilson had reported that. Not Finch, Annabelle thought: she didn't want anything with Finch. After all, as Donna had said, it would be hard to be the wife of a crazy minister who screws the girls in his own Sunday school. And to be one of the girls, that would only be worse.

Annabelle, in the upstairs hall of her own dark house, heard the oil burner switch on. A few seconds later the furnace fan began to blow hot air through the newly installed ductwork. She was standing near a grate and the hot air searched her out, made her nightgown billow and tongued her legs.

She walked back to the bedroom, looked out the window to the church spire once more. In the moonlight her eyes were a dark and luminous brown, and her hair hung like a cowl about her cheeks and shoulders. Each time she exhaled, the window briefly misted. Thirty-two years old: her life seemed to be slipping by, sneaking free from her the way Isaac used to at midnight, the way the unborn foetus had bolted from her womb.

"Bad luck," the doctor had said. "Nothing to worry about. And besides, you have your own life to live."

Climbing into bed beside Allen, Annabelle tried to think of what her own life might be. Perhaps it was her career, her glazed dinnerware that was sold in certain gift stores every Christmas, or by special order at a very high price. Or her family: her mother, an eccentric woman with a narrow, pinched face and an unpredictable tongue; and her father, a retired schoolteacher with a perfect memory for *Reader's Digest* jokes, bridge hands and euchre odds. Or perhaps it was her husband who counted — Allen, the clever lawyer who had the bad luck to be caught doing something stupid, now putting in the time to heal his reputation and his finances — then there would be the inevitable move to the bigger city, a new law firm; by then he would be perfect, seasoned and mature. They would both be perfect, Annabelle thought, perfect, professional and careful: a couple that knew how to live, a couple that knew what mattered to them and where to draw the line.

Not much of a life, Annabelle thought. But just the same, the ache in her stomach was gone, and as she snuggled next to Allen, a feeling of contentment settled through her. Finch? She had already learned her lesson with Isaac.

When she woke up it was late. The bright morning sun streamed through the opened curtains and Allen had left for work. Hurriedly, Annabelle dressed and rushed outside, feeling as soon as she opened the door the shock of summer on her face and neck. She breathed deeply, then hesitantly placed one bare foot onto the grass. The sun was so warm that it dried her feet even as she walked across the wet lawn to her flowers. The trellises had kept the newspapers in place, but they were sodden wet and had been driven into the ground by the rain.

She pulled the papers away. At first she thought the flowers had been killed; they were pressed down, their petals flat against the soil. But then, as she straightened them, she saw the stems had only been bent; soon her whole row of flowers was standing brightly in the sun.

Annabelle was just balling up the sopping papers when she saw Donna coming towards her from across the street. Donna was wearing jeans and a T-shirt and seemed to have lost ten years overnight.

Annabelle remembered waking in the night, her dream about Isaac, the tugging in her stomach, the doubts about Finch and Allen. Then there was a new warm breeze, she could feel the sun's heat reflecting from her beautiful stone house, and the night sealed over.

Seven

*A*t the back of the lawn, untrimmed grass rose jagged against the white-painted fence and around the base of the small apple tree. Scattered through this fringe were bright yellow butter-cups. Annabelle, sitting contentedly in her studio, watched them waver in the breeze that was coming across the lawn and through her screened windows.

With the warm and perfect weather, Annabelle felt that she had finally begun to settle into a rhythm of work. For one thing, she had taken the top off her work table, a project she had been vaguely planning for years, and replaced it with a new piece of wood she had painted a bright and cheerful blue. Then she had covered the coat of acrylic paint with several layers of plastic varnish. So instead of having a scratched and pitted surface that kept absorbing water from the clay as she worked, she now had a perfectly hard surface that was easily cleaned.

And on this new and promising surface, after a frenzied few weeks of churning out another round of dinnerware, she had accelerated work on the mosaic begun during the first part of the winter. Now every morning she made her figurines. And there was something about being able to sit at her work table and doodle with clay that made her want to get up in the morning, to be at work with a fresh cup of coffee and a view of her newly green backyard. Sketched on one of her whitewashed walls was the finished plan for her first mosaic. She had spent almost a week drawing it in pencil, rubbing out and redrawing when necessary, once painting over a whole section, until she had given birth to a wonderfully mottled and dense surface, pencil lines everywhere. In the same wry spirit she had talked to Allen about it, she had signed it, in tiny letters near the bottom right-hand corner, *my Guernica, A.J.*

But in fact she thought of it as something entirely different, not Guernica or Spanish or foreign at all but as the town of Salem. Its entire past, present and future would be shown as a sea of figures from different generations riding on no other surface but each other. On her wall had grown a self-sustaining mass of pencil lines, erased intentions, areas whitewashed in and out of existence, limbs, heads, breasts, hips, in a dance so unbearably interconnected and clear that when Annabelle regarded it for more than a moment, the fixed figures would start to waver; then rumours and gossip, whole sagas would begin to shoot out of the picture like sparks from a fire, and she would have to let the image blur, set again, go back to lying at peace.

To some she had already assigned names. The stocky bearded man from the newspaper office was Jacob Beam. Now when he tipped his hat and said, "Good afternoon, Mrs. Jamieson," she could say, "Good afternoon, Mr. Beam," never missing his name for a moment because she had him right here, at home, to practise with. And when she went for an ice cream, she could smile and say, "Thank you, Mrs. Fitzhenry," and how was Mrs. Fitzhenry to know that there was a figure of her, stooping shoulders and all sitting with her arms akimbo in a wooden frame in her study. Even the newspaper boy was there, young Ralph Paul with his lick of hair brushed to the right over his face and the grey canvas *Whig-Standard* bag hanging over his stomach. Would they all think, if they knew, that she was practising voodoo against them? Or would they dismiss it as a harmless variation of the way they recreated each other every day with gossip and exaggerated stories?

Donna Wilson said all small towns were like this, that she herself didn't repeat rumours though she didn't mind hearing a good story, but even the tongueless Donna Wilson had now told her so much that Annabelle couldn't meet someone on the

street, couldn't say, "Good day, Mr. Beam," or "Good afternoon, Reverend," without the decades of scandals and lies,
improprieties and webs of deceit that this person was accused of
coming to her mind. So that the actual person that she was
greeting, the washed-out, innocent-looking personage in the
street, always seemed nothing more than a mere and insub-
stantial shadow of the stories that had preceded. Mr. Jacob
Beam and Mrs. Lennie Fitzhenry had, for example, been suspected of dealing in more than newspapers and ice cream. It was
even said that "one night Lennie Fitzhenry sockoed her
drunken husband halfway across the kitchen and told him if he
ever interfered with her Jacob she would do a lot worse." This
Donna Wilson had told her.

"What would be a lot worse?" Annabelle had asked Donna.
"Killing him?"

Donna had laughed. "Oh God, no, people don't kill each
other here, you must really think we're savages. *Leaving* him is
what I meant."

"I don't understand," Annabelle had said, puzzled. "Why
don't they split up? If they hate each other and they're both
involved with other people, wouldn't they be happier apart?"

But as soon as she said the words, she knew they were
wrong, because in a town of three hundred people what was the
use of separating and regrouping with someone else? It would
only confuse the children and encourage the real-estate sales-
man.

"I would never leave Charlie," Donna said. "Never."
Annabelle had always thought the Wilsons, with their neater-
than-neat house, their three outdoor Christmas trees all strung
with coloured lights, their two perfectly mannered children,
were totally happy and committed to each other.

"I hope not," Annabelle had finally said, as Donna glared at
her with uncharacteristic intensity, daring her to contradict.

From the next room Annabelle could now hear the telephone ringing. The sound was low and muted — when she had
started to work on her pottery again Allen had suggested that
the telephone repairman could accomplish this — and now,
instead of being an intrusion, Annabelle regarded the telephone

as a nicely independent purring cat that needed no response unless she felt like it. This morning, as during most mornings, she didn't. So with her newly moistened hands and some cool clay taken out from under its covering cloth, she began to make a figure of someone hunched over, on his knees, talking on a telephone. That was the wonderful thing about this new project, everything that happened could be used.

"Just like therapy," she had said to Donna Wilson.

"Therapy?"

"I mean everything fits in," Annabelle had said.

Donna, her bleached blonde hair tightly bound in curlers, had just nodded and said, "Oh yes," then reached over for one of her own excellent shortbread cookies.

The telephone stopped, then started again, and this time Annabelle didn't find it quite so easy to ignore. Only her mother, she knew, telephoned once, hung up, then started again; and if it was her mother she could do the same trick over and over for hours, until finally Annabelle broke down and answered.

"God, Annabelle, what are you doing?"

"Oh, Allen, I'm sorry. I thought it was my mother."

"If you're not too busy today, I was wondering if you could do me a favour."

Annabelle hesitated. The wet magic of the clay, the cool yellow luminous world that she was creating were suddenly reduced to her own dirty hands and the fact that she didn't have a job. "Sure," she said. "What is it?"

"There's a document I need delivered, and my secretary is off today, so I can't go out. Do you mind?"

"Of course not. I'll just clean up here and be right over."

"Clean up? I thought you said —"

"Never mind, I was just thinking of going outside."

Although she had owned it for a month, Annabelle was still surprised to see in her driveway the white MG convertible with shiny wire wheels and a hard black top that could be removed for summer driving. There were deep leather seats, a recessed dash, a motor that snapped to life with the first turn of the heavy steel key and then roared so loudly when she floored the accelerator that she could feel the vibrations of the frame right through her body.

"It's a present," Allen had said. "You can't turn down a present."

"Cars are obsolete," Annabelle had protested moodily. "I could never afford to give you a present like this."

"You could give me something better," Allen said, then stopped, his face flushing. What he meant, of course, was a baby: these days he was almost prepared to take up knitting. Every second night, the exact frequency recommended by the doctor, they wrestled for the pregnancy in the big, shag-carpeted bedroom. And every second night Annabelle found herself looking out the window to the high wooden spire of the church; and hoping this would release whatever was being held back.

"It's for the Reverend Finch," Allen said when she got to the office. He handed her a thick envelope. "I want him to sign it and send it back with you."

"Finch?"

"You know, the Reverend. I have directions to his place. It's not hard to find."

"I didn't know you were seeing Finch," Annabelle said.

"Yes." Allen leaned back at his desk. "Is something wrong?"

"Is something supposed to be wrong?" She clenched the envelope in her hands, trying to keep them from shaking. If he was going to play games, to dare her, then she would have to call his bluff.

"Are you feeling sick? Look I'll drive it out tonight."

"Don't be silly, I'm absolutely fine. I'll see you later." And for a moment she saw that puzzled look he sometimes got, that puzzled lawyer's look that was trying to fit the facts together, to come up with enough evidence to close the case.

The bright morning had given way to a warm afternoon, and as she drove out of Salem on the winding blacktop Annabelle opened the window and let the fragrant June air whip through the interior of the car.

She had felt guilty about the white MG when she saw it in

the lane. But she liked to drive it and she had passed the turn-off for Finch's place long before she looked at the map. Instead of turning back right away she stayed on the blacktop, heading a few miles farther towards the big lake. On previous drives she had found a dirt road that wound up to a rocky bluff overlooking the water.

It was a long way down to the lake, a real lover's leap, and she couldn't help wondering if the youths of Salem ever dared each other to take the jump. There was a story she had once read, the story of an extraordinarily beautiful young woman with hosts of local suitors. She lived in a provincial French town and finally a very determined gentleman from Paris heard about her and travelled to see if her face lived up to her fame. Instantly, he fell deeply in love with her and said to her that he would do anything she pleased, if only she would marry him.

"I don't know," she had said. "I'm so bored."

"I love you madly," he had insisted. "Don't you love me?"

"Of course," she had replied wearily, "I love you, but you have to prove your love to me."

"Anything."

So she had described a lover's leap, a cliff by the sea from which he must jump to prove his love. Enthusiastically her Parisian suitor, a handsome young man from an excellent family, with an assured and brilliant future, had run down the road until he came to the cliff. He had looked over it to the green foaming sea and been overwhelmed by the great distance she had asked him to jump. But my love, he thought, my love will protect me. He looked again at the water smashing against the cliffs, at the seagulls wheeling in the currents of air, and then, holding his hand to his heart, he leapt.

Meanwhile the beautiful young woman, whose family, though provincial was also excellent in its way, woke up from a lifetime of lethargy and realized that she was desperately in love. At the same moment she realized that during her years of boredom she had sent dozens of other suitors to a similar task, and all had drowned. She even recalled that the head of the local militia had come to plead with her not to take the life of so many future soldiers; unfortunately, while making this plea, he had been so struck by her face that, uniform and all he had rushed to dare where others had failed.

In her extreme moment of wakefulness the beautiful young woman sprinted through the streets to the cliff's edge, only to arrive just as her latest was fluttering towards the sea. "François," she screamed. "I love you. If you truly love me, for my soul alone, you will survive." He drowned. The young woman dressed in black thereafter and always wore a veil. When they buried her they found the veil had become unnecessary: her face had grown dried and withered, old like anyone else.

This, Annabelle had always thought, was a lesson to those who would swim out of season. But standing on the outcropping, feeling the fresh breeze in her face, she felt exactly in-season herself, exactly ripe and ready, and she wanted a baby so badly that her whole body was bursting for it.

She sat for a few minutes on the rock and smoked a forbidden cigarette. All day she'd felt cramps trying to grip her stomach: the sign of another period, another missed month. As usual Allen would smile and pretend that nothing had happened. And as usual they would both go back to counting the days by twos.

"God," Annabelle said aloud, "God, why not me?" She was starting to be convinced, as Donna Wilson had suggested, that if only she sincerely desired the baby, it would happen.

She got back into the car and drove back to the turn-off, then followed a series of dirt roads until she came to the mailbox with FINCH stencilled in fading black letters.

In the driveway, which was deeply rutted, the car twisted and threatened to bottom out. She stopped in front of the house; it was a very small very freshly painted white frame house surrounded by well-kept bushes and lawn. It looked, Annabelle thought, like a real minister's house, and suddenly the stories she had heard about Finch, even her own impressions, began to melt away. She got out of the car and took the envelope from the seat beside her. And then, seeing no movement from the house, she slipped her coat over her shoulders and put Allen's envelope in its pocket.

She was still standing in the drive when the front door opened and a young girl came out to the veranda.

"Hello," Annabelle called.

The girl was silent.

"Is your dad home?" She recognized the girl from the church.

The girl was advancing across the lawn now, looking at Annabelle, then the car.

"Is your dad home?"

"He's in the barn," the girl said. She was pretty, with her mother's white skin and Finch's black eyes. "It's back there." She pointed to a huge wooden building about fifty yards away. Then she looked down at Annabelle's feet, at her nyloned toes sticking out of her light summer sandals.

"I've got the flu," she said. "I'm supposed to be in the house."

"It's all right," Annabelle said, trying to reassure this girl with a smile. "I'll get there myself."

As she walked she was aware of a new and complicated array of smells, of the intensifying heat of the day, of the girl re-entering the house and slamming shut the door as she did.

When she hit the first wet patch Annabelle gasped and jumped away, only to land in another. Suddenly the whole barnyard was a sea of mud and cowpies, and Annabelle realized why it was the girl had looked questioningly at her sandals. She looked down at her feet, then continued on until she had reached the back of the barn and the wide-beamed entrance-way. Feeling like the suitor in her story, she put a hand on the door to steady herself, then crossed into the barn.

She had stepped from one country into another.

At first she was aware of nothing but dark shadows and the thick smells washing over her. Then gradually the shadows took on layers, rust-coloured beams and hand-squared posts appeared, a row of milking stalls filled with clumps of sodden hay.

She swayed momentarily in the entrance, eyes still confused by the darkness; and then finally she took a second step into the dark interior. It was filled by a dank mist laced with the odours of stale milk and cow manure. At the far end of the huge barn, an electric light burned dimly, and beside it, on the wall, was a broken white patch of light that she realized must be a window, the only one in this whole building.

At least, she thought, trying to keep her sodden shoes out of the cow patties, the only *transparent* window in the building. But there were, in fact, windows in front of each stall; these were covered with layers of dust and clinging dirt that glowed the colour of tobacco juice. When she was halfway down the aisle she heard a sudden snort, a sharp intake of breath. Terrified, she stopped and jerked her head towards the sound. An ancient horse, his thick neck drooping with cords of muscle, his red coat flecked with tips of silver and white, was looking blindly in her direction. From the shadows his mane suddenly emerged, tossing to the other side of his massive neck; it was a thick and lustrous red, and it had grown long as a woman's hair.

"Hey-yuh, Sean," came a voice from the back of the barn. The voice belonged to Finch; in his own barn his voice had the confident tone that it took on in church.

"Reverend Finch," she called back, "it's Annabelle Jamieson."

"Good day, Mrs. Jamieson. We'll be right with you."

"I've brought a letter for you, from my husband." She felt as though she was shouting into a huge and invisible telephone.

"Right with you, Mrs. Jamieson."

She still had not seen Finch, though she could hear that his voice was coming from the lighted stall, but now, as she advanced a few more steps, she saw a shadow detach itself from the stall become a figure and move rapidly towards her.

Annabelle started to scream, then jammed her fist in her mouth.

"Mrs. Jamieson."

"Mrs. Finch."

"You're shaking, Mrs. Jamieson. Would you like to sit down?"

Annabelle looked around, wondering if Maureen Finch meant that she should simply smooth out her coat and sit on the manure-soaked floor. She took a deep breath, trying to push out her stomach as she drew in the air. Then she extended her hand to the woman in the wheelchair.

"Mrs. Finch, it's good to see you again."

"Good to see you, Mrs. Jamieson."

"My husband couldn't come this afternoon," Annabelle said. Then, realizing how disconnected this explanation must sound, she added: "I've heard wonderful things about the Sunday school."

"Thank you, Mrs. Jamieson."

Annabelle realized that Maureen Finch was still holding onto her hand, and that something warm and wet was sliding between their palms.

"You'll have to excuse my hand, Mrs. Jamieson. We've been trying to free a calf from its mother. I'm afraid it's a bloody business."

Annabelle, despite herself, pulled back her hand and wiped it on her coat. In her other hand she had the letter for Finch.

"Excuse me, Mrs. Jamieson, I don't suppose you're used to these things in the city."

In the months since she had met Maureen Finch, Annabelle had never stopped feeling sorry for her. But now the voice that had softly wished "Good Sabbath" was more metallic than the chair; and the face that seemed stone solid in the church was here white and pasty. She had heard that Maureen Finch had once been a nun, but had quit the convent to marry Gordon Finch, a Protestant preacher. And then, she had also heard, Maureen Finch had gotten sick with arthritis and turned more righteous than God Himself.

"Maureen," Finch called, "now where have you gotten to?"

"I'm talking to Mrs. Jamieson."

"Well both of you come down here. You know, Mrs. Jamieson, I couldn't run this farm without my wife."

In a deft motion Maureen Finch spun her wheelchair around.

"I'll take the letter down for you, Mrs. Jamieson."

"It's all right, Mrs. Finch I don't mind walking."

"I was thinking about your shoes, Mrs. Jamieson."

"Don't mind about my shoes. Can I give you a push?"

"My husband usually keeps his women away from the house, Mrs. Jamieson."

Before Annabelle could reply Maureen Finch had put her

hands on the glistening rubber wheels and sent herself spinning down towards Finch's end of the barn. Annabelle walked slowly after her, half-formed phrases crowding to her tongue.

In contrast to the rest of the barn, the stall was absolutely clean, even the wood was freshly whitewashed, and it was filled with hay so green and sweet-smelling that Annabelle, for the first time in several minutes, could fully catch her breath.

On the floor of the stall was an enormous, swollen cow. She was lying on her side in the green hay, one large brown eye open towards the ceiling, and she was panting, a low regular sound that Annabelle now realized she had been hearing from the moment she had entered the barn.

The cow's face, which was turned slightly towards her, was all black, and amazingly pretty. Save for the blood at the nostrils she might have been a cow in a poster.

"Mrs. Jamieson," Finch said, with a grin, "you've caught us in our manger." He was kneeling beside the cow. In his coveralls he looked even bigger than usual, and he was smoking a pipe. She realized that she had never seen him except in the most formal of circumstances. She liked him better here, at his own place. *His women.* She wondered how much of the gossip about the Reverend Finch was true.

"This cow's been trying to have her calf for two days now," Finch said, "and now we're going to have to help her." In the shaded side of the stall next to Finch there was a jumble of ropes and pulleys. Annabelle remembered a picture of a calf being pulled out of a cow by block and tackle; she had always thought that this was a medieval practice, something from the Middle Ages of animal history that corresponded to the Inquisition and the Crusades.

"She used to be such a pretty cow," Maureen Finch said, "a nice slim-hipped cow, but she got into a pasture with a bull that was too big for her."

"It happens," said Finch.

"She's paying the price," Maureen Finch said.

"Now," Finch said, "she's only an animal."

"We are all only animals," Maureen Finch said, "but some of us know better."

"Mrs. Jamieson, I should tell you that my wife is famous for her wit." Finch stood up. The light from the barred window passed over his dark bearded face, making him for a moment a giant prisoner in this giant barn, and as he stood behind his wife's chair, one muscular hand resting on the stainless steel, he looked at Annabelle directly for the first time. Again, as on the street three months ago, she felt a wave of desire passing from him to her, saw his deep eyes stare as if he truly believed that he had the power to simply force her to his will, as if he would just step forward, right in front of his wife, and crush her against one of the hand-squared beams of the barn.

Annabelle hesitated for a moment, dizzy, trying one last time to convince herself that Finch and his wife were a perfectly normal couple. And then, as she was starting to extend the letter towards him, the cow gave out a grunt so deep and so loud that Annabelle felt as though she herself had surrendered.

From lying on her side, the cow had gone to kneeling, and as the first grunt was followed by a second, Annabelle saw a small hoof emerge from the cow's vagina.

"Put her head in the yoke," Maureen snapped, but Finch was already doing it, pushing the cow's head forward through the metal hoop at the front of the stall, so her mouth was suspended above water and hay. Again the cow grunted, but this time more quietly, and Annabelle could see her skin shudder. The calf's hoof stayed where it was, then part of it was swallowed up again.

The cow took a mouthful of hay and began to grind it slowly between her jaws, rotating them against each other with the slow deliberation of millstones, a loud grinding sound that filled the whole building.

With the cow now safely secured Finch knelt behind and wrapped one of his huge hands around the remaining portion of the calf's hoof.

"Doesn't it just come out?" asked Annabelle.

"It's supposed to," Finch said, "but this little sucker's been in and out all day. If it doesn't get born soon it's going to die." And then with a movement so sudden and forceful that Annabelle felt her insides give way, Finch yanked the hoof with one hand while thrusting the other up into the cow, as if he would jam his arm in up to the elbow. While the cow's rear end jerked in surprise, her head was totally unconcerned, and she took a new sheaf of hay into her mouth and began to grind away while Finch, now grunting himself, emerged with a second hoof.

Maureen wheeled to a corner of the stall where she got a chain with a pulley at one end. This she handed to Finch who, without comment, took it from her and began to fasten the chain to the calf's exposed ankles.

Then he took the pulley and attached it to a huge hook screwed into one of the beams.

Annabelle, transfixed, was right against the stall now, her elbows over its wooden gate, one wet shoe on the cement and the other resting on a crossbar. The low amber light of the interior, the barred patch of white on the wall of the stall, Finch's bearded face leaning intently into the rear end of the cow, these had become the elements of a new world as she breathed in the thick smells of milk and birth that enveloped them all now in a deep, hypnotic fog.

Annabelle looked at Maureen. She too was staring at Finch, her eyes wide and her mouth dropped open, and gradually elements of fear were beginning to mix into the softening mask of her face. As Finch leaned back and tested his weight against the brace she winced, and instinctively put one hand to her stomach; and for one last moment Annabelle felt sorry for her, wondered again how it was that this beautiful woman in the wheelchair survived the life of immobility while having to take care of two children and contend with the obstreperous and crazy Finch.

"Give it to her," Maureen whispered, "put it to her now." Maureen's emerald eyes turned towards her and Annabelle smiled weakly. Maureen smiled back. "The bitch," she whispered. "Now's the time." One of her wet hands lifted up from the wheelchair and came to rest on Annabelle's wrist.

Finch, his long arms spanning the gap between the cow and the beam, slowly began to turn the crank.

The hooves, like diver's hands clasped together; straightened out; a length of the legs then emerged and with them a brief shower of blood. But through and above the occasional metallic clanking of the chain was the grinding of hay as the cow continued to eat. Finch paused briefly, caressing the calf's legs.

"Faster, Gordon. Don't take all day."

Finch gave the chain one more crank and there was a swelling at the end of the cow, then a sudden sucking sound as more of the calf was released, the rest of its front legs and its head now coming into view. The eyes were closed and the whole face smeared with a thick, transparent liquid.

Now the cow, still eating, straightened out her head and neck and grunted. She shifted uncomfortably, moving away from the beam so that Finch, about to start cranking again, was thrown off balance and more of the calf was pulled out. The cow started to struggle to get up and suddenly one foot was on Finch's groin and her weight was sliding into him. Annabelle felt Maureen's nails claw at her wrist, the pain made her breath catch; then Finch had dropped the chain and rolled away. In the same motion he was on his feet, behind the cow, pushing her back to the ground before she had her balance, the half-born calf dangling grotesquely. Before Annabelle could even wonder what was going to happen to the calf, Finch had shoved his hands into the cow and was pulling using his own shoulder as a brace, pulling and grunting as the cow settled back to her hay.

The calf's eyes were closed, its lashes a blue-grey fan on its wet cheeks. As Finch pulled, the calf's face peeked out from where it was squeezed between his arm and his chest, but it didn't open its eyes, didn't show any expression at all.

"Hurry, Gordon, it's going to suffocate." The vise of Maureen's hand closed ever more tightly. But there was no need to exhort him; Finch was already scarlet with exertion and his breath was coming loud now as he strained against the cow. Finally he began rocking back and forth, his arms still extended into the cow's womb, the calf's head in a hammerlock, rocking back and forth and pulling so hard at the calf it seemed its neck would surely break.

"Sucker," Finch grunted, and with one final violent tug he wrenched the whole calf free of its mother, falling back into the hay with his effort, the calf still in his arms, connected to its mother by a thin, torn sheet of bloody afterbirth.

With the freeing of the calf, Maureen's grip had also loosened. Finch held the calf away from his chest, first showing it to Annabelle and his wife, then gently setting it on its feet where, afterbirth now fallen away, eyes still closed, it blindly moved towards its mother.

"It's out," said Finch. He sounded exhausted, as if it were from his own guts that this animal had been torn. He unlocked the cow's stanchion, so she could move towards the calf, then turned to Annabelle and opened the stall door. He pointed towards a bucket and a terrycloth towel.

"Wash it," Finch ordered, "then rub it down with the towel."

Annabelle hesitated, looked at Maureen whose face was once more waiting and impassive, then stepped inside to the calf. Unlike its mother, which was spotted with large areas of white, the calf was almost completely black. Only its four feet were exceptions — they were a snowy, newborn white. These Annabelle washed first, tentatively holding each one as she did. But soon her shyness was gone and she was kneeling in the hay, firmly holding the calf to her with one arm while with her free hand she wiped over the warm, silky skin, rubbed it all over once and then, without having to be told, rubbed its chest and ribs so its heart would beat stronger and its breath would bring it to life, give it the strength to keep its feet, to search out its mother's teat and open those eyes that still stayed closed, so content and so dreamy it might never wake up.

Later she remembered that, told Allen about it: the feeling of the calf warm and new against her, its first moments of life beating out to the tense rhythm of her breathing, its first sounds the low crooning of her voice in its still-moist ear.

"Maureen," Finch said, "I think we should offer Mrs. Jamieson a cup of tea."

"Of course," said Maureen. "A cup of tea." Annabelle looked up to see Maureen spin her chair around; with a quick push she was off, gliding down the barn with the sound of a bicycle on wet pavement.

"Excuse me," Finch said. His voice was low and threatening, the way it sometimes became during a sermon. "I'll have to help her to the house." Then he strode off rapidly towards Maureen, who was fixed in the white light of the barn entranceway.

Alone, Annabelle stayed kneeling by the calf, kneading its chest until the heartbeat was familiar to her hand, stroking the silky fur, playing with the new pink ears. She was still holding the calf when Finch returned. Looking exhausted and grey he propped himself against the side of the stall and began refilling his pipe.

"You look tired."

"The cow started bawling at four o'clock this morning. I didn't think we'd save the calf."

Annabelle turned its face towards her. Its eyes were still closed, its breathing shallow. Only a few minutes had passed since Annabelle had embraced the calf and been overwhelmed by its warmth. The sudden feeling of blind mother-love was still in her, but the calf seemed to be fading, slipping back into the dream it had never really emerged from; and looking down at it Annabelle couldn't help remembering the way Finch had torn it from the mother, the way its sleepy dreaming face had not even awakened in the force of his hammerlock.

"I don't know," Annabelle murmured. "It's not breathing very deep."

"You can still lose them," said Finch, in a matter-of-fact way, "even after a few hours you can still lose them easy. Happens all the time."

Not this one, prayed Annabelle. *Don't lose this one.* She wanted to hold it closer, to hug and squeeze it until its life caught with the force of her own. She wondered if her own baby would be like this. She patted the calf nervously with the towel, tried to set it close to its mother.

The cow, on her feet now, seemed completely uninterested and had gone back to nosing through the hay. The light bright pink of her tongue was so beautiful as she took the choice bits of hay into her mouth that Annabelle couldn't resist reaching out her hand to it; then the tongue rasped over the skin of her palm and she laughed with delight. The first lick was followed by a second and the cow started to try to work her way up Annabelle's arm.

"She likes me."

"You and your salt," said Finch. "Bring the calf to her teat." The cow's bag was swollen, and Annabelle self-consciously took away the hand the cow had been licking and wrapped it around one of the long, liver-coloured nipples. Then she pulled the calf towards it.

"Pull the teat," Finch instructed. "Let the calf smell the milk."

But the calf suddenly stumbled towards it's mother, mouth open, and the connection was made without Annabelle doing anything. In seconds the calf was an expert, its throat stretched straight to receive the milk it was greedily sucking down. And then finally, for the first time, the cow turned curiously towards her calf, looked at it sucking away at her own underbelly, and pushed her nose down towards it, the pink tongue now out again, slowly licking the black fur along the ridge of the calf's spine.

Annabelle stayed kneeling in the straw. The cramps she had been feeling earlier had returned and were now mixed with crying: her face was wet — her cheeks, her upper lip, her chin and the hollow of her neck where tears always collected. The calf moved away from the cow and Annabelle reached out for it. Then, with her arms around it, she cried as if she would never stop, crying the way she had when she woke up in the hospital after the miscarriage, tears flowing so thick and so fast she was afraid she was crying not water but blood.

"It's all right," Finch said. His voice was low and Annabelle realized he was crouching by her side, slightly behind her. In town his nearness had only made her want to run. Now his tone was intimate, for the first time not part of some show but words meant only for her. She kept staring ahead, afraid to turn around, wishing only that he would put his arm around her.

"Maureen's waiting on us with our tea," Finch said. Then, miraculously, his hand was on her shoulder, so large and so heavy that Annabelle felt she would collapse. For one moment she let herself imagine how wonderful it would be to lie down in the soft hay of this very stall and have Finch's whole weight over her, just lie in the soft yielding hay with his weight over her and the sound of the calf's sucking in her ear.

Then he was at the door of the stall holding it open for her. "We'd best go inside."

She got to her feet, brushing at straw and wisps of hay as she stood. The cow and the calf, indifferent, carried on with drinking and licking.

"It's all right?" Annabelle asked.

"It's all right." And then his arms were around her and she was leaning against his chest, her face against the rough denim of his coveralls, weeping. Images of the miscarriage kept coming back: the walk to the bathroom, the nightgown soaked in blood, the taxi ride to the hospital, the sad sterile face of the woman doctor who'd attended her in emergency and told her not to worry, that she'd be pregnant again in no time. Annabelle clenched the bib of Finch's coveralls, smelled the deep, sweet-sour smell of dirt, old clothes, and skin. Shook her head and stepped away.

"I'm sorry."

Finch's arm was over her shoulder and he was leading her towards the door of the barn, towards an emerging patch of blue sky and blinding light.

"I almost forgot why I came." She reached into her coat pocket and extended the letter towards Finch. "My husband sent you this," she said. "You're supposed to sign it and send it back."

The moment Finch's arm came away from her back, to take the letter, she craved it again.

"Look at the envelope, it's totally soaked." Now in the growing light she looked down at herself — at her coat, her slacks, her shoes. All were smeared with blood and afterbirth and covered with wisps of hay and straw.

They were at the doorway of the barn and the sky was an explosion of blue and yellow. Finch had his hand on her shoulder again and the touch was now so familiar and so good she smiled up at him, smiled with her whole face and watched his smile coming in return. His teeth were strong and squared, with tiny gaps between, and with his dark, fringed beard and his coal-black eyes he looked like one of those lunatic prophets who spent whole lifetimes in the desert praying for a sign.

"Well," said Finch. For a moment Annabelle thought that he was going to kiss her. Her heart was already leaping to him, but though the pressure of his hand increased, he was only turning her away from him, towards the house.

"Well," said Finch, "you may not be much of a messenger but you make one hell of a midwife." He laughed and she started laughing with him, joining him for the sound of their two voices mixing together. As they laughed and walked towards the house, Annabelle could see the beautiful white face of Maureen Finch watching from the window, waiting.

Eight

*I*n the afternoon it had rained, and though the sky was now perfectly dear, water was still gathered in the ruts and potholes off the driveway. Finch had arrived home just before the schoolbus, and while the children were walking up the drive, he sat at the large kitchen table thinking about his visit with Allen Jamieson.

Valerie, who was the eldest and would be turning eleven next month, was instructing Clare in the mystery of puddles. By the time they came into the house, they were elaborately spotted with mud. Finch was standing at the kitchen counter, chopping vegetables into the cast-iron pot he used for stews.

"Take off your boots," he said, without turning, "and then go up to see your mother."

"Da?"

"Hurry up now."

"Da." Valerie had called him Da when she was a baby, unable to add the final *d,* and she still did whenever she was up to something.

She had a piece of paper in her hand, rolled up into a scroll and streaked with mud on the outside, and she was pushing it towards him. Like Maureen she had red hair and very fair skin, but she was still a tomboy, all bones and skinny arms and legs. After the first few days of sun her face was covered in freckles, and now, nearing the end of June, her nose and forehead were already peeling.

"Look at it, Da. Look at it."

She was starting to laugh, the way she did when she thought she had done something cute, and as he flattened out the paper she grabbed at his arm. It was amazing how untouched she was by Maureen's illness and his own unpredictable temper.

"Look Da, look. Last night Mama said you were a devil so I drew this in art today."

It was a picture of Finch, standing in front of the house. He was wearing his coveralls and bulging from his head were two horns. In one hand he held a pitchfork in the other, a red bushy tail.

"Who told you to do this?"

"No one, Da. I wanted to." Her voice was beginning to break, and Finch, suddenly repentant, gathered her in his arms.

"It's wonderful, Valerie. It's a wonderful likeness." He hugged her for a moment, then took her shoulders and held her out away from him.

"But, Valerie, do you know who the devil is?"

"Oh, Da, I didn't mean *that.*"

"All right, then. Up you go."

Maureen's room was right above the kitchen so as he rushed cooking dinner and laid the table, he could hear the murmur of their voices. This, it sometimes seemed, was as close as he and Maureen could come to mutual comfort; listening to each other through the kitchen ceiling. Finally, he took the coveralls from the hook beside the kitchen door, drew them on, and walked out to the barn where the cattle were waiting to be milked and fed.

It had been dark for hours when Finch returned to the house. The waxing moon spread a silvery sheen through the sky, but from the house itself there was only one light: the yellow glow of his wife's reading lamp.

Finch quietly let himself in the kitchen door. Then he lit the kerosene lamp that waited in the centre of the table. There was electricity of course — after his wife had gotten sick Finch had even installed a furnace so that Maureen needn't be cold if he was gone for a few hours — but after his evening walks Finch liked the softer light of oil.

From the cupboard Finch got a clean bowl. Then he went to the oven and helped himself to the stew he had cooked for supper. The children had gotten their own dinner, as they often did, and now Maureen's tray and their own dirty plates and glasses were piled in a messy heap on the counter beside the sink.

As he ate, Finch drank from the jug of milk he had brought into the house. In April and May the milk had the green briny taste of spring grass, but now, as the clover thickened, it was getting so creamy and smooth he would sometimes milk one of the cows by hand, just for the warm summery taste of milk squirting straight from the teat to his mouth.

When the bowl was empty, Finch wiped it dry with a piece of bread and butter, then reheated the morning's left-over coffee. And when he was finally sitting in the dim kitchen puffing on his pipe and enjoying the feeling of warmth spreading out from his stomach and chest, he sighed so loudly with the task that lay ahead that he startled himself, his own complaining voice like that of an exhausted animal.

The sound of his distress was a signal; not only did Finch stand up to drain his cup, but he also heard his wife shifting in her bed. He blew out the lamp and softly padded up the stairs.

"How are you tonight?"

"I'm fine," Maureen said. "You were out a long time."

"I went for a walk after I milked the cows."

"You should get help."

"It's a small farm to support a hired man." Finch was still standing in the doorway, as he always did until Maureen invited him in. They had, he thought, invented politeness in the absence of love.

"Your hair is looking nice," Finch said. "Did Valerie help you?"

"Her and Mrs. McConnell," Maureen said.

She was in bed, wearing one of the dozen white nightgowns she had gotten for her wedding, and her red hair was loose, curling around her shoulders and framing the white skin of her face and neck. At one time the gifts of night-gowns had been a joke between them and Finch had threatened that in his passion he would tear them away until the silk and linen of her beautiful wedding nightgowns littered the house like so much confetti.

"You could come in," Maureen said. "Would you like a drink?"

"Sure," Finch nodded. "That would be nice."

He stepped into the room and walked over to Maureen's dresser, which was where she kept her perpetual decanter of sherry and two matching crystal glasses — wedding presents. Also on her dresser, surrounding the glasses and in jumbled rows behind them, were the bottles and vials of pills that Maureen took for her arthritis. But the pills didn't affect the truth: were Maureen to do what she used to, were she to climb up on Sean and gallop, she would die of the pain.

Finch poured two small portions of sherry, took Maureen's and placed it in her outstretched hand, then backed away to the red-padded armchair where he always sat for these late-night conversations. It was a relic from the days when Finch's uncle had owned this farm, and in Maureen's room it was the only trace of Finch's past.

The other sitting place in the room was Maureen's wheelchair. In it she could travel around the upstairs, including the bathroom where she was still able to lift herself onto the toilet or into the bath. On Sundays and when there were visitors, Finch would carry the chair and then Maureen downstairs, where she could participate in the cooking and eating of dinner, and on Maureen's good days, during the summer, she would ask Finch to carry her chair outside. For many years she had actually managed to plant and weed a kitchen garden from this chair. But this habit, along with certain others, had gradually given way to more and more days in her room, a sign Finch thought not of increasing illness but of her growing estrangement first from him, then even from her own children, so that now he thought she was happiest sitting passively in her room, reading the Bible or talking on the telephone.

"Cheers," Maureen said. She raised her glass to Finch and smiled. Her face and neck were fuller than they had been, and there was the shadow of a double chin, but Finch still found her beautiful. That, in addition to his unwanted errand, made it difficult to smile back at her as he raised his glass, then sipped at the horribly sweet sherry that Maureen insisted on. At one time, at least, the sherry had its compensation, because the invitation for a drink had always been part of the ritual — politeness again — that preceded a night in bed together. But as those nights had become spotted so far apart that the intervals were measured first in months, then years, the drink had become established as an occasion of its own, a substitute so innocent that Finch sometimes wondered if the doctors were giving his wife some kind of anti-sex hormone. A new medical discovery that made her independent of what ever it was that drove everyone else into each other's arms.

"A few weeks ago," Finch said, "I went to see Mike Taggart."

"Mike Taggart?"

"He was an old friend of my father's. Says he used to go drinking with him."

"That's nice, Gordon. You should see your father's friends more often."

"He said the Tillson girl is pregnant. Nellie Tillson, up on the Fifth Line."

"Is that right?" Maureen asked. "She used to be in the Sunday school."

She looked at Finch, and he was amazed once again to see how the eyes in such a soft and creamy face could be such a hard green, a judging Irish green.

"She's too old for Sunday school now," Finch said. As if this was news to Maureen. "She works at Mandowski's store."

"I know."

Finch looked at his wife. It had to be told. "She wants to file a paternity suit," Finch said. "She wants ten thousand dollars. Mandowski's already been to see a lawyer."

Maureen was sitting straight up in bed now, totally alert, and Finch could see the little ditto marks that formed between her eyebrows when she was thinking about something. Occasionally lovemaking had made her concentrate that very same way.

"What happened?"

"He swore an affidavit," Finch said, "claiming that he caught me with the Tillson girl in the old stone church opposite the old Beckwith place."

"Gordon, you —" She stopped and Finch could see the hate on her face: it twisted the skin around the already old eyes. Then her expression was impassive again and she breathed deeply, crossing her arms and holding her hands to her opposite shoulders as though, Finch thought, she was afraid that the evil ways of her husband might attack her virgin breasts. There were times when he had been so contemptuous that he had exploded into hitting her. But not any more.

"That would be a sin, Gordon, a mortal sin." Her voice was controlled, but he could hear the hate in it anyway, in the tone and in the heavy way sin fell from her mouth. Like a Catholic gravestone.

"Mandowski did it," Finch said. "I went to see him at the store."

"You went to see him?"

"I just wanted to talk to him."

"It's all over the township," Maureen said, "that you tried to kill him."

"He pulled a gun on me."

Maureen laughed. Her looks had stayed on through the years and the illness, but her laugh had changed from a fresh and wonderful sound that made him laugh inside with her, to a metallic and jangling noise that only made him nervous. He reached automatically for his pipe, but it and his tobacco were downstairs; there was no smoking in Maureen's room.

"Gordon, God, Gordon, you should know enough to stay away from young girls."

"It was Mandowski," Finch insisted. What he meant was that he was sure it was Mandowski who had actually gotten her pregnant. A fine point he was not yet ready to explain. "She wants ten thousand dollars."

"Do we have ten thousand dollars?"

"Of course not."

"We could mortgage the farm."

"It's blackmail," Finch said. "Mandowski hired her so he could look down her dress and now that he's in trouble he wants to put it to me. And to the church."

At the mention of the church Maureen, as always, stiffened.

The loyalty she had once had for her husband, for her family, had gradually eroded, but Finch knew that in at least one perverse way his marriage had succeeded: Maureen's support of the church, her desire for it to succeed and keep its place in Salem, had only grown stronger. Sometimes it seemed to Finch, as he preached, that the purpose of Maureen's stony stare was not simply to embarrass him and to make him remember, at the most eloquent heights of his piety, that she knew better — God and she knew better — but actually to strike him down, to stop him in mid-flowery-sentence, so that she herself would be forced to carry on, to mount the pulpit, wheelchair and all, look out on the two hundred souls that gathered every Sunday, and herself declare God's harsh Catholic truth.

"You could resign," Maureen said, "before you drag the church through the mud with you."

"I'll not resign."

"Then pay."

"I'll not pay."

"Did you do it?"

Finch hesitated. Maureen's face was so cold now; she was staring at him as if he was the most evil man on earth, as if he was truly the devil his daughter had drawn.

"No," he said. "I didn't."

"Will you swear on the Bible?" Maureen took the Bible from her bedside table and passed it to Finch. "Gordon, do you dare swear on the Bible?"

Finch set the Bible on his lap. Then he laid his large right hand over the cover. Under his palm the leather was worn smooth and soft, polished by his wife's constant touch. He remembered one night after their engagement when he had met her drunk. "Oh Lord," he had joked, "rebuke me not in thy wrath; neither chasten me in thy hot displeasure." But even the forgiving Lord would not take lightly an oath made on the Bible.

Finch lifted the Bible up; his fingers instinctively caressed it. Then he raised his eyes to Maureen's: that hard, judging look. He gripped the Bible, decided. The muscles of her face looked like iron beneath the white skin. The point of no return had passed without his seeing it.

"I swear," Finch said, "I swear that I did not make the Tillson girl pregnant." In the silence that followed a thin layer of sweat formed between Finch's palm and the leather.

"You bastard," Maureen finally whispered. "I hope your what-for falls off if you're lying." She held out her glass. "Get me some more sherry, will you, Gordon?"

He stood up. He set the Bible down on his wife's night table, suppressed the urge to wipe his hand on his trousers, took the glass that she held carefully so their fingers wouldn't touch, and walked to the dresser. in the old days, a fight like this would have meant that he would sleep downstairs for a week. Now he slept downstairs all the time, so he had nothing left to lose.

He poured the sherry, gave back her glass. Her eyes had turned away now and he looked down as he talked.

"I went to a lawyer," Finch said. "He said that a paternity suit is impossible to prove."

"Impossible?"

"Almost impossible." Finch hesitated. "I told him this afternoon that I wasn't afraid to go to court."

"And I suppose that everyone in the township must know by now," Maureen said.

"It's the new lawyer, that Jamieson. They've been to church a few times."

Maureen was silent, sipping at her sherry, and Finch found himself watching her reflection in the window. The psalm he had joked about with Maureen had gone on to say, "For my loins are filled with loathsome disease." Even then he would have known better than to mention that line. Now the reflection was moving, preparing to speak.

"You can't go to court," Maureen said. "You can't go. I'll think of something." For a moment Finch thought her voice had gone soft, that she was going to break and cry. There was a sudden response in his own chest, a knife of sympathy and desire.

Then he saw her hand move. She switched off the light and the room went black. "Good night, Gordon."

Finch sat still for a moment, grateful that there was darkness to hide his pity for her. Gradually the black window turned a soft, living velvet. He looked to Maureen, saw the curve of the blanket over her hip. She was facing him. Finch stepped forward, then kneeling beside the bed took her hand and kissed it very carefully. Her hand moved up, rested briefly on the side of his face. The wave of pity broke in him, but the hand withdrew.

Finch went downstairs, his feet finding their way through the living room to the small porch he had insulated against the cold. It was the same room he had had when he worked for Benjamin and Mary; even the same braided rug was on the floor.

The night after he first made love to Maureen Newell he had known that rug well enough. He woke in the middle of the night, his chest on fire, hardly able to breathe. Only in his sleep had his own stupidity hit him. The silly happiness he had felt all evening was entirely gone, and groaning and cursing himself he had rolled off the bed and onto the floor.

There he dug his knees into the corded wool and laced his fingers together to pray. Maureen Newell had been a gift, a perfect, white-skinned virgin of spring. "A wife," his teacher had said, "a minister needs a wife." And who would make a more beautiful wife than Maureen Newell? But ministers' wives weren't made out of the farm girls he had known, girls who didn't mind getting lost in the trees.

Maureen Newell with her high, shining boots and her galloping horse was no farm girl, she was a woman to be won and not taken. In the middle of the night it had come over Finch that for ten minutes in a ditch he had thrown away everything; he had been such a fool that afterwards he hadn't known anything but the delicious happiness of conquest.

But even as he was repenting and the skin of his knees was being corrugated with the rough ropy texture of his aunt's braided rug, his mind was unable to resist the image of Maureen Newell stark naked, Maureen Newell with her hair grown down to the ground, her red coppery hair twined around in a devil's cape, cherry-red nipples protruding like devil's horns.

"Desire," his teacher had said. "It can be a blessing or a curse."

He spent the night on his knees, alternately swamped by his need for Maureen and remorse for ever having laid eyes on her perfect skin. When he finally fell asleep the sky was already growing light and only an hour later he woke up to his uncle's hand on his shoulder, shaking him awake for breakfast.

The whole day he stumbled through his chores, and by the time of the afternoon milking, he was almost sick with anxiety.

Usually Finch was a fast milker, but that day he was so nervous the cows sensed it, and he found them shifting away from him, or trying to lie down when he wanted to milk them.

"Nice day for a walk," Ben said.

"Might rain." In fact the sky was grey and black, so dark the barn light had to be on at four o'clock in the afternoon.

"If a person was going to walk," Ben said, "they might as well set out now."

"Doesn't matter," Finch said, "a walk is a walk."

There had been a time when walking up and down the rows of cows at milking time, slapping at their rear ends and looking at their swollen udders, had seemed obscene. Boys made jokes about women and their horses, about hired men who snuck into the barn at night. He was a hired man now; he wondered if boys made jokes about the minister's son who lived with his uncle, the minister's son who was in love with a Catholic girl.

The rain held off long enough for him to reach their meeting place. When it started he waited for a while longer under the spread of a huge elm tree. Then the drizzle thickened and he stood up to go. But not home: he couldn't face the carefully neutral looks of Ben and Mary, the carpet where he had sworn that he would forego this meeting.

Instead he walked towards Maureen Newell's house. When the wind sprang up or a branch snapped he was convinced that she and Sean must be trotting down the road, searching for him, ready to save him from the disastrous scene that would surely follow when he actually mounted her step and asked for her at her door.

But he didn't see her or Sean until he was finally walking up the maple-lined drive towards the big house that Maureen's grandfather had built. "Brick," Maureen said, "because brick doesn't burn. Even kerosene and rags can't touch it."

As he came up the drive, Sean whinnied in recognition. He

was in a paddock beside the house and he galloped excitedly towards Finch, tossing his head and bucking. For a moment Finch stopped, looking at the horse and waiting for Maureen to appear. He thought he saw a shadow move behind a lace curtain. Lace curtains: in this county the Catholics lived in brick houses with lace curtains, took piano lessons and were secretly elegant; the Protestants lived in plain frame houses, had tongues so thick they could hardly say their own names.

Finch walked up the steps of the white wooden porch. The railings were wrapped with climbing vines and he wondered what it would have been like to court Maureen in the evenings, to sit among the vines with their mysterious flowers and look out at a clear summer's night.

There was a screen door, which Finch opened, and a wooden, windowless door behind it. On that door Finch knocked. Then he let the screen door close while he waited.

After a moment he heard a step, a step too slow to be Maureen's, coming towards him. It hesitated at the wooden door, there was the sound of a bolt being unfastened, and then the door opened. Finch saw a woman — she was about the age of his Aunt Mary — peering at him curiously. She was leaning on a cane, the hand that surrounded it had swollen knuckles, and with her free hand she reached out and, just as Finch thought she was going to open it, locked the screen door.

"I've come for Maureen," Finch said. He realized how shabby he must look, with his rain-soaked clothes plastered to his skin. He tugged nervously at his beard and stood up straighter. "I'm Gordon Finch," he said, "Bob Finch's son, and I've come for Maureen."

"I know who you are," the woman said. She was still leaning on her cane and she made no motion to let him in. Her features, like Maureen's, were finely made; and her once-red hair had coarsened and was streaked with grey. "You're the minister's son and you look just like your father used to."

"Thank you," Finch stammered, wondering if this was meant to encourage him.

"But you're too late for Maureen," the woman continued. "I'm afraid she's gone."

"Gone? When will she be back?"

Finch saw her smile, a kind of smile he had never seen a smile so extraordinarily gentle that it was, in fact, absolutely cruel.

"I'm sorry, Gordon," Mrs. Newell said.

His name hung in the wet air. Then gradually, like some old piece of laundry, dissolved in the drumming rain.

"When?" he demanded, but he knew he had lost. "I've got to see her."

"I'm sorry. I really am terribly sorry." Then she turned her weight on the cane and began to limp back into the darkness of the house.

At two o'clock in the morning Maureen Newell Finch was still awake in her room. A discreet ten minutes after Finch had gone downstairs, she had climbed out of bed to sit in front of the mirror, her hands wrapped around the silver handle of her great-grandmother's brush.

As she waited for the night to loose its grip on her, Maureen might have almost guessed that her husband was dreaming of their first meeting. With her eyes closed, she dreamed it too: Finch, like herself, drunk on the hope of her passion. If she had given him half of what she'd wanted to. If he had let her approach him in her own slow way.

That much her mother had been able to warn her about, though she had seen Finch's face only once.

"He's a Protestant," she said. "He's a minister. He's a man that takes what he wants."

"If I love him?" Maureen had asked. But she had already seen the priest.

"It would be a terrible crime," her mother had replied. "To give your own self to a man like that. I would rather be dead."

Years later, when her mother was dying, and knew by intuition or by rumour that Maureen was still in love with Finch and was not only seeing him secretly, but was writing him secret letters and getting secret letters in return, and was planning to marry him as soon as the earth was thrown on her own dead face, she spoke of the day Finch had come in the rain.

"He was dark," she told Maureen. "He had a dark face just like his father's and he was soaked right through to the skin. I should have let him in, I guess. Until the rain passed. You could let him into your house, and it wouldn't be a sin. Not just into your house."

Maureen knew the story from all sides, even her own. She had gone to confess, leaving her mother to deal with Finch. And then she had gone to Toronto, as the priest had instructed, and trained to be a nursing sister. The heat of the summer had pressed down with the weight of the priest's stale breath and the black light of his confession booth; and then finally it was fall and the cold winds swept down from the north. She was glad to see the leaves go that year, glad to see every reminiscent bit of colour finally swept away. But one afternoon she walked to a drugstore, bought a greeting card with an envelope, then went and sat inside a restaurant to write him a letter. The words came easily, she had already made the story so perfect that even she half-believed it:

Dear Gordon,

I should have told you that I was planning to come back to Toronto to continue working for the Church. I used you to test my strength to resist temptation and that was wrong. My only marriage can be to Jesus Christ and my flesh must be bound to Him. Six months remain of my probationary period here and after that I will, if all goes well, take my permanent vows. Please don't try to find me. I know what I am doing.

Yours sincerely,
Maureen Newell

As she looked at the words on the page, the perfectly formed first-in-her-class letters on the deckled page of the flowered card, her belief, for at least the one moment of the ink's drying, became absolute. Then she stepped outside and mailed it, knowing the instant the red mailbox drawer swung shut that she had, once and for all, broken the hold of the Church. Green eyes, her father had said, yes; but surely she wasn't supposed to spend her whole life praying.

Now her green eyes were shut, the long auburn lashes glued to her cheeks by dried tears.

She opened them slowly, wheeled to the bathroom where she splashed water on her face, then wheeled back to the secretary. In one of the drawers, locked, were all the letters she and Finch had written: an inheritance, like the story, intended for her daughters.

Nine

*T*wo weeks after she'd delivered Allen's letter to Finch's barn, Annabelle saw Finch again. When she did, she realized that she had been thinking of him the whole time. *This is it,* she thought. The words passed through her mind slowly and separately, as if a fatal accident was being announced.

"Mrs. Jamieson."

"Mr. Finch."

"A fine day for driving." He was looking down at her white MG, which was parked in front of Mandowski's store, and as she followed his eyes Annabelle felt her throat jam tight with tension. She looked up and down the empty street.

"Could I help you with your groceries?"

He had taken the two bags from her arms and was lowering them towards the passenger seat when her voice broke free.

"Would you like to go for a ride . . . now?"

She was so surprised at her own words that she instantly turned from Finch and began to get into her car. Even as he followed suit, Annabelle did not look at him. Instead, praying that Mandowski would not be choosing this moment to look out his window, she drove quickly around the corner and onto the highway that led out of town. Only when they had left the last house behind did Annabelle remember that Allen had said he would be eating dinner in Kingston that evening, with a client.

Finch was the first to speak: "A fine day, Mrs. Jamieson, but I'm afraid it's going to rain."

"Finch." She was still on the highway, she was driving to the lake she had visited on her way to Finch's farm, and she let one hand drop from the steering wheel to Finch's knee. She was surprised to find the cotton cloth of his trousers soft and clean.

His large hand came down towards her own. She had so often seen it descending harshly to the church lectern that she almost expected an oaken crack to reverberate through the car. "The other day in the barn, you were very brave."

"I was frightened," Annabelle said. "I'm still a city girl." His hand had enclosed her own, and she felt frightened again.

A few minutes later she was sitting on the cliff top with Finch, in the white MG. Their hands had separated and Annabelle found herself distracted by the thunderclouds that were taking possession of the sky. Some were moving faster than others, black, low-flying clouds that barrelled in over the lake, waggling their wings like young airplanes ecstatically eager to smash themselves to bits on the facing cliff.

For almost a full hour the clouds collected, and while she talked with Finch, Annabelle tried to hide her nervousness behind a stream of cigarettes. Finally the air grew so dark and humid that even the cliffs were reduced to a faint and hulking shadow. Moments later, lightning rose up from the centre of the lake, two jagged white fingers splitting the sky into a perfect V. The thunder followed, a single deafening clap that shook the car and made Annabelle bite her tongue.

"Finch."

"City girl," Finch said, unconcerned.

But the thunder began again and Annabelle leapt from the car and started running across the open meadow; as she ran, the rain began to fall in thick sheets, and by the time she had reached the shelter of the woods, she was absolutely soaked. Only then did she turn to see if Finch had followed. He had, at his own speed: he was ambling along the cliff top, making a slow promenade while the rain beat against him. "Finch," she shouted, but her voice was lost in the sound of wind tearing through the leaves, and despite everything she had to laugh at the wonderful strutting vanity of the man: Finch, the crazy fool, anything to show off; if she asked him now he'd surely jump.

By the time he had finally joined her under the tree, Annabelle was sitting with her arms folded across her stomach, drunk with fear. Finch pulled her to her feet and kissed her roughly, pushing her hard against a tree so she felt her back scrape against the bark. His mouth covering hers made her want to gag: struggling, she tried to free herself. But Finch's hands were like heavy chains on her shoulders; they held her easily, keeping her trapped against the tree. Then he moved his mouth to her throat like one dog asserting mastery over another. Annabelle felt his teeth on her skin; then there was another explosion of thunder and in her terror she pressed her throat into Finch's mouth, wanting to be simultaneously penetrated and torn open, nailed by lightning into the wet ground.

Suddenly Finch stepped away and ran out into the rain. Crying Annabelle followed him. In the meadow behind the rock cliffs he let her catch him, then he threw her down into the wet grass and ran away again. "Finch," Annabelle screamed. *"Finch."* She was on her knees and the warm rain was driving into her eyes. Finch: how could she ever have trusted him? Then the thunder began to roll again and she collapsed face down on the ground, dirt grinding into her mouth. She felt like a squirrel trapped inside its own hoarded nut. But the shell had been breached and with each crack of lightning each thunderclap, it was forced further apart. Lying curled tight to herself she gradually unwound with the sweet and delicious sensation of her fear bleeding away.

But it was too soon when Finch descended. "Finch," she protested, but one of his hands was pressed against her mouth while with the other he searched out the small of her back and lifted her to him. And then as lightning tore through the dark clouds Annabelle felt dissolving inside her the last barrier against losing control against Finch, against that chasm of terror that she had glimpsed with Isaac and that she had covered over with her civilized and ironical life. She wrapped her legs around Finch, gathered him to her until her thighs cramped with pain; finally her skin, electric with fear and lightning, joined to the grass and the earth and they were all writhing together under Finch's crazy pumping.

"City woman," Finch whispered later.

Annabelle smiled. Her face felt new, as though a mask worn too long had been torn away.

"Mrs. Jamieson?"

"Yes."

"This is Reverend Finch speaking. I was hoping you could come to our meeting about the orphans."

"When would that be?"

"Thursday afternoon."

"That's not possible."

"Are you certain, Mrs. Jamieson? The church needs you."

"I'm sorry, that's not possible."

"Is he there?"

"You must have the wrong number." Hanging up.

"Who was that?" Allen's question.

"Well, don't let it spoil your dinner."

She walked back into the dining room; the beautiful July evening sun was a golden cloth on their table, illuminating Allen's fair hair, shining through the crystal like angel's light.

But later that night, while Allen performed his bi-daily ritual, what she saw was Finch's face, his eyes black holes, as Allen shadowed over her, forcing her to groan, to squeeze her eyes closed and turn away from the watching spire.

Annabelle was sitting in her studio, working on her mosaic, when for the first time it occurred to her that by some miraculous fluke she'd made it: she'd found some balance between the two men; and she was suspended between them, moving back and forth as if these few weeks of deception could last for years. She had never practised deception before, but of course deception wasn't a fair word because although she hadn't told Allen — and of course would no more tell Allen than tell her mother — Annabelle reassured herself that what she felt for Finch had nothing to do with Allen. Even if her feelings were love, it was a private love: a harmless affair that had finally moved her from the city to the country and was a matter for her own conscience.

But her conscience, unfortunately, was hurting these days.

After each visit with Finch, as she drove home so happy that her heart purred with the motor of her white MG, she would tell herself how wonderful it was that she felt satisfied, that she had gotten from Finch what she needed and might, in fact, not see him again except to view him in his pulpit.

The idea that the relationship with Finch was not actually a drama that would need to be resolved, but was only a series of encounters — a series of encounters that might already be over — would ease her guilt. By the time she started to ask herself just who she was trying to fool, her mind would slip back to planning the next meeting with Finch.

Dark blues and browns, streaks of red: Annabelle had been glazing the background for the relief, glazing and firing, and the workroom which had been dominated by the grey of raw clay was beginning to take on a stronger, more erratic look, clumps of colour waiting to meet the sun as it worked its way around the windows.

She was drinking her second cup of coffee and kneading the clay, working out the air. From time to time she broke off a morsel and made experimental little forays: today she wanted to do the grocer, George Mandowski, and for some reason Annabelle pictured him standing against the wall, wide but not entirely corpulent, an unctuous look on his face as he stood with his arms outstretched, his big belly exposed, waiting to be crucified. Mandowski the martyr, but what had he done? Annabelle put down the clay and picked up her pencil wanting to sketch his face. Donna Wilson had said that he had been the only foreign boy in the school and that he had married the girl who spent every Saturday night flat on her back.

Annabelle's eyes were closed. She wondered what Donna Wilson would say if she unburdened her conscience and told her about Finch and their meetings near the lake. This afternoon, for example, she was to see Finch there. These days were so blue and clear: when Finch emerged from the woods Annabelle's blood would start to race and she felt as if she herself, running towards him, was making the great lover's leap.

The way she had felt, Annabelle suddenly remembered, as she had leapt into the disaster with Isaac — the disaster she had promised never to repeat because at the very least she would stay faithful to her work.

Pushing back her stool Annabelle threw her pencil onto the table and walked quickly out of the studio. Mandowski: how could she do Mandowski when she couldn't even keep his face in her mind? Grabbing her purse in the hall she swung out the door and into her car. Soon she was in the General Store, and since Mandowski was out of sight, she decided to salvage something of the morning by getting the shopping done.

Nellie Tillson, as always, was at the cash register. Her face was flushed with the heat and when she pursed her lips to check the figures, her mouth looked so soft and inviting that Annabelle expected some man to leap from behind the stacks of cans and drag her to the floor.

As Nellie packed the groceries, Annabelle looked down at her stomach. It was definitely bulging, pushing out at the loose sweatshirt that she wore. But there was no ring on her wedding hand, nor could Annabelle recall any talk of Nellie Tillson getting married.

The next customer — a tourist in Bermuda shorts with a gauze boating cap on his head — was impatiently trying to get through. Annabelle took up her shopping bag and hurried out of the store.

Then she saw him: Finch. He grabbed at her and Annabelle lost her balance, almost fell. Nothing had changed the way he clenched his hand around her arm.

"What were you doing in there?"

"Finch, let go."

"What were you doing?" His voice insistent and forcing.

"Finch." She hated to meet him in town. The very sight of his shoulders in his black suit made her churn and flutter, and the miraculous balance was just another fragile shell waiting to be broken. *Finch, go away. Please go away.*

People were looking at them now and Finch had stepped back. "Mrs. Jamieson," he was saying, "what a pleasant surprise."

"Mr. Finch."

"Mrs. Jamieson, may I help you with your groceries?"

"No, thank you, Mr. Finch."

"Mrs. Jamieson, I insist."

He was still holding her arm and she knew that people were watching them from inside the window of the store.

"Thank you, Mr. Finch, that would be very kind." She had pushed the bag towards him and he had taken it, releasing her arm. She knew it would bruise, and as she walked to the parking lot with Finch she was so angry that she was already rehearsing her conversation with Allen, telling him that the insane minister had grabbed her on the street again, importuned her about the orphans from Thailand. Impossible, he was absolutely impossible.

And then, as they were entering the parking lot: "Mr. Finch, you are never to grab me like that again."

"You are never to go into that store again," Finch returned.

They were at the car. The top was off. Yesterday afternoon they had driven along dirt roads, their shirts open to the wind and sun.

"Put my groceries in the car, please." She remembered hitting Finch and the look of surprise on his face. Now she wondered what it would be like to be strong enough to squeeze Finch around the neck the way he had squeezed her arm.

"Promise," demanded Finch.

"Finch." She could feel her temper starting to go.

He put the bag in the passenger seat. There was no sign of the smile she loved, only his dark beard looming over her. "Mandowski is the lowest —"

But she didn't hear any more, because as he started to talk about Mandowski he renewed his grip on her arm and when he did, Annabelle's temper exploded: her free hand shot up, she slapped him so hard that the little spikes of his beard dug like splinters into her palm.

"Annabelle."

But she was in the car; her foot to the accelerator she skidded out of the parking lot and down the street.

Later in the afternoon Annabelle left her house again and drove the white MG to meet Finch at the rock cliff. Fear beating in her like a trapped bird, she collapsed into his arms. Safety was the weight of his muscled hands on her back, the growl and thunder of his voice when she pressed her ear to his chest. Holding her tight Finch said that he would never grab her arm again. Finch: she was drowned in his presence, she was so relieved that she agreed never again to go into Mandowski's store. Lying on the grass, naked in the afternoon warmth, they both promised, promised once and promised again, never to show their private faces in the town.

"We're in danger now," Finch said. "People will be watching."

"Let them watch."

"Let them see nothing but the Reverend Finch and the good Mrs. Jamieson."

"The Reverend Finch with his pants down," giggled Annabelle.

Finch lay on his back in the thick grass. Viewed closely his usually shadowed eyes were softened by the sun and Annabelle, hovering above him, examined the glowing healthy whites, the transparent black surface of the pupils. They were flecked with bits of brown, rusty metal shards: this is the place, Annabelle suddenly thought, where Finch buries his dead. She moved back, getting the view of the whole face: the tanned, leathery skin beginning to web around the eyes and the corners of the mouth; the strong, wide bones that defined each feature; the black beard sparsely laced with grey that framed the chin and jaws.

With a stalk of grass Annabelle traced the frown lines that connected nose to chin, the hollows of his eyes, the strong, wide cheekbones. After the dark V of his neck Finch's skin was white as sheets "The notorious lecher Finch," Annabelle laughed. "You're such a prude you're afraid to open your shirt in your own fields." She drew the grass down his white chest, followed the matted hair to his stomach, going up again to the thickly muscled shoulders, the huge arms with their blue veins pushing at the surface of the skin.

The arms reached up to enclose her but even as she was sinking into Finch, Annabelle was wondering what the price was, and when she would have to pay it.

When she got home, the day, split apart by comings and goings, lay behind her like something dangerously shattered.

She was pacing nervously in the kitchen, cooking dinner for Allen, and as she slapped together a casserole of chicken and mushrooms — for the second time that week, she realized — there was a tension across her back and shoulders.

The chicken was in a glass dish, and the sliced mushrooms covered it like the remains from a battlefield.

"Finch," Annabelle whispered. All the unspoken anger still lived inside her. Finch had grabbed her arm in front of the store as if she were a cow about to be thrown into its place. As if she were one of the women Donna had told her about, one of the town women who couldn't keep their skirts on when the preacher came to visit.

She sprinkled rosemary on top of the chicken: the smell was vaguely soothing. Then she took a jar of paprika and dotted the whole casserole red.

As she picked up the dish to put it in the oven, the anger started through her again; her arm jerked, the chicken heaved up into the air. For a moment the whole concoction hung suspended — chicken, mushrooms, little straws of rosemary and powdered paprika.

Then miraculously it fell together again, and Annabelle slid it into the warm, glass-doored belly of her new stove.

Finch: he had turned her into one of his women. She could feel his weight still on her, his teeth pretending to clamp onto her nipple, could hear their voices as they swore to be careful in the future.

The Reverend Finch with his pants down. Annabelle paced into the living room and looked across the street at Donna Wilson's house. She was cooking dinner for her husband. If Annabelle stepped outside she would be able to hear Donna, hear the noise of the children playing.

Or she could go into her own backyard, look at the garden which in turn was overlooked by houses on either side.

There was the walk down her road to the lake. There, along the shore, the town had laid out a short cinder path for tourists to stretch their legs and look at the lake while resting from their time in the shops.

Or she could stay at home, where Allen would shortly be arriving.

It was six o'clock; the afternoon light was still warm and golden in the living room of her postcard stone house.

She had spent almost six years with Allen, recovering from Isaac and learning how to protect herself; now Finch was putting her back again, back to where she had been when Isaac had called her bluff by arriving on her doorstep with a suitcase and announcing that he had left his wife and was moving in with her. Not only had he quit his family, but he even promised to drink nothing but beer and to cook every second night.

"A man who doesn't know how to cook is helpless," Isaac said. "I know. I was married for thirteen years and I never cooked a meal." He was making his speciality, scrambled eggs.

"Thirteen years?"

"That's right," Isaac said. "Our anniversary was last week." He turned away from Annabelle to the stove.

"Did you get her a present?"

"Sure," Isaac said, "I got her a fur coat."

"And now you've left her for me."

"That's right. Now I've left." Isaac was looking straight at her, standing tall and rigid at the stove; and now his eyebrows jerked up, as if to remind some invisible audience of the ridiculous life he was leading, the incredible words he was saying.

On their first night Isaac had shown Annabelle a picture of his wife: a dark-haired, smiling woman with a round face and soft eyes that matched his own, but he had never complained about her, never said anything at all except that she was very independent and could live without him. For some reason Annabelle had taken this to mean that she had lovers, but now she wondered if Isaac had left behind him an innocent woman with three children to care for.

"Do you miss your children?,"

"Of course."

"Do you intend to see them?"

Isaac nodded.

"When?,"

"Oh, I don't know. Maybe next week."

"Will you see your wife?"

"I guess so."

All this time Isaac had been stirring at the eggs and now, Annabelle noticed, a faint trail of smoke was beginning to rise from the stove. Meanwhile Isaac was reaching into the refrigerator for another beer.

"What does your wife think?"

"About what?"

"About us."

The brown smoke was turning black and Annabelle, unable to restrain herself, got up from the table and went to the stove. Isaac was leaning against the wall, crying.

"Isaac, what's wrong? Do you miss your family?"

"It's not that," Isaac got out, between sobs. She had never heard of men crying, let alone wailing like Isaac, who could break into tears five times a day.

"What is it?" She put her arms around him. Poor Isaac, he was so sweet that she sometimes woke up in the morning bursting with love for him, wanting him so much she could swallow him whole.

Isaac finally turned and wrapped Annabelle in his arms. "I haven't told her," he sobbed. "I said I was going to New York for a week to buy jewels."

"You what?" She could see the apartment darkening, as though the sky had wiped out the sun. She had her hand on the skillet, preparing to swing at him if he tried to kiss her, when she felt the hot metal burning into her palm. She dropped the pan and clutched her burnt hand to her chest.

"Annabelle, I'm truly sorry." He had fallen to his knees and was clinging to her legs. Annabelle shuddered at his touch, found herself kicking out at him convulsively as she backed into the dining room.

"What," asked Annabelle, "were you going to do if she came to the store?"

"She never comes to the store."

"But what if she did?"

"I don't know." He looked up at her, his face tearful and beseeching like that of a beaten child. "I guess I'd tell her I was back."

"Well" said Annabelle, "you can go tell her you're back right now."

She was sitting on one of the oak chairs she had sanded clean; the heel of her hand was pressed against her heart.

"I could stay in a hotel," Isaac said. "We could try again tomorrow."

"You can stay anywhere you like, but if you're not out by the time I count to ten, I'm going to call the police."

Isaac was still on his knees. "I know it was wrong," he whispered, "I'm sorry."

"One," Annabelle said. "Two."

Isaac struggled to his feet. "I'm sorry. Didn't you hear me say I'm sorry?"

"Three," Annabelle said. "Four."

He turned from her and went to the bedroom. She could hear him muttering to himself, but at the count of twenty-six he reappeared with his suitcase bulging. By this time Annabelle wasn't saying the numbers aloud, but was hissing them as her burnt palm pulsed. In her lap she now had the telephone; the directory was at her feet, opened to Emergency.

"Forgive me," Isaac begged.

"Go."

"Goodbye," Isaac said. "I forgive you." And then he turned his back, opened the door, and started down the stairs.

When she had heard the Datsun pull away, Annabelle walked to the window. According to the watch Isaac had given her, the new reconciliation watch that was even more expensive than the first, that fitted so lightly she could hardly feel its weight, it was twelve minutes to nine. She slipped off the watch and prepared to throw it down to the pavement.

Soon Isaac would arrive at his house and tell his wife and three children about his wonderful adventure in New York. Perhaps he would even stop at the airport to pick up some presents. Annabelle took the watch from the windowsill and put it back on her wrist. Keep a souvenir, her mother had once told her. Something to remember.

Now Annabelle looked at her watch and remembered: it was five thirty, in a few minutes Allen would be home for his supper. Annabelle reached into the cupboard for dishes to set the table with and took down two plates with faint beige figures etched onto the sides. This had been her project before the mosaic, doing dishes with rings of dancing figures, holding hands like the human chains that had been found in the old cave paintings.

They had been intended to symbolize, Annabelle had told Allen, the connections people had to each other — the connections of which they themselves were unaware. When Allen finally came in the door, Annabelle was in her studio, sketching him with his hands extended: one to Isaac and the other to Finch.

Ten

"Mrs. Jamieson."

"Mr. Finch."

"Mrs. Jamieson, I believe, and aren't you looking lovely today."

"Mr. Finch, you'd flatter a woman to death."

"Mrs. Jamieson, honest men are made to praise beauty when they see it."

"Good day, Mr. Finch, at the lake at three?"

"Good day, Mrs. Jamieson. At three."

Walking blithely home from the bank, so happy it was an effort to keep from sprinting in the warm morning sun, Annabelle considered just how well things were working out. There had been the fight, to be sure, and sometimes when she saw her face in the mirror it looked so different and so young she couldn't believe that Allen didn't know how much she had changed. But the stream of effortless encounters with Finch had continued, and the early intensity had given way to a series of long and mellow afternoons.

These afternoons were like the summer itself, which as it drew into its last month seemed determined to wipe out all memory of winter. No longer could Annabelle think that each visit with Finch might be the last. Instead, she said to herself, when summer ended and the cold fall days began, the affair would gradually diminish with the weather; exactly how this might happen, and how she would give up the excitement of

Finch for the narrowness of Allen, was a mystery she didn't want to solve.

Back at her house, Annabelle went into her studio to work at her figures. The sketches of Mandowski had been completed, and now it was time to make the clay model. When the shapes resisted her understanding, she liked to make the naked bodies first and then to dress them. With Mandowski, she began with the legs. Some heavy people had pipestem legs that miraculously supported their spherical bellies and chests: Jacob Beam, for example, had bowed legs so thin that the sharp edge of his shins could be seen cutting into his pants, making the loose cloth billow behind them.

Jacob Beam was a thin-boned man who had grown a belly, grown it in the same way he had grown his beard. But Mandowski was thick all over, lumps of muscle and fat joined together on big bones so that every movement was constrained. Annabelle had the clay of Mandowski's legs in her fingers, and now she found herself shaping it; making first the stumpy cylinder, then using her fingernail to define the knee, the calf, the thick square thigh.

In the old days, she knew, people who wanted to paint or sculpt figures took classes in dissection. She had studied art for a year in university: to draw the body, the teacher had said, that is the noblest thing. The museums of Europe were, in Annabelle's mind, filled with the sketches of famous artists, perfectly executed little drawings with arms and shoulders twisted, hands and feet projected to the viewer's eye. But to cut into corpses would have been too much. Though she had imagined often enough: the stainless knife drawing across the grey cold skin, layers of flesh and muscle bloodlessly exposed.

Her hands were trembling. She spread out her fingers and pressed her palms together. When she and Isaac had finished, she had gone back to university and taken — along with the karate — a night course in pottery. The karate had been to protect herself from Isaac, should he keep returning; but the pottery had been a practical version of the romantic teenage idea that she would like to be an artist.

After the first week she had a dream in which she was

attending a lecture in anatomy. The air was thick with antiseptic and formaldehyde, and rising steeply towards the vaulted wooden ceilings were rows of benches for the eagerly watching students. Lying on the table in the pit of this enormous room, his dead grey skin waiting for the knife of the instructor, had been Isaac.

Long incisions were made, great flaps of flesh cut free and pulled back, until finally Isaac, reduced to bones and muscle, was surrounded by the grey cape of his own skin. Only his genitals were intact. For these the instructor now reached and Annabelle, choking on the deathly smell that now filled the room, had closed her eyes and screamed, "Run, Isaac! Run!"

She had woken up relieved to hear the summer night breeze rustling through the leaves of the tree outside her window.

Remembering the dream, Annabelle crushed Mandowski's legs between her palms and reached for a cigarette. As she did, the telephone rang.

"Don't get caught," were the first words her mother said. Annabelle, afraid that her mother was referring to Finch, was paralyzed.

"Annabelle? Are you there?"

"I'm here, Mother."

"If you're going to get in trouble, Annabelle, don't get caught."

Annabelle stabbed her cigarette slowly into the glass ashtray on the telephone table.

"I called this afternoon, but there was no answer."

"I went for a drive," Annabelle said, wondering how much exactly her mother could know.

"It happened last night, right in my own apartment. Annabelle, I never would have believed it. Your own father."

Annabelle lit another cigarette.

"At least he could keep it a secret."

"Keep what a secret?" There was a cold cup of coffee beside the telephone, which she now reached for and nervously sipped.

"What are you drinking?"

"Coffee."

"I won't tell you that you drink too much coffee."

"All right," Annabelle said. "Don't tell me."

"Anyway I was calling about your father. I'm afraid he's going to spend all his money on that floozy of his."

"He doesn't have a girlfriend," Annabelle said. She could hear her own voice shaking with relief. "Anyway, you're just afraid of losing the money he gives to you."

"I earned that money, Annabelle, I deserve every cent I get."

"More," Annabelle said. Her heart was still booming with the false alarm.

"It's lucky for me that you and Allen send me something too, or I don't know what I'd do." She paused, and Annabelle knew that, her act of contrition done, she would now resume. "Anyway, I am worried about that floozy."

"What floozy?"

"Rachel Parsons, you know who."

"Oh, for God's sake, Mother. Rachel Parsons is no floozy and no girlfriend of father's."

"You don't think Ben Parsons does her any good."

"I don't think she cares, Mother. She's sixty-two years old and she likes to eat."

Instantly Annabelle knew she had said the wrong thing, and as her mother launched into medical statistics proving that sexuality only increases with age, Annabelle looked out the window.

"Anyway," her mother said, "did you ever see *Cat on a Hot Tin Roof?*"

"Yes, I did." This was a new one.

"With Elizabeth Taylor?"

"Yes, Allen took me to it at a drive-in."

"You remember the scene when Elizabeth Taylor pulls up her skirt and starts to take off her nylon stocking."

Annabelle concentrated, and then the scene came back to her. Elizabeth Taylor, young then, a ripe peach ready to be peeled. "I remember," Annabelle said. "But I think she was pulling it on."

"Never mind, you remember the scene, don't you?"

"Yes," Annabelle said.

"Well last night your father was over, we were playing bridge with the Parsons, and Rachel Parsons got up from the table, then stopped in the middle of the floor, as if something was bothering her, the floozy, then looked at your father, lifted up her skirt, and slowly took down her stocking. Annabelle, I was so shocked I couldn't move."

"Maybe something was biting her."

"Annabelle, this is no joking matter. In fact, I'll tell you, your father completely lost control of himself."

"What do you mean?"

"You know what I mean. After all I'm not blind."

Annabelle lit a new cigarette. Her mother was crying into the phone.

"Well, Annabelle, do you believe me now?"

"No, Mother. I think that's a disgusting story."

"It's not disgusting," her mother sobbed. "It's true."

"Sometimes even true things are disgusting."

Annabelle's mother stopped crying. "No, Annabelle," she said, very firmly, "there is absolutely nothing that is disgusting about your father. If you had known him the way I did you would appreciate that. He's a shell now, just a shell of what he was."

"You're right, Mother, you're absolutely right."

"You don't have to get smart, Annabelle, but I am right about this. I know your father better than he knows himself." A pause. "Anyway, I just wanted to talk with you about him. How are you?"

"I'm fine."

"And Allen?"

"He's fine too."

"Give him my love."

"Yes, Mother."

"Goodbye."

Annabelle set down the phone, then walked outside to her backyard, wanting the full force of the sun on her face. For a moment she had actually believed that her mother had somehow discovered the truth about Finch; her throat felt dry and sore from the cigarettes she'd smoked. She was living a double life now: the summer days were perfect but her nights were filled with uneasy dreams. It was only after Allen had left for work that she could catch her breath, then she would wait all day long to see or hear from Finch.

And if she got caught? She was concentrating so intently on this fear that she didn't notice she was no longer alone. Donna Wilson had crossed the street and was standing beside her, looking at the grass that was growing to seed along the north wall of the garage.

"Well," said Donna.

"Well," Annabelle replied. *Well* was always Donna's opening remark, delivered in a way to make clear that she knew Annabelle was in the midst of some inadmissible train of thought.

"I saw you looking at your garage," Donna said, "and just thought I'd better come and help you hold it up."

"You want some coffee?"

Annabelle turned to go inside. She liked Donna Wilson, she truly liked her. The blonde coiffed hair, the blue, china-doll eyes, every pore on her face meticulously cleaned and tended: Donna was like the indoor garden of a naturalist trapped in the Arctic. Annabelle started walking, hesitated for a moment at the back porch, then led the way around to the front so they wouldn't go through the studio and past the Salem mosaic.

"Haven't seen you for while," Donna said. She had brought some her own perfect shortbread cookies. They were on the table between them, set out in a shallow bowl that Annabelle had rejected from one of her Christmas dinnerware sets.

"It's been busy." The afternoons with Finch had filled the past few weeks; time had fled by like a child's summer.

"Busy," Donna repeated.

She knows, Annabelle thought, and before she could even begin to frame a reply her skin reacted, a blush so fierce and instant that she could see the scarlet on her arms and wrists.

There was a silence, which grew longer, and as Annabelle waited for Donna to continue her stomach began to drum.

"I hear you had words with the Reverend outside the grocery store."

"He can be a pest," Annabelle said. It had happened two weeks before; she had thought the danger must be past.

"I hear you hit him pretty good," Donna said. She grinned and for a moment Annabelle thought that the secret had been kept after all. Perhaps this would turn out like her mother's phone call: another elaborate scare.

"He was bothering me."

"He's been more than bothering you." Donna helped herself to more coffee from the pot. She had a delicate way of wrapping her fingers around the silver handle that always caught Annabelle's eye. "Everyone knows," Donna said. "You might as well have put a picture in the paper."

"Knows what?" Still hoping. Looking right at Donna, hoping to face her down.

"Annabelle, how could you be so dumb?"

The churning in her stomach had stopped and now there was a brief and total silence, as though she had walked into a glass wall.

Then feeling returned to her skin. It was tingling and uncomfortable: her neck chafed against her collar; her nipples felt tender and raw against the cotton of her shirt; even the skin behind her knees was uncomfortably hot. And then her stomach started again, a white heat springing through it, instantly boiling with tension. She wrapped her arms around herself, bent forward so that her stomach pressed into them.

Donna reached across the table and put her hand on Annabelle's. The small tanned fingers caressed her own; each of Donna's nails was a perfect little pond of hardened polish. She warned me, Annabelle thought, now she thinks I deserve this; but when she looked up she saw that Donna's mouth was trembling.

"Annabelle, don't you care?"

"I do," she choked out, "I do." But though she wanted to, she couldn't feel very much. Even the tears that welled up wouldn't flow; they trickled grudgingly from the corners of her eyes, one by one. Donna's hands tightened over her own and Annabelle began to hear a fine buzzing in her skull a warning sound. It's all over, she thought again. It's all over. Finally she was crying freely, her mouth twisted and her cheeks stretched, crying and gulping back her tears at the same time.

"Do you love him?"

"I don't think so."

"Why did you do it?"

"I don't know," Annabelle said. She was still crying and the words came out half-strangled, making her want to laugh. Then the story began to spill out and she told Donna about Allen's telephoning her, the way she had hated being interrupted. The warm afternoon drive out to the farm where she had gone into the frightening darkness of the barn — only to see Maureen Finch whistling towards her in her stainless-steel wheelchair. Then there had been the silky warmth of the calf, the thick dense smell of milk and blood. Birth: the violent energy had been a storm forcing them together, joining them. And Maureen had known and was egging her on the whole time, daring her to take the chance, to lay her life open to guilt and gossip, to risk destruction as she herself had been destroyed.

But when it had all been told — the birth of the calf, her own miscarriage, Finch's arm around her shoulder as they stepped from the barn back into the yellow afternoon sun, the moment in front of the store when she invited Finch to come for a ride — Annabelle found herself wondering if this affair would become like the one with Isaac: a tearful comic drama with herself as the victim.

Finch: she preferred him to not-Finch for the same reason she preferred summer to winter: he made her feel alive.

"Does Finch's wife know?"

"I think so," Annabelle said.

"A bitch. And what about Allen?"

"I haven't told him."

"God," Donna said. She leaned back in her chair and wiped tears from her own cheeks. "What an old lady I am, crying like this. It's none of my business."

"Yes, it is."

Annabelle's throat was raw and tired. The morning sun had climbed high in the sky so that it shot through the sheer white curtains and warmed the pine top of the table where they were sitting. Annabelle felt the sharp pain in her chest begin to ease:

and her eyes, which had resisted crying, were now melted into a warm and throbbing pulse.

It was three weeks since the afternoon on the cliffs; since then she had woken up early every morning eager to start a new summer day and work on her crazy but entertaining project. For the first time since she had moved to Salem she had stopped worrying about the ringing of the telephone, and when her mother did call she sometimes got through the whole conversation without a cigarette. There were days, it was true, when she was furious at Finch, and when she was sure she would never see him again. There were days when being with Allen was so smooth and calm it made her want to scream with frustration. But the truth was that for three weeks her mind and body had been fully engaged, alive, spinning with plans, deceits, loyalties, betrayals, projects so vast and beautiful they could never be accomplished, visions of her own ridiculous work and this tiny, turned-in town that made her want to have a thousand hands, a thousand bodies, a thousand lives to live.

"That's it," Annabelle finally said. "I'm happy."

"Happy," Donna repeated incredulously. And then she looked at Annabelle with a stare so puzzled and intent that Annabelle thought the two of them would soon be crying again.

"Oh, Annabelle. I'm so sorry. It's going to be so hard.'

"I know."

"What's he going to do about Nellie Tillson?"

"Who?"

"She's showing already," Donna went on. "They say she wants to take him to court."

"Nellie Tillson? Isn't she the cashier at Mandowski's store? And," she went on, amazed at the steadiness of her own voice, "doesn't she sometimes teach in the Sunday school? Why would she want to take Finch to court?"

The telephone began its muted ring. Annabelle put her hand down and braced herself on the pine table, the old table she and Allen had bought in Ottawa and that she had sanded down and finished. "We should go outside," Annabelle said. "It's such a beautiful day." She stood up, unsure of her balance, conscious of a sudden bead of sweat on her upper lip. Donna's visit began to seem like a series of battering waves; yet while she had been smashed apart, Donna survived untouched. Her hair bounced from her shoulders in perfect blonde curls as she moved around the table and took Annabelle's arm.

"I'm sorry," Annabelle mumbled. "I'm not taking this very well."

"You should sit down."

"No. We have to go outside." She broke away from Donna and walked quickly to the front door. She pushed it open.

Allen was striding up the walk, his jacket over his shoulder and the white sleeves of his shirt rolled up to the elbow. His face wore the same smile it had when he'd said he was going to be doing some work for the Reverend.

"It's such a nice day," he said, "I thought I'd surprise you." *Keep your eye on the birdie* flashed through her mind, and as she stumbled and pitched forward she kept her eye on Allen's smile, watched it as she lost her footing, and kept watching it as he sprang forward and gathered her in his arms, swung her up so quickly that as she passed out she saw his face coming towards her like a speeding train.

Eleven

Annabelle woke up with a fever throbbing through her. Her first thought was that she must have missed the meeting with Finch, but to her surprise this safe bed seemed more desirable than the shadow of her white MG.

She turned her head on the pillow and smelled the fresh cotton. It was a soft, sweet smell, and it reminded her of the thicker, richer smell of the barn. With the memory of the barn came the remembered feeling of Finch's strong chest beneath her cheek, the deep sound that his heart made when she pressed her ear against it.

This made her want to cry but there had already been so many tears with Donna that only a bittersweet ache was left. She smiled at Allen across the room but then wanted to close her eyes when he smiled back. She wondered if this new feeling was hatred for Allen, for Finch, or only for herself.

The fever was the kind she used to have as a child. It had a distinct cycle, and the first stage was a giddy rush of heat through the blood. She sat up but as she put her feet to the floor she wobbled and fell against the side of the bed. Allen, who had been reading by the window, sprang to help her.

"It's all right." The fever was like a river ripping out the past and forcing everything and everyone into one tiny room. Her mind felt as if it was stretching and straining, wanting to find a place to push out the way Nellie Tillson's pregnant belly pushed out over the smooth black counter at Mandowski's store.

And as Annabelle thought about Nellie Tillson, about her corn-yellow hair and the loose sweatshirt she wore to cover Finch's child, the second stage of the fever's cycle began — the heat burst through to her skin and she was drenched with sweat. When she was a child her mother used to wrap her in a sheet, and Annabelle on her way to the bathroom took a sheet from the closet and held it to her chest.

Allen had followed her down the hall and was standing behind her as she leaned over the sink, brushing her teeth.

With the sweating came the panic, as with thunderstorms, but this panic was more intense because it was her own body that threatened to fall apart. When she had finished brushing her teeth she took two aspirins from the small bottle in the medicine cabinet. The glass of water seemed almost too much to hold, and she had to set it carefully on the white porcelain. Allen's face in the mirror was utterly known: even in the reversed image of the mirror his fair hair and rounded features made the perfect lawyer's mask.

"Annabelle." His face was calm enough, but his voice was losing control. She turned and looked at him sharply. He backed suddenly away.

"You know about Finch." Not a question.

"Yes."

"Oh, God." She walked by him in the hall to the bedroom where she climbed back into bed. She pulled the blankets up to her neck: her heart was booming in her chest, against the insides of her eardrums. She reached to the bedside table for her watch, the same watch that Isaac had given her. It was eight o'clock now; the time for her meeting with Finch had long passed. Had he waited? Had he leapt despairingly into the lake?

With Isaac she had been a fool and he had been cruel to her. But despite all the tears it had been a comedy and life had continued. She'd had the compulsory disaster with a married man; he'd gotten an easy trip through the arms of a young woman.

But if the relationship with Finch was also supposed to be a comedy she hadn't yet seen the joke. And then suddenly Annabelle felt like one of the figures in her mosaic: a pawn for

Donna's mischievous plans; a stranger for Maureen to hate; a city woman to titillate Finch; a desperate wife for Allen to manipulate.

Allen was sitting at the window again; he was watching her with the same detached interest as, in her dream, the students had watched the dissection of Isaac.

"You knew," Annabelle said, "that day in your office."

"No."

"Yes, you did. You knew about Finch and Nellie Tillson the day you gave me the letter, and you knew Finch was after me, too. You sent me out there just to see what would happen."

"My secretary was sick."

Annabelle was sitting up in bed, holding Isaac's watch. "You really are disgusting. You just wanted to see what would happen."

"You've got it wrong," Allen said. "I thought you might like the drive. I had just bought you a car, remember? I didn't know about you and Finch until Finch came and told me this morning."

Annabelle's knees slammed together. Her stomach was clenched and her body was so confused that her thighs were beginning to ache. Finch must have gone straight from the bank to Allen's office. "I don't believe you."

"It's true. He said that he had made the final decision not to settle out of court with Nellie Tillson. He said that he knew that if he confessed his sins to God, then God would forgive and protect him. Then he asked me if I would forgive him."

The drumming in her heart speeded up; each beat shook her whole frame.

"What did you say?" She only meant him to repeat it so she would have more time to think.

"I forgave him," Allen said. "He said that if God could forgive him, I could forgive him too."

It was ten minutes after eight. Annabelle put down the watch and reached for a cigarette. It felt large and foreign between her fingers, the way cigarettes used to feel when she stole them from her parents and smoked them secretly in the bathroom. *God had forgiven him.* She imagined the two men happily praying to this kind and understanding God: mouths wide and beaming with joy, down on their knees on the cheap nylon broadloom of Allen's Salem office.

"Did you sing hymns?" she asked.

Allen didn't reply. His face was composed, waiting. He had her now. He was like one of those overgrown boys in her public school who used to make presents for the girls, matchboxes full of grasshopper legs. "You'd better go downstairs," Annabelle said. "I have to think."

Allen got up: Annabelle noticed that his hands were red. He's been twisting them together like an old woman, she thought; he's rubbed it in my face and now he's ashamed of himself — and for a moment she was afraid that they would both lose control. But Allen simply turned and left the room, carefully closing the door behind him.

It was only when he was downstairs and she could hear him pacing the length of the living room to the liquor cabinet that it occurred to Annabelle she too could have begged to be pardoned, could have wept and gone down on her knees.

She looked about the room. There was this bed, a pine four-poster they had bought before they got married, and two matching dressers. Beside the window was a rocking chair, also pine, and a chest. All these they had found together, driving on weekends to country auctions. Then they had spent long evenings stripping off the various coats of paint and enamel, laughing at the strange bad taste of the rural people who had covered this wood with layers of pink and orange and green when underneath lay the rich golden grain. But now seeing the carefully resurrected past littered about the room, she felt suddenly a fool. After all, it was the people of Salem and other such towns who had originally built this furniture, who painted it odd pastels, who had their houses filled with all the little jim-jams and remnants that she and Allen so enthusiastically collected. Finch had said that his father, and before that his grandfather, had been carpenters: perhaps between lecheries and betrayals it was they who had found a few spare moments to knock these piece together out of some pine, nick-nacks to keep their wives' mouths shut while they wandered the fields in search of higher entertainments. Another time she would have told Allen of this wonderful discovery: that they were keeping the town's graveyard, and they would have stayed up for hours, laughing and talking.

Despite the long stretches of perfect weather the nights were getting shorter now. The affair with Finch was ending with the summer, just as she had predicted. Through the window she could see the spire of the church, keeping its indifferent watch. And far below, across the street, the Wilsons' house glowed, all lights on as the children ran through the halls, protesting their bedtime.

She was feeling better, in the plateau of her fever. For a couple of days or even a whole week she could go through this cycle, until the fever burned itself out. The last time it had caught her was after Isaac. Not the night he told her about his family, but a week later, when he had come to her apartment at four o'clock in the morning, using the key she had given him, and tried to climb into bed with her. That had been the most unexpected, the most frightening moment ever: this sudden shadow in the middle of the night, the hand on her shoulder: she had screamed in such loud terror that one of the neighbours had called the police.

Annabelle put on her working jeans and a T-shirt. In this uniform she felt safe enough to go downstairs and stand in the doorway of the living room. Allen was sitting in a corner chair, waiting. For a moment Annabelle wondered what she was going to do. Allen's face was turned to her, distant and inquiring. Her white MG was parked in the driveway. If she wanted, she could pack a suitcase, go out to her car and drive away. Of course there would be the problem of a destination. Finch, no doubt back in the bosom of his family, had already been forgiven by God Himself; surely he would not want to trespass again. She could go back to Ottawa to her own family; no doubt her mother would take her to dinner at a restaurant and remind her, over a suitably charming wine, that all men were fools, though it was best to get one who could afford alimony. Or finally she could live alone again. She could drive to a city she had never been to and live without Finch, without Allen, without her mother.

"I need a drink," Annabelle said, "and some supper too." She was surprised at her own voice, which sounded small and submissive, and at her own words too: she had given away more than she intended. But Allen, without hesitating, got to his feet and began to walk with her towards the kitchen.

She couldn't touch him, couldn't bring herself to embrace or be embraced by him, and as she moved about the kitchen, taking things out of the refrigerator and setting them on the table, she was continually conscious of Allen's presence, of his body shifting around hers, making way, leaning over her shoulder as she searched inside the crowded refrigerator, reaching to the top shelves of cupboards for her. And even when they touched, as if by accident, she pulled away, trying to pretend that this was normal.

Finally, as they were sitting down at the pine table she and Donna had occupied that morning, Allen broke the silence.

"Will you give up Finch?"

Annabelle kept chewing. On her plate there was the tuna salad she had just made: fish mixed with chopped onions and celery. The smell of the fish rose from the plate to her nostrils and reminded her of her own smell after she and Finch made love. She wondered if Nellie Tillson smelled the same way, if somehow Reverend Finch had a way of making his women smell like tuna fish.

"You forgave him," Annabelle said. "Haven't you forgiven me?"

There was some tuna fish on her fork, which she started to raise to her mouth but then, smelling it again, put down on her plate. She pushed her plate away.

"Annabelle." Allen's voice was sad and accusing.

"Don't talk to me like that."

"I'm sorry."

"I can't be pushed around between the two of you, like some common —" She stood up and walked to the kitchen window. *Slut* was the word on her tongue, but she wasn't going to give Allen that too, not even in return for the white MG. She was starting to sweat again and now she noticed that the front of Allen's shirt was stained. The windows were open but there was no breeze, only close, still air that seemed to be moving in with the growing darkness, choking the house.

"Is it humid or isn't it?" Annabelle muttered.

"I know."

"Freeze the whole winter and then spend the summer sweating until three o'clock every morning."

"They say it's the pollution," Allen said in that consoling tone he always used to deflate her when she was winding herself up.

Annabelle sat down again. It was truly insulting that Finch had gone to Allen's office, and having already exposed his little problem with Nellie Tillson, implicated her too. If he wanted to apologize, there must be a lot of people in line ahead of Allen. Or perhaps the contrite Reverend had been seeking out every one of the cuckolded husbands and outraged parents, confessing his sins to each so that his misery could be shared. Perhaps her own turn had been coming up this afternoon. For which, she remembered once more, they had had a date, an assignation, an arrangement, as naked as weather and mosquitoes would permit, to fall from grace.

"You know," Allen said, "I didn't ask Finch to come to my office and tell me that he had seduced my wife. And I didn't ask you to get involved with the crazy minister of a two-bit church, for Christ's sake —"

"Allen —"

"And if he came and spouted so much nonsense to me, well at least he had the nerve to tell the truth."

"Real white of him."

"Christian," Allen said, "and it truly was."

Annabelle pushed back from the table. *Christian.* She wondered if Allen too had noticed the smell of tuna. "Finch isn't a Christian," Annabelle said. Her voice was loud and brittle, the way her mother's used to sound when she attacked Henry MacLeod, the way it used to sound when it meant to say, "You absolute idiot, you don't know anything."

"Finch isn't a Christian," Annabelle said again, trying to keep her tone reasonable. "He's a pagan. A con man. A total primitive. The only things Finch cares about are fear and desire."

"Desire," Allen repeated, "and is that what attracts you to him?"

"No." She stood up and scraped the tuna into the garbage. Then she turned around to face Allen; soon they would start to say things that couldn't be forgotten, let alone forgiven.

"I slept with Finch because I wanted to."

She saw Allen fighting for control, his fingers interlaced, his knuckles turning white. But he had let her say it. This was why, Annabelle reminded herself, she had married Allen. Someone who wanted to care for her, to possess and protect. That was what she needed. She extended her hands across the table.

"Let's go upstairs," Annabelle said. "It's time for sleep."

But bed was no relief. The fever had come back, its hold firm on her again, and she lay close to her own edge of the bed, sweating profusely in the dark room. She could feel the stickiness of her cheek against the pillow. And when Allen's hand came, exploring her back, she lay stone still unable to respond.

"I'm sorry," she finally whispered. "I'm too sick." She should turn around, she knew, turn around and tell him that she loved him, wanted to keep him, needed to be with him, but she was possessed by the heat and the need to escape. Finally, aware of her open mouth silently mumbling, she dozed off.

It must have been early morning because the inside of Mandowski's store glowed with a yellow-white light it never had in the afternoon. In this brilliance the aisles were unnaturally wide and even the food itself was explosively bright. She had pushed her grocery cart towards the brightest of the lights when the quiet, empty feeling of the store suddenly changed and Annabelle felt herself surrounded by other shoppers, women from the town. Now the aisles were too narrow and she was constantly having to move away from the disapproving stares of the curious. They looked at her as if she were now somehow less than a person, simply a stranger to be hated and avoided.

She had no friends in this town, she realized, no friends at all and then, conscious of Donna Wilson slipping away at the corner of her vision, she looked up to see Mandowski. Grotesquely fat, arms outstretched, he was coming towards her.

"Mrs. Finch." His face was the grey of raw clay, and his smile of welcome so frightening that she turned to run.

But there was nowhere to go.

Behind her were the women, their faces horribly contorted. *"Sssst. Sssssst."* Their hisses filled the store. As if they would like to have her trapped in a sealed room, strapped to a chair while they turned on the gas.

She turned back to Mandowski. He had come closer to her and his face wavered in the bright tight, his cheeks and forehead shining in the glare, ballooning as his mouth opened wide.

"Mrs. Finch," he trumpeted. "Mrs. Finch, I believe."

"Mrs. Finch," the women took up. "Do we have the new Mrs. Finch?"

Mandowski's arms were as open as his mouth and he was standing, frozen, his lips cherry red and his skin a porcelain pink. "You've broken the code," he suddenly screamed. "You've broken the code."

Annabelle turned to run but the women behind were advancing, chanting, "Mrs. Finch, Mrs. Finch," and their breath was like a warm, sour tide. She turned back to Mandowski. One of his arms had broken off. Then she charged. She rushed at him with her shopping cart, pushed like a sail by the women's breath, and bowled right into his stout, brittle legs, sending him flying back with the word *Finch* spitting out of his mouth like a distasteful worm.

"Mrs. Jamieson," Annabelle shrieked. "Mrs. Jamieson."

When Annabelle woke up she was lying on her stomach, the sheet wrapped like fingers round her neck. She struggled up on one elbow and reached over to the bedside table for a cigarette. The fever seemed to have gone now but the night air was thick and close, as if the whole town were blanketed with the bad omen of her dream.

She had been sweating and now was covered with dried perspiration. She would smoke the cigarette and cool down, compose herself. *Mrs. Finch.* Her lighter flared in the darkness and she saw briefly her own hand, the tips of her fingers. She drew the smoke deep into her lungs, held it there. She remembered looking out at her white sports car: nowhere to go. She exhaled and flared the lighter a second time, holding it to Isaac's watch. It was exactly three o'clock in the morning. She decided to sit up and as she rolled over she saw him.

The blocky figure slowly rose from the chair by the window. Arms extended towards her, shadows hung round the face and shoulders. Annabelle's hand shot out to the bedside table. She missed the switch and the lamp skidded off the table, fell to the floor with a heavy crack.

Then the overhead light went on; it was only Allen, wearing the beige pyjamas that her mother had given him for Christmas.

"For God's sake, what are you doing?"

"I couldn't sleep." His voice was low and reasonable. Annabelle wondered how long he had been sitting by the window, staring at her. He sat down beside her on the bed and she had to stop herself from drawing away. He reached his hand out for her forehead.

"You feel better," Allen said. "Maybe you've broken the fever."

The bed sagged with Allen's weight. The night was so hot and close. Now she remembered Mandowski, in the dream, telling her that she had broken the code. Annabelle adjusted the pillow behind her back, tried to move a little away from Allen. In this heat even his very presence in the room was impossible to bear.

Evil: this night was so dark and heavy that a person could almost believe they had been possessed. Allen's hand was reaching out again.

Suddenly Annabelle was afraid he was going to press her face down, smother her into the pillow. She breathed deeply, already feeling the weight of his hand on the back of her neck, her nose crushing into the soft feathers. Then she jerked away from his hand, just as it reached her shoulder, and swung out of bed. Allen, innocent Allen. Allen, who wanted only to protect and possess. Allen, who sent her on errands to Finch's farm. Good-hearted Allen who claimed he didn't know a thing but sat like a ghost at the window, staring at her while she slept.

It had been her idea to move to a small town, but now the small town had moved into her.

"What's wrong?" Allen asked, innocent and aggrieved.

"I don't know." Angry. Pulling on her clothes.

"Where are you going?"

"Oh for —" She realized she hadn't the strength to shout or even the will to break whatever fragile bonds were left between them.

Outside the air was cooler and the stillness that had been so oppressive in the house was broken by a breeze rustling intermittently through the trees. Annabelle stood for a moment, catching her breath, and then suddenly afraid that Allen would follow, she started walking quickly towards the corner.

The town was silent. All the houses were dark, except for the yellow glow of a few plastic doorbell buttons, and the streets were empty of traffic. Gradually her pace slowed, and by the time Annabelle found herself standing in front of Mandowski's store, looking at the display windows of canned goods and baskets of summer fruit, she wondered how she could have had such frightening dreams about this innocent store. She climbed the steps for a moment, and stood in the place where Finch had grabbed her arm.

When she had slapped him the bristles of his beard had dug into her palm but his head had been heavy and rocklike; it had barely budged at her blow. Perhaps even then God had given him a *carte blanche.*

Annabelle backed away from the store and crossed the street. Soon she was at Allen's office, the century-old stone building with its modern frosted-glass door. Allen had instantly adapted to this town, its unspoken customs and ways, its webs of old loyalties and feuds. He had disappeared into the weave of the place without resistance or fear. She looked down the street towards the hotel. For the first time in months they had missed a beat of their schedule. She tried to imagine having a baby in Salem, a child to be nurtured in this small, closed network of streets and stores. A child to make the walk from church to hotel, from innocence to evil. Everyone takes that walk, Finch had said, but I choose to go the other way, the hard way. Good old Finch, the righteous Reverend Finch, son of the carpenter from Kingston. Annabelle turned and began to walk towards the church.

If I can make this journey, she said to herself, if I can take every step from here to the church and stand on its stone steps, then somehow I'll have started to redeem myself. She laughed. Redeem myself, God, I'm being a child. She stopped, took a step backwards towards the hotel, then resumed her walk towards the church. Stopped. Back and forth. What a wonderful game, a marvellous six-year-old's game, this whole town laid out like a board of Snakes and Ladders, a game of Heaven and Hell for her to march about, each movement towards the angels accompanied by a tug from the devil.

At the end of the block, facing the church, was a library that only opened two afternoons a week; and outside the library was a facility much more frequently used, a stone bench. Here she sat down and lit a cigarette. She was just beginning to feel peaceful and to wonder if she would actually be childish enough to go stand on the church steps, when the footsteps were upon her.

"Mrs. Jamieson."

"Mr. Beam?"

"Jacob Beam at your service, ma'am."

She shifted on the bench, partly to give room to sit down but also to get away from the overpowering alcoholic smell that surrounded him like a large and humid cape.

"Perhaps you didn't wish to be interrupted."

"No, sit down." If he grabbed at her she would be able to outrun him; in his condition he was doing well to stay awake.

"Thank you."

She had heard about Beam and Mrs. Fitzhenry, and now Annabelle looked past him to the Fitzhenrys' store. It was only a few steps away. Perhaps Beam had just emerged from some unspeakable debauch. On the other hand, his office and everything else in this town were also only a few steps away. It would be, as Allen had said, a long time before they had to take a bus.

"A fine evening, Mrs. Jamieson. We should be grateful for evenings like this."

"Excellent weather, Mr. Beam."

"My wife says it's been humid, but I say the close weather is good for the mind. The Egyptians used to claim that water stimulated the brain, did you know that?"

"No."

"I used to study the Egyptians as a young man, Mrs. Jamieson."

"That's too bad," Annabelle said, then realized how inane it sounded; what she had meant was that it was too bad that a man who had studied the Egyptians should have to lose his youth and become famous only for his adventures with Mrs. Fitzhenry.

"The Egyptians were a great race, Mrs. Jamieson. What they built has endured."

"The stone houses of Salem," Annabelle said, "will probably outlast the pyramids."

"I shouldn't be surprised." And then he sighed so loudly that Annabelle couldn't help looking directly at him. The stocky, thickly bearded Beam was closer, in this night, to the figure that she had been shaping in her studio than to the innocuous man she waved to daily as he passed her in the street. He was wearing a shortsleeved shirt with the top button undone, and from his neck and chest sprouted red hair as thick as that of his beard which, she now noticed, grew straight down his throat to the hollow of his collarbone.

"Mrs. Jamieson, I've often thought strange things must be going on in that brain of yours. If you don't mind me saying."

"Of course not, Mr. Beam."

"I've seen you walking up and down these streets like a woman who has found herself in a zoo. Do you find this place so strange, Mrs. Jamieson?"

"Not so strange."

"Then what do you think about, may I ask? If you'll pardon an old man his curiosity."

"Think?" And then, unable to resist him: "I think about *things*, Mr. Beam, the good and the bad of things."

"Things," Jacob Beam said. "The good and the bad of things?"

"Evil," Annabelle blurted out.

"Evil, Mrs. Jamieson?" But his voice had lost its drunken tone, and he was leaning towards her, his bearded face peering into hers. She realized that Beam must know about Finch, and about Nellie Tillson too. "Surely you haven't let the local gentry talk you into such ideas, Mrs. Jamieson, because there is no such thing as evil."

"What is there?"

"Just us," Jacob Beam said. Then he laughed and Annabelle realized he was not so old after all, just a disillusioned man in a small town who had coated himself with layers of fat, hair and alcohol.

"Just us," Jacob Beam said, "though in the long run, who knows, maybe that's worse."

Then he was on his feet, teetering ever so slightly, one stubby arm extended.

"Mrs. Jamieson, may I see you to your house?"

She rose with him. Across the street were the steps of the church, unattained. To explain her little game of redemption to Jacob Beam — he who had already dared and lost with the Fitzhenrys — would be too ridiculous. Reluctantly she turned away and began to walk home.

Twelve

*T*he sky was milky blue, veiled with a light August haze that warned of the hot afternoon to come. The first cutting of hay had long since been taken from the fields and the second crop now inched its way along slowly, the thin reeds of grass baking brown in the parched earth. But the farmers who had planted corn stood outside every morning and looked happily at the sky. The stalks were eight feet high in some fields now and the kernels were gradually turning to the fat, yellow colour of the sun.

It was, Maureen Finch thought, the kind of summer that used to make her tomatoes cluster like grapes on the carefully staked plants.

Now Finch and the children kept the garden and the tomatoes grew sparse and low to the ground. Sometimes, to shame him, Maureen made Finch carry her outside. Wearing the white, wide-brimmed hat that kept her face from burning she would spend an hour on her knees, crawling painfully down the crooked rows and throwing weeds onto the surrounding grass. But her knees couldn't support her, and her fingers soon ached from the constant grasping and pulling.

She missed the deep, fecund smell that would escape from the broken soil, and she missed too the warmth of sun and the exercise that gradually loosened her muscles and her bones and made her feel, no matter how faintly, the echo of her own once active body.

Through the screened window of her bedroom, this

morning's air carried only the warm, bland smell of the front lawn and the maples that surrounded the house. Green, they smelled green: and as Maureen Finch looked out her window a panorama of greens was what she saw: the bright, watered green of the lawn; the yellowed green of the hayfield beyond; the far-away dark green of the trees that lined the far side of the field and made a long wavy line on the horizon.

By instinct Maureen swivelled towards the barn; Finch was just emerging and starting for the house.

She turned her chair to the secretary where she had been looking at the old letters. Not his letters to her: those she left locked away until her heart was stronger. But her letters to him, those voluntary missiles that had boomeranged and destroyed her own life: the first letter that she had sent from Toronto; the second that told him she was coming home to take care of her ailing mother; and then the third letter, the one where she had signed herself away.

Dear Gordon,

When you asked me to marry you last night I was too surprised to answer. I won't pretend I didn't think the question was coming but I didn't think it would come so fast.

Marry you? Yes, Gordon, I'll marry you, but not in shame or secrecy. If I'm going to be your wife I want to be a whole wife, to support you in everything you do, including your ministry. I still don't know what faith is, but I'm convinced you have it in you, and feel it, and I'll lean on you for that, Gordon.

There's only one thing, Gordon. I can't marry you while my mother is still alive. She is absolutely opposed, because you are not Catholic, and she says it would kill her if I cross her feelings in this way. Please understand.

Yours,
Maureen Newell

Mrs. Newell lived for six more years, but until the day she was in her coffin, Finch's only meeting with her was on the rainy afternoon he had come searching after Maureen.

"She doesn't want to see you," Maureen said.

"We can't wait forever."

"Jacob waited fourteen years."

"In those days, men lived longer. And at least he had the sister. What if I make you choose between us?"

"I can't choose," said Maureen. "I didn't choose her to be my mother. It just happened. She did her duty and I'm doing mine."

At the funeral they stood side by side. The whole township knew about them but they didn't dare touch hands. During the service Finch was so tense that he had to clap his fist against his chest until the gentle clatter of dirt against the fresh-cut pine allowed him to draw a breath.

"Thank God it's over," Finch whispered.

With her mother safely underground, Maureen squeezed his arm. Her skin was still white and smooth as cream, but the six years had laid tiny wrinkles in the corners of her eyes.

Chaste the whole time.

She could hear Finch banging around in the kitchen, then the plodding footsteps crossing to the hall coming slowly up the stairs. Finch moved around the house like a bitter old woman.

"I brought you some tea."

"Thank you, Gordon."

He came beside her and set the teapot on the secretary. He was wearing, she now noticed, not his coveralls but his black suit.

"You going to town today?"

"Uh-huh," Finch grunted. "You said Mrs. McConnell was coming today."

"She is."

"I'll be back in time for the milking."

He had edged back towards the door and was talking without looking at her; nor did she look at him. They both gazed through the window as though that familiar view was enough to share.

"You're seeing the lawyer again today?"

"Uh-huh."

"Try to talk properly, Gordon. It wouldn't hurt."

Silence.

"While you're in town, why don't you take the girls to the library?"

She turned now and looked at Finch. He hated taking the girls. They spoiled his going-to-town afternoons, which he used for philandering with the local ladies. The latest, she knew, was Annabelle Jamieson, the lawyer's wife. But the jealous reaction wasn't as bad as it used to be; even if they were supposed to be going to the lake every afternoon. But getting Nellie Tillson pregnant was something else. It was just that she had hoped that Valerie and Clare could be protected. Surely their life was hard enough.

"I could take them," Finch said.

"You could."

"I will."

"Thank you, Gordon. Would you like some tea?"

"A small cup. Before I go."

Maureen reached out to her desk. There were always clean cups and saucers here because in the afternoons, after the yellow schoolbus had brought them home, the girls always came up for a cup of tea and cookies. This year they would have lots to talk about, because this year the schoolbus gossip would be all about the court case, about the minister who got taken to court by one of his own Sunday school pupils: a paternity suit. In a few years Nellie's child would be old enough to go to school herself, and instead of hearing whispers on the bus her daughters could see the child itself, a little living trophy of their father's popularity with his parish.

"Gordon, what have you decided with the lawyer?"

"He says I can win the case."

His voice, Maureen noticed, was tired; in fact these days he seemed to be just dragging himself around: his voice, his slow step, the look of defeat his face was always slipping into.

"I thought you wanted to keep it out of court."

"I do," Finch said, his tone rising. "Of course I do."

"Won't she settle?"

"Settle?" Finch said. "There's nothing to settle."

"Gordon."

Since he had told her about Nellie Tillson's lawsuit, there had been only the one time, the first night, when she had asked him to tell her the truth. And she had been sure then that he was lying. Now he was standing in the doorway, the place he always occupied during their arguments, his weight settled into the frame of the door as if hoping that when all else failed he would be supported by the lumber cut by his own grandfather's hand.

"It's blackmail," Finch said. "It's that goddamn Mandowski who's behind it."

"Gordon, your language."

"He's put her up to it."

"We could mortgage the farm."

"And why should we do that?" Finch had stepped into the room now and was facing her aggressively. "If we give her ten thousand dollars everyone in the county is going to know about it. And we're going to be slaving to make that money back while she rings up the numbers in Mandowski's store, her belly sticking out to the cash register, telling everyone that she's ten thousand dollars richer because George Mandowski put it to her nights when he drove her home.

"Can you prove it?"

"It's my word against theirs," Finch said. "Jamieson claims I can't lose."

"I don't know." Maureen looked down into the teacup, at the leaves floating just below the amber surface. A court case. Nothing could be worse. And if Finch was lying? Didn't they have blood tests? And if he was telling the truth? By the time Nellie Tillson's lawyer finished, every rumour in the county would have been aired in long and legal detail and everyone with a grudge against Finch would have told their story. "No. I don't want it to go to court. It can't."

She swung her chair towards the secretary, ready to pour herself more tea. It was amazing to think that locked into its drawers were dozens of love letters from Finch, each filled with the voice of virtue and hope.

Finch sighed. Before she was sick, he always used to sigh

like that: when she asked him to speak properly, or to keep himself from blowing his nose at the table, or to perform any of those other little niceties that distinguished human beings from their hairy predecessors. In those days her remarks and Finch's sighs and groans were scattered through their days like a sea of punctuation marks: now they were both more restrained, their truce had grown so elaborate that whole weeks went by without more than a few necessary sentences.

"I'd best be going."

"Goodbye, Gordon." She held out her hand: it was one of their customs to touch after a disagreement, to try to cover over the wounds that were far beyond healing.

But Finch bypassed her hand, leaned over and pressed his mouth against hers. Maureen let the once familiar saltiness of his lips penetrate her mouth, and her hand, in spite of itself, slid up to hold his shoulder. The bristles from his beard bit into her cheeks: if Finch had known how she had longed for that, how she had remembered every touch and taste and smell of him. There was no reason now, the doctor had said, but it hadn't been for doctor's reasons that she had stopped. His hands were on her shoulders, working down towards her breasts.

"Gordon."

She had lowered her hands and now she seized one of the wheels of her chair and pulled away from Finch, forcing him to stumble forward to keep his balance.

Finch looked at her without apologizing, wiped his mouth with the back of his hand.

"Gordon, before you go, please carry me downstairs. I believe even Mrs. McConnell might be growing tired of my new wallpaper." She looked up at him calmly, trying to keep the fear from her face. One day soon this whole masquerade would grow too precarious and shatter. Finch had provided the costumes, but she could decide when to send the guests home.

It was about that decision, and the prospect of the court case, that Maureen thought as Finch gathered the girls and got them ready for the trip to Salem. When the car had pulled out of the driveway Maureen Finch, feeling comfortably alone, wheeled back and forth from the living room to the kitchen, her hands now trained to make turns and manoeuvres that had once seemed impossible.

It was her own form of pacing, wheeling restlessly about in the chair, and sometimes, catching herself rolling nervously through a room, she had to laugh at her body's perverse desire to stay mobile. For though the muscles of her legs and hips had atrophied, the exercise of wheeling the chair, and the constant use of her arms and shoulders, had made her upper body far stronger than it ever had been even when she had been riding Sean every day. And despite the fact that she could hardly stand on her own two feet, Maureen still believed that once more, before Sean died, she would ask Finch to saddle him up and lift her into the saddle. Leaning forward and burying her hands in his long mane she would have one last gallop, one last thunder of hooves through the fields with her hair streaming out and her shouts and laughter spurring him on.

Upstairs was her wicker chair; it had been her mother's once and was still the most comfortable of all. For downstairs and the barn there was the canvas and steel portable. There was also, downstairs, a pair of crutches in the hall. For years she had used them daily but now she only tried them if she was alone.

Pulling herself up to get the pads under her armpits was easy enough, but once standing, her whole weight ground down upon her knees and ankles. That was the pain she couldn't endure. Today, it was bearable: she was sweating and she would never let Finch or her daughters see her face twisted and slick with tears, but she could move, on this particular morning, without the pain being so sharp that it made her collapse. After dragging herself up and down the whole length of the kitchen, she crossed the front hall and went into the living room.

This was Finch's territory. Once, in happier days they would sit here at night planning their family and their future. Even after things started to go bad and they slept apart, she would sometimes take pity on him and on her own loneliness, and late at night she would come downstairs and cross this living room in the light of the moon or by touch in the pitch darkness, cross this living room as she was crossing it now, and go into the small porch where Finch made his bed. There she would slip in beside him, the arthritis already so advanced that the mere climbing in would twist her hip and start the tears, and while Finch would take her in the darkness the tears would run with self-pity, pain, and finally the relief of having breached again the wilderness that was growing between them.

On crutches now, Maureen Newell Finch stood in the doorway of the porch, hovered in her husband's doorway the way he more often stood in hers, looked at his narrow bachelor's bed, the small cupboard where his clothes were heaped, the knitted coverlet that had warmed this bed for the more than twenty years since he had returned from the seminary to work for his aunt and uncle.

There had been a time, he had told her, when he prayed every night on the braided rug that lay still, its different colours worn and washed into one, at the side of his bed. Did he pray now? Maureen wondered. What did he ask God to forgive? And when he listed his sins, how did he know where to start? And if he prayed, or if he didn't, did he know that she made prayers of her own, that sitting in her wheelchair every morning she would first watch him make the passage from the house to the barn, walking like a man moving from one life to another, and that then she would close her eyes and recite the prayers of her youth? The Catholic prayers she had once tried to give up for him. Did he know that she longed for confession, the close safe darkness of the priest's box where she could whisper out her sins of pride, her refusal to give her husband his rights, and, worst of the worst, her failure to bring her daughters up in the Church? Her daughters who were still heathens in the Church's eyes? With her eyes closed, praying, she could feel the beads slipping through her fingers.

She stood in the doorway to Finch's room: he had won his monkhood, in his own twisted way he had taken the world around him and squeezed it until it fitted the shape of his soul.

Maureen turned and began making her way back to the kitchen. At the centre hall one of her legs gave way but she caught the stair railing with her hand and she didn't go down. Then she started again, one step at a time, resting for long moments using her shoulders and crutches to do the work. When she finally had reached the kitchen, she put her hands on the table and used it to support her weight while she lowered herself to safety. Which reminded her, safety, of a report she had read in yesterday's paper about convicts escaping from the penitentiary.

She sat and looked out the window. After a few minutes had passed she took the telephone that was on the table and called Mrs. McConnell, saying that she wasn't feeling well today.

Then she called the grocery store.

As always, Nellie Tillson answered, her high, young voice filling up the morning.

"It's Mrs. Finch, Nellie."

"Oh, hi." *Oh, hi.*

"I have the list, Nellie. Do you have a pencil there?"

"Yes, Mrs. Finch."

In the silence Maureen could hear Nellie's breathing, close and intimate.

"And Nellie, the Reverend's in town today. Could you ask Mr. Mandowski to bring the groceries by on his way to lunch?"

"Yes, Mrs. Finch."

When Mandowski arrived, Maureen waved at him through the kitchen window and so he came in without knocking, first bringing one carton, which he set on the floor beside the kitchen table, and then, after nodding to her, going back to the car for the second. That too he placed on the floor. Then he stood in front of Maureen, smiling and holding his hands clasped in front of him the way she remembered him standing when he was still in the church choir, before his voice had changed, singing solo with a soprano so clear people used to joke it was a shame he couldn't stay that way.

"It's good to see you, George. Will you have a cup of tea?"

"I can't stay." But he pulled up a chair. Mandowski was one of her weapons against Finch. Of course, that was unsaid. It was also unsaid that he came only when Finch was in town, and that his chaste visits were supposed to counterbalance those activities of Finch's that went equally unremarked. What she had told Finch was that she had been willing to give up her church for his, but she couldn't turn her back on all her old friends. Not that Mandowski had been exactly a friend, but he had been an admirer. When she was a girl he was already an awkward and bulky adolescent, but she had observed him watching her often enough, turning towards her in the church when he thought she wouldn't notice.

"You look well."

"Thank you."

"You always were the most beautiful girl in the church."

Maureen laughed. It was amazing the way George Mandowski complimented her: unbidden words flowed from his mouth, sweet as the maple syrup he sold in his store — which was thinned with water and then bulked again with brown sugar.

She had seen Mandowski only once since Finch had told her about Nellie Tillson. That time, in a roundabout way, she had spoken to him about it, hoping to make him back down. But his face had hardened and he had pushed back his chair, saying in that absurd drawl of his, "It's a man's business, Maureen."

"Bullshit," she had answered, enjoying the shocked look on his face. "It's my business, too. What happens to Gordon happens to me too, you know, and to my children."

"I'm sorry, Maureen," Mandowski came back, starting that fool's drawl of his again, "but a girl's been wronged and it has to be set right."

"She's no daisy herself." At that, Mandowski had flushed.

"If I'm offending you," Mandowski had said, "I'll leave your house."

"Don't talk like such a fool, George. I'm just saying that what happened to that girl might have been done by anyone, and what's being done now isn't going to help her, it's going to hurt Gordon."

"She needs the money," Mandowski said. "Who's going to marry her now? And as for your husband, well —"

"Well what?" Maureen had asked. But Mandowski had stayed silent while his red face grew brighter. And then finally she had rolled back her chair from the table and let Mandowski stare right at her instead of sneaking his looks over his tea. She would make him do as she pleased, but not yet.

"Goodbye, George. Thank you for bringing the groceries."

"There's things I've seen," Mandowski had insisted, his eyes boldly on her. It came into her mind that she could reach up and undo one button of her blouse.

"I don't want to hear about them."

"Goodbye, Maureen."

"Goodbye, George, thank you for bringing the groceries." This in spite of herself, because she wasn't ready to give up on him.

He was still breathing hard after the exertion of carrying in the groceries. Panting, his white shirt patched with sweat, and his hefty neck and face florid in the August heat, he was beginning to show his age.

"Well," Mandowski said, "It's nice to see you again. After the last time I thought I wouldn't be welcome here."

In high school George Mandowski had been famous for his ability to talk like Western movies, but it was a habit he still clung to and it was even said that every summer night possible, he took Therese and his children to the drive-in, just to keep his accent in shape.

"The truth is sometimes hard to take."

Mandowski nodded.

"But I did want to ask you a favour, George."

Mandowski leaned forward. His eyes, Maureen noticed, were pink around the irises as if he had been crying or drinking. She wondered suddenly if Mandowski still went to confession. He opened his mouth to talk and Maureen caught a glimpse of his tongue.

"Now you know I can't change my mind about that other business." A new note in his voice, pleading beneath the hardness.

Maureen paused, searching for the exact point where Mandowski would begin to understand.

"George, if I ask you something, can you keep it to yourself?"

Mandowski nodded.

"Promise?"

Mandowski nodded again, his face eager and intent, his

small eyes boring in on her: old pig eyes, that was one of the names they had called him behind his back, because his eyes were tiny and round. He pulled a handkerchief from his pocket and wiped it across his forehead.

"George, I want you to get me a revolver."

"A gun! I can't do that. Anyway, what do you want with a gun? Are you planning to shoot someone?"

His voice was so concerned and earnest that Maureen laughed.

"Kill someone? George, who do you think I am?" She picked up the newspaper that was on the kitchen table, folded to the story about the convicts who had escaped from the nearby prison. "Look at this."

"I know," Mandowski said. "I heard about it."

"Listen," Maureen said. She rubbed her palm against the newspaper. " 'Six men escaped last night from the Millhaven maximum security prison. All were armed and are considered extremely dangerous. Area residents seeing strangers are asked to call the police.' "

"I know," Mandowski said. "I've been telephoning Therese twice a day to make sure she's all right."

"Well," said Maureen, "when Finch is in Kingston there's no point in him telephoning me. And if they come on me, alone, with the girls, what can I do? In a chair like this."

"They wouldn't come up here," Mandowski said. "They're probably caught by now."

"Every summer there's at least one or two breakouts. And I'm here alone most days, with the girls. It's not myself that I worry about, George, but the girls —"

Through the window there was nothing to be seen but the driveway, acres of bush and fields.

"I'm not saying you're being silly, Maureen, but people are getting awfully worked up about those convicts." His pink eyes growing redder, calculating.

"Look at their faces," Maureen said. Six close cropped heads were lined up on the page, each looking trapped and desperate. The way Finch used to look some nights, standing in the frame of her doorway, putting off the inevitable moment when he would have to acknowledge that she had dismissed him, that it was time for him to turn his back and walk down the stairs to his own bed.

"I wouldn't want one of them here," Maureen returned, "with my daughters."

"And you in that chair," Mandowski added piously. He looked appraisingly at Maureen, the calculations finished, ready to write up the bill. "You wouldn't know what to do with a gun," Mandowski added. The pink tongue darted out, licked his lips. Maureen watched him. She was thinking that he looked like an undertaker greedy to be measuring the body to the coffin.

"I'd just wait until he came close, then I'd pull the trigger."

"He's a desperate man." Mandowski's face flushed and he looked away, wiping at his forehead with his handkerchief. "A man like that would do anything."

Maureen felt the breath catch in her chest. Sometimes it seemed Mandowski hated Finch more than she did.

"You can't be much of a shot," Mandowski said. He was looking out the window now.

"No."

Mandowski, still looking out the window: "There's new kinds of pistols, with mushroom bullets. You hit someone with one of those, it blows them apart."

Maureen became suddenly aware of her hands. Beneath the blanket, they were clutching each other so tightly that her knuckles hurt. She closed her eyes and saw a blurred image of a body being torn apart, skin and bone spraying about the room, blood like —

"You must be pretty strong from that chair," Mandowski said, "I suppose you could handle it."

She opened her eyes. Mandowski was holding the handkerchief to his throat.

"I could."

"All right," Mandowski said. "I've got something I can loan you for the rest of the summer. Unless you want to get a permit?

"No."

"All right."

Blood like a fine rain on the walls.

Thirteen

Finch stepped quietly out the door, squeezing it carefully shut behind him. For a moment he paused on his own front porch, looking at the field that led down to the road and, hanging above it in the southwestern sky, the yellow waning moon.

With his first steps across the grass his back straightened and the last layers of sleep fell away. Amazing that with everything that had happened he could still need an alarm clock, but in the evening he had dozed off with the merciful quickness of a child and now, in the middle of the night, his dreams still surrounded him, a soft palpable cloak that sweetened the cool August breeze and made his walk slow and liquid.

As he passed the barn Sean whinnied restlessly. But Finch carried on, not caring if Maureen heard the horse, knowing that she thought it normal enough for him to go on these late-night walks: what else was a man to do at forty-two years of age when he slept like a child in a bed so narrow and barren it would hardly hold his own turning body.

The dew was heavy. In the light of the moon beads of moisture shone with quicksilver brightness, turning the slope into a hill of shining knives.

The image startled him and hurt his eyes.

He stopped for a moment, wriggled his toes inside the thick protection of his boots, then began moving up the hill behind the barn and past a knot of his own sleeping cows.

Although he had climbed to this plateau hundreds, even

thousands of times, his heart was pounding furiously and Finch became aware that his limbs were heavy and sluggish. He dreamily wondered if the moon was shining inside him, if through his veins were flowing its heavy silver rivers.

Finch's heart beat louder, a painful warning dirge. He turned back to the house and outbuildings. The tin roofs gleamed and in the drive there were two silvery brows, the rear fenders of his girls' bicycles. No lights were on, his family was asleep, and if he wanted he could think this whole scene was set a hundred years ago, that he was a pioneer who had carved this homestead into a protected valley of the land, a living valley that he now guarded from the awful dangers of the dark.

There were nights when he could sit here for hours, looking down on the hollow and trying to find a way to think of it that would settle his restless mind.

But tonight this house was only the place he had escaped. The iron net was closing and his only answer was a last and hopeless meeting. "Why?" she had asked when he telephoned. His hands had flexed, imagined unprompted the quick way she moved towards him, the sudden burst of tears when she cried out.

He climbed the rail fence and set out across the stubbly hay-field that separated the main pasture of the farm from the woods and the river that ran down its centre. In the winter that river had shot clouds of spray into the surrounding trees until their branches were frozen into sparse, icy dancers, frozen in the moonlight. Now the maples and the cedar had carved their own universe out of the summer sky. The breeze that had moved so slowly through the field was here a hollow echo in a cathedral and the sounds of rustling leaves tumbled majestically through the trees, mixing with the noise of rushing water. Air that had surrounded the leaves all day in the brilliant sun was now falling to the cold ground thick with oxygen; Finch sucked it in, greedily searching for the secret space that lived between one day and the next.

Desire, yes: it was pumping like an old engine in his chest, pushing the freight of his heavy silver blood, pushing him towards the morning. He got up from the rock and descended the bank to the river where he knelt and cupped his hands to drink from the water sluicing through the rocks. It was so icy and pure he could suddenly feel the separate spaces between his teeth.

Upriver was the gleam and foaming of the rapids, rocks and whitewater illuminated by the moon. But whereas in winter with the surrounding snow and its own faster flow the river was a rushing white force, now its mystery was more subtle, buried in the shadows of overhanging trees and sweet grasses growing long on the bank. In this long and lemon grass Finch now lay down on his stomach, letting the dew soak through his shirt. Then suddenly he stretched out and submerged his whole head in the water, letting the force of the stream batter into his skull until he was dizzy.

By the time he got to the cliffs it was five o'clock in the morning. If he had not forgotten himself he at least felt distracted from most of his worries; and the sight of Annabelle waiting on the cliffs, her silhouette black against the gradually lightening sky, gave him the peace he had been searching for all night.

He came up behind her, stood for a moment at her side, looking out with her at the lake. Then as she turned to him he put his hand on her shoulder; as always there was the surprising sensation of living bones beneath his palm, the electric way she moved under his touch, leaning now against him, her lips on his neck.

Finch dropped his hands down to her waist, let his thumbs rest momentarily on the small saddles of her hipbones. Then he slid his fingers in towards her spine, pushed to make her arch against him.

"Finch."

"I didn't think you'd come."

"I wasn't going to."

She had with her a large straw bag and now she bent and took out a blanket which she shook out onto the grass.

"City woman," Finch murmured.

"Don't talk."

Finch lay on his back, his arms around her. Her weight

pressed into him, dissolving the slow exhaustion that had dogged him for days; and the phalanx of problems he had thought so important broke apart, drowned in the rush of desire, the sweet feeling of need that would be satisfied.

"Finch, will you make me a promise about tonight?" Her face was above his, the dark eyes in shadow, her narrow features looking sharp in the night. He had been attracted to her right from the first, though she didn't have the looks of Maureen or even Nellie Tillson. She was, he thought, neither beautiful nor ugly: she was like a part of himself, a secret twin who was beyond being judged, beyond even understanding, a secret fact of nature as opaque to him as was his own inner self. All he knew about her was that she was electric, she was available, and her restlessness more than matched his own.

"Finch, will you make me one promise? Just make love to me tonight, this last time, and then you have to let me go. No more desperate meetings, no more grabbing me on the street, no more anything."

Finch closed his eyes. He was usually the one to arrange endings. "Maureen knows," he would sigh, and the rest would be understood. "I need you," he said to Annabelle. "You're all I have." He was surprised by his own words. Even with Maureen he had never begged.

Annabelle rolled off his chest and sat beside him. He kept his hand on her back; it was so narrow that his fingers could span the distance between her shoulders.

"There's your family, your children, the church."

Finch stroked her back. In his father's house he had wished for a stranger to release him; with Annabelle his wish had been fulfilled.

"Why did you tell Allen?"

"I had to," Finch replied. "There were too many secrets. It was like being in a cage."

But the confession hadn't been planned. It had been a sudden inspiration, right in Allen's office. The idea had come to him and it had instantly felt so pure and so right that he had simply leaned over the desk, looked into the complacent and self-satisfied eyes of this man he had been cuckolding, looked into his eyes when he was supposed to be swearing more affidavits and lies, and had said: "Mr. Jamieson, we all sin; I have sinned with your wife."

Sinned, Finch had heard himself say, and knew that with his own words he had not only ended the affair with Annabelle Jamieson but that he had also begun his final confrontation with the town.

The lawyer's face hadn't changed for a moment: it was as if another piece of evidence had been thrown across the glass-topped desk.

"Do you hear me, Mr. Jamieson? I have sinned with your wife."

And with this confession the pain that had been knotted inside him for weeks had started to ease. He had waited for Allen Jamieson's reply; the response of this man with his lawyer's mantle and his dark and oversexed wife held the key to his future. Or, Finch asked himself, had he already used Annabelle Jamieson to throw away the key.

"I hear you, Reverend Finch. And I believe you."

"Will you forgive me, Mr. Jamieson?"

There had been another silence but Finch, fascinated with what he himself was doing, was totally absorbed in staring at the lawyer's face, trying to read it as Annabelle must, to find the clue to the mask of blandness.

"Why should I forgive you?"

"Because I need you," Finch said. The lawyer's face stayed frozen and Finch wondered what it would take to melt it. "I need you on my side. Because you are a Christian and you should have compassion for those weaker than yourself. After all, Mr. Jamieson, I have prayed to God and He has forgiven me. Perhaps, if you have compassion, God could forgive you too."

The mask broke and there was a ghost of a smile, the expression of someone who was looking at the scene from a great and lofty distance.

"I forgive you," Allen Jamieson had said. The smile still lingered. "Now tell me the truth about Nellie Tillson."

Finch had started talking but he already knew that his confession had been wasted on this lawyer: nothing was changed.

There was no secret key to the future. He couldn't even find the door.

Now that they were together Finch's desire for Annabelle had changed from nervous tension to something deeper, a cloud inside his body that was beginning to fill his chest, to block his breathing in the old way it used to with Maureen. Desire: after the confession to Allen Jamieson, Finch had spent the whole afternoon thinking about his desire for Jamieson's wife until finally he remembered a sermon in which his father had said that desire, like Gaul, was divided into three parts: greed, passion, and lust. That had been just like Bob Finch, with the white sign of God in his hair, to make his little half-elegant, half-educated jokes: and Finch could remember listening to his father winding his way around his little sayings, rambling in and out of the Bible, anything to hold the congregation — but of course he had learned the same trick when he needed it.

Greed, passion, and lust. Greed to possess her, to know she was in the power of his two hands, greed for the absolute ownership of another person, if only for a few seconds; but there was passion too, a true and noble tidal wave of his own self that went out to that part of her who was his own twin, from the dark side of himself to her own shadowed needs. Then there was lust, which was beyond his control; it was a force that he eagerly gave in to, a force like the changing light in the sky or the delicious sound of poplar leaves — but stronger, irresistible, because it was the curse that ruled his life. It had nothing to do with other people, was only a blind compulsion to satisfy what could never be satisfied, to drain away the tension and need.

Nellie, Annabelle, Maureen: sometimes their names and those of the others blended into a jumble in his mind, a rock valley of half-separate syllables. Once that had bothered him, now he was pleased that a past that might have been empty was filled instead with memories and hours stolen from forbidden bodies.

Finch propped himself up on one elbow and began to undo the buttons of Annabelle's blouse. She had a child's body: small breasts, a flat stomach framed by ribs so delicate that he couldn't resist putting his mouth to them. He let himself smell the familiar flowery fragrance of her skin then, with his tongue, he began to travel along the fragile ridges of her ribs, first the ridges and then the tiny valleys between until his tongue was dizzy with the taste of her and had come to a rest in the salty flats where the skin of her belly met the leather belt that held up her jeans. This he now undid, and the button beneath, then slid his hand down to the place where she was warm for him, where she was no girl needing him the way he needed her.

Once he had slept this way, his head on her belly, breathing his breath in and out of the tangle of nakedness. Remembering that, Finch turned his head away, unable to bear the knowledge that this was the last time, that the memories he had already were going to have to serve. And anyway, what use were memories when the future was doomed to be blank and empty?

The first time he had seen Annabelle in the church he had noticed her eyes, the way they drank him up, and her hands gripping the pew. A city woman, Finch remembered thinking. He hadn't known many city women, hadn't felt city hands drawing him close.

As he kissed his way from Annabelle's belly to the hollow of her throat, Finch was thinking too of Nellie Tillson who had started all this, Mike Taggart with his insinuating old man's voice, George Mandowski who had kept it so tightly strangled in his pants that even his face was turning red. "Your father always paid," Mike Taggart had said: the old man had paid in money but nothing else; he hadn't paid, for example, with a wife who was colder than metal and a town that was turning against him with the same sure completeness of a turning season.

Now Annabelle's hands were on his neck, moving down his back, and he came closer to her, crawled up so her fingers could reach where they wanted; soon their clothes were on the ground and they were wrapped together, naked in the blanket. Finch dug his toes into the wet grass, letting the earth give him purchase as he moved up into her, waiting for and then hearing that first low breath she always gave, the animal sound when she changed suddenly from the city woman who was out of place in this town to an extension of his own shadowed self.

Hearing the husky drop in breathing triggered something in him too, so that he pushed himself at her, wanting her, needing to go deeper, holding her back and forcing her towards him to give the feeling of being taken up and swallowed; and as she moved under him Finch began to feel as though he were swimming, swimming the many-channelled river of Annabelle, of Maureen, of Nellie, swimming the river of all the women who had given themselves to him. And this swimming appeared to him suddenly as a long and endless ceremony, a mating without purpose: because it wasn't the children that he was driven to, though he did want them, or the climax, though that too was necessary and was starting to work its way between them, but just the ritual itself, the slow and constant swimming, the long climb through the water: all he wanted was that it should last forever: all he wanted was that his body and hers join with the spirit of the river: all he wanted was that the river finally find his soul and release him from the life he had been condemned to.

Under cover of the moonlight, a thin skein of clouds had drawn over the sky, and when the light of the sun, which was itself well below the horizon, began to reach into the cloud, it stained the sky pink and silver, a large spreading stain that travelled right to the peak of the clouds and there began to change colour again, the silver growing, into a hollow grey-blue veil that hung between the two lovers and the day. Finch, lying on his back and watching the night dissolve, felt whatever had held him to Annabelle was dissolving too and that when the full light came they would be separate again, lost.

In this light her skin was the colour of sand, her lips and her nipples a delicate pink, answering the pink call of the dawn. He was lying on his back, his elbows spread wide and his hands laced beneath his head, and while he lay there Annabelle was kneeling above him, delivering clusters of tiny kisses. With his skin humming to the touch of her teeth and tongue, he watched the changing light as the sun reached towards the horizon: it silhouetted her breasts, threw new pools of yellow light in the hollows of her belly, played long and elaborate tricks with the outline of her back, her haunches and her legs. With her sand-coloured skin against the slate sky she was like a figure in the desert, a warm and moving sphinx. As she started him wanting her again, there was nothing in his mind but these comforting images of sand and light, and when finally he wrapped his arms tightly around her, he was out in the middle of the desert two thousand years ago, out in the middle of the desert with the yellow sun drumming and the sand's heat flaring around him. He was stiff and sore with wanting her, and with every thrust he felt her flesh parting around him as if he were a long, painful column passing backwards into time. Then the soreness eased, her breathing pulsed hot against his cheek and he felt her hands tighten in the small of his back, her thin city hands clawing, cleaving him to her.

The heat burst and there was a flood of yellow light and warmth so strong that it forced open his eyes: and while they were fixed on the white fingers of the sun, the humming that Annabelle had started on his skin exploded into his groin.

The waves passed through him, every muscle in his body cramped and then released.

The moment passed and Finch was only himself again, the Reverend Gordon Finch, son of the praying carpenter from Kingston; and lying on top of him shivering in the cold morning air was a woman he hardly knew.

Finch rubbed Annabelle's back, trying to warm her.

And then they stood up and dressed themselves again.

Now the sun was over the horizon, and the lake was visible below: a large, irregular oval mist steaming from its surface into the surrounding pines.

Annabelle had refolded the blanket and returned it to her straw basket which, in turn, was put back into the passenger seat of her sports car. The smooth white finish was covered with dew, and in it Finch drew a heart pierced by an arrow. GF, he initialled in its centre.

AJ, Annabelle put beside his. And then she sketched a tree trunk around the heart, a tree trunk with a surrounding arch of branches and leaves. Watching this, Finch remembered that

Annabelle had once told him that she had gone to art school, that she did pottery in the house while her husband worked. At the time, hearing this, Finch had felt sorry for her. Now he was sad to think that she would continue to live a life he knew nothing about, sad to be reminded that despite the power he liked to think he had, he hadn't touched her at all, hadn't for one moment penetrated the actual life of this woman. The house that she lived in and the boundaries of her life would from now on be as unreadable to him as had been her husband's mask.

She put her hand on the car door, ready to go.

Finch stepped away.

"Goodbye, Finch."

He had nothing to say, not even her name.

"You'll be all right?"

Finch nodded.

She was looking at him, waiting. Finch looked past her, down to the lake. The water was like silver, mist shooting up into the sky. Later in the day it would be blue, grey, even tinged with green, and with each change in the wind its surface would wrinkle or break in response. When night came the darkening colours would also find a home there, and eventually deep layers of blue and purple would mix in the surface, until finally it was simply a black and invisible well.

"Finch, I can't just — Finch. Finch, please look at me."

He had to wrench his head away from the lake.

"Finch, will you remember me?"

Her face was like a bird's in the morning air: a hunter's nose, eyes bright and scanning, even her tears shone like bits of glass.

"I'll remember you," Finch said. He felt so sad, driven down so deep into himself. When this affair was finished, when the gossip and the anger had washed over, he would be here still, looking out over the lake. And where would this woman be? In her white car and protected by her husband's mask, she would have driven to another town, another life.

"You could do me one favour," Finch finally said.

"What?"

"Come to church. Not next Sunday, there's a visiting minister next Sunday, but the Sunday after. Could you do that for me?"

"I think so."

"The next time I preach." Finch said. "I want to look out there and know I have at least one friend."

"All right," said Annabelle. She smiled at Finch but he could only see her hunter's face, the dangerous fence of teeth. "I'll come."

Now he saw her fingers moving towards the handle.

"Goodbye," Finch said.

She stopped and stepped towards him; perhaps she wanted one last kiss, but Finch turned and began to run, jogging slowly across the wet emerald meadow behind the cliffs, then sprinting to gain the safety of the woods.

In the shadows of a large pine he stopped and turned to watch Annabelle. She climbed into her car and started the motor. It coughed at first, then roared as she gunned the accelerator, sending smoke spewing across the rock. Then she backed up and drove down the dirt trail that led to the road.

Finch stayed in the woods for a few moments, facing the empty clearing, wanting to go out one last time and look at the lake. But there would be, he knew, nothing to see; it was too recent and too raw. He noticed now that his fingernails had dug into the pine bark, and when he pulled them away there was the sudden sweet smell of gum. Annabelle Jamieson had loved him in that same sweet way. She had shared the summer with him, but now the summer was over and he was left alone. As Finch started to walk home every step was so painful that he could have believed that his heart was actually and literally broken, bleeding real blood from the inside. Perhaps that meant he had loved her too. "City woman," he said aloud, but the words didn't comfort him. Instead, as he walked, he thought about his own broken heart, his bleeding heart emptying into and filling the red lake of his own slow dying.

Fourteen

At the very end of August, Annabelle's mother telephoned to announce that she was coming down to spend the Labour Day weekend with them.

"She always picks the worst time," Annabelle said to Allen. "You'd think she had some kind of radar."

"Now," Allen said, "she hasn't been here for months."

"You don't know her."

They had been at breakfast when the telephone rang, and while they discussed the event Annabelle got up to add more coffee to their cups. As always the sound of her mother's voice irritated her, yet going to the telephone it had not been her mother she had feared, but Finch.

It was almost two weeks since that final meeting at the lake, and Annabelle, though she had counted back to discover that over the whole summer they had met less than a dozen times, found herself afflicted as though she had withdrawn from a drug. Nervous and irritable, she had begun to smoke cigarettes the whole day through; she had also instigated, as a new routine, the serving of gin and tonic before dinner: a liquid transition to help her over the jolt of having Allen, solicitous and wary, walk into the house with his eyes sweeping every corner as though there were yet more evidence to be uncovered.

"I should go to work."

"I'll walk with you. I need to get some envelopes."

Since the night Allen had told her of Finch's confession,

whole areas of conversation and activity that had once been taken for granted were now studded with little landmines of possibility, silently bowed to and reconnoitred with care. Yet when she was with Allen she dreaded being apart from him, and every morning she found an excuse to walk with him to work. But once separate and alone, the prospect of having to face him again, to be once more in the aura of that calm containing presence, was equally terrifying.

Only in the night could she feel safe; with the lights out she could lie in the orbit of his body's warmth, breathe in his sleeping smell, and even bear the sight of the inquisitive spire.

For this visit Annabelle had asked her mother to come at lunchtime. Of course, she arrived late. By the time her old-fashioned blue sedan pulled up in the driveway, Annabelle had already resorted to a gin and tonic to soothe her nerves. At the sound of her mother's car she rushed upstairs to brush the liquor off her breath; and by the time she got down to the front hall, her mother was inside, calling for her.

"Did you just get up?"

"I was combing my hair."

She kissed her mother, avoiding her mouth, wondering what she would think of the smell of gin and toothpaste.

"Show me where you work," her mother suddenly said. "You kept it a secret on my last visit."

"It's such a mess."

"Oh, come on, you send me all those lovely things every Christmas and I never know where they come from."

"Just one Christmas."

"Annabelle, what are you hiding?"

The noon sun exploded through the glassed-in porch, shining on Annabelle's work table so strongly that her figures looked alive in the brilliant golden light. As her mother advanced towards them Annabelle stayed in the doorway watching the play of the light on the brightly glazed surfaces.

Her mother picked up one of the figures: it was George Mandowski: he had finally been captured — wide, stumpy legs, a round belly and a belligerent expression on his face. Annabelle watched her mother holding Mandowski, at first bringing him close for inspection, then pushing him away, her lips and eyes screwing up in distaste.

"Who's this?"

"No one," Annabelle said hurriedly.

"What an awful little man."

He's not little, Annabelle thought, but didn't say.

"Why would you make an awful man like this?"

"Oh, I don't know. Let's go get Allen for lunch."

"Just a moment." She had put down Mandowski and picked up Jacob Beam. His beard, which should have turned out red had cooked to a slightly orangey colour in the glazing and his mouth, small enough in real life, looked like a cherry held in invisible lips. "Now this is better. I like a fellow who wears a waistcoat." She turned it in the light. "It must have taken you forever to paint all their clothes."

"I guess so."

"But they're so cute." She picked up a tall lanky figure in khaki green, a mechanic who had once fixed the little MG, tuned it and made it run smoothly when it started to sputter. "What are you doing, making a whole town?"

"That's right," Annabelle said. The mechanic, Pat Frank, had asked her if she was a tourist. When she'd said no, he had asked her what she was.

Her mother surveyed the figures, more than two dozen so far, and then her eye fell on one of the pieces of the relief, an abstract, swirling field of colour where more figures were placed. Some were in little islands of their own colour and shape; others stood in groups, posing for one another as if caught in a slow and intricate dance.

"Good God, Annabelle, is this what you do all day? What happened to all those lovely dishes you used to make?" She laughed and turned towards her daughter. "I mean, Annabelle, what are you going to *do* with these people?"

There was a silence while Annabelle's mother examined the figures again, the parts of the mosaic that were already finished, the sketches on her work table and wall.

"Well, it's quite something that you're doing here. There's

no reason why you couldn't sell these, you know. Like toy angels. I think there's a shop, in Ottawa near the market, that handles this kind of thing. Is that what you're going to do?"

She looked at Annabelle, her eyebrows raised to wrinkle her forehead. She was still a handsome woman: her features strong but delicate, her confidence undimmed.

"We should go to lunch," Annabelle finally said. "Allen will be getting hungry."

"You haven't answered my question."

"I know, Mother. I know."

Two months ago her mother's behaviour would have made her want to scream, but after two months of Finch and Maureen, and of intrigue turning to disaster, her mother's sallies and barbs were almost a welcome change. Standing in the studio where her mother had tried to ridicule her work of several months, Annabelle wanted to cross the floor and hug her, put her arms around this prickly, demanding woman and squeeze her until they both cried.

Now her mother had put the figures back on the work table and turned her inspection to Annabelle.

"You're looking well," she finally pronounced, "tired but well."

That night, when Annabelle was alone with Allen, her mother's presence in the house made her feel so rebellious that she insisted on making love, pursuing Allen across their marriage bed and holding him until her body was wrung out and exhausted. Lying on the damp sheets she stretched and arched her back. For almost a whole day now the thought of Finch had been nothing more than a shadow, a clock ticking in the background. Perhaps, like a familiar clock, he would gradually become inaudible, a fixed part of the scene no longer to be noticed.

She took Allen's hand and laced her fingers through his. This was new, the idea that wounds might heal, broken bonds grow strong. "Do you think we might get better?"

"Of course."

"Truly better, so that things could be as they were again?"

These days Allen was supposed to know everything. She

would ask him these questions and then look into his face for the answer. Even his fingers seemed longer, stronger than her own.

"Things change," Allen finally said. He gripped her hand and made her knuckles hurt. But not, Annabelle thought, as much as Finch had hurt her, because from Finch she hadn't known what to expect.

"You can't go back," Allen said.

This was, Annabelle remembered, exactly the sort of statement, the perfect archetypical Allen evasion, that used to annoy her. But not now. Allen held all the power now: her own reserve had all been spent that first afternoon in the barn. But Allen was implacable; while she lost control he never wavered, only grew thick and opaque, as if something unexpectedly sensitive in him was being darkened by exposure to too much light.

"I love you," Annabelle whispered.

"I love you."

Annabelle drifted towards sleep. *I love you.* Finch had broken her open; why was she saying these words to Allen?

On the Sunday morning of the visit they went to church. "After all," her mother had declared, "in Europe people always go to church when the family is together." Annabelle at once envisioned a postcard her mother had sent two years ago when she was on vacation: a Swiss village with the snow-covered mountains overlooking a quaint wooden church surrounded by well-dressed and comfortable-looking citizens.

"All right," Annabelle finally agreed, looking helplessly at Allen. It was, she now remembered, the Sunday Finch had asked her to attend; and it would be the first time they had been to church since Finch's confession.

A sleepy morning peace lay over the town but the cool breeze and the sharpness of the colours warned of the season's turning. The excitement Annabelle always felt with the onset of fall was for some reason connected, this day, with the consciousness of her mother's aging: not that she seemed old, but her body, thinner and drier, appeared to be poised on the edge. Annabelle, linking her own arm to her mother's, wondered how this proud and irritable woman could ever have gone through the indignities of pregnancy and childbirth.

Later Annabelle would remember this particular stroll through Salem's streets, the peculiar tranquility of the day. And she would remember, too, how the light struck the stone church, turning the ancient limestone a bright yellow-grey and making the painted spire rise even higher towards the sun: as if, by its very shape, this old building could try to split apart the sky and reach towards God.

They were a few minutes early but the church was already crowded. At first Annabelle imagined that the attendance had increased because this was Labour Day Sunday, the last Sunday in the country for most tourists and cottage-dwellers. But as she and Allen and her mother found seats in their usual place, a long polished pew about halfway back on the right side of the church, the side that was the farthest away from Maureen Finch's habitual station at the front, Annabelle saw that the church was filled with townspeople and local farmers. She was just about to comment on this when she saw Nellie Tillson.

Her long yellow hair was worn loose, down to the shoulders of her gauzy blue dress; and with her parents on either side, gravely escorting her, she looked like a shotgun bride as she made her swollen way down the centre aisle. To their neighbours Nellie Tillson's parents waved and spoke softly, but Nellie herself kept her mouth closed and her eyes to her feet, which were encased in a pair of pumps so white that Annabelle was reminded of the day of her own wedding.

"There's Nellie Tillson," she said to Allen, across her mother who was sitting between them. Allen, who was already holding the prayerbook and wearing that slightly uncomfortable look he always got in church, just nodded and smiled at her.

"Who is Nellie Tillson?" Mrs. McLeod asked. But before Allen could answer Annabelle pointed to the front, where Maureen Finch was being wheeled in by her husband. The ghostly white of her face and hands outshone even Nellie Tillson's shoes.

"Look at her," Mrs. McLeod exclaimed. "How extraordinarily beautiful she is."

As there burst within Annabelle a sudden rush of panic and jealousy, she was jostled by a large woman sliding in to sit beside her. He doesn't usually bring his women home, Maureen had said; but once, it was true, their marriage must have been whole, and the hatred that filled Maureen Finch must have been mixed with love.

Now Annabelle regretted having come. Finch had mounted the pulpit, looking as powerful and as confident as ever. His eyes ranged over the congregation — taking in Nellie Tillson, Annabelle saw, without even pausing, sweeping by her bridal splendour just as they swept by Annabelle herself. And just as the Reverend's eyes took count of his congregation, his wife's did not: Maureen was sitting rigid, her hands gripping the rubber wheels of her chair. Her red hair, which wound like flames coiled and restrained against her head, and her white indoor skin combined into a howl of distress, echoing through the church.

At a signal from Finch the hymn began and at least for a few moments Annabelle could escape from the tension by singing. But after the first hymn her stomach began to hurt so much she wondered if it could provide an excuse to leave. She wished desperately that she was sitting beside Allen instead of between her mother and the large and stolid farm woman who smelled of the barn and who kept, though staring straight ahead, shifting her massive freckled arm over the wooden arm-rest and into Annabelle.

On the far side of the church Annabelle saw Donna Wilson; and she in turn saw Annabelle and waved. She looked, Annabelle thought, like an illustration from the cover of a magazine, and Annabelle wondered what thoughts were going through her mind, how she, after all her jokes about Finch's bedroom eyes and her arranged meeting with Finch in her living room, viewed the fact that Annabelle had somehow lost track of the rules, had gone too far and been caught. "I am weak and you are strong," Annabelle sang. If the words of hymns and the Bible had had any left-over, uncontemplated meaning from her childhood, they seemed now nothing more than a gigantic and ominous threat: a promise not of salvation in heaven but of God's revenge upon those who strayed, and the sound of her mother's strong voice, which she had not heard singing in church for years, was only another ominous sound, a note in the rising chorus of dread by which Annabelle felt entirely surrounded.

The farm woman beside her had firmly established her pink arm on the rest and Annabelle was squeezed uncomfortably close to her mother. She, mistaking this for affection, had linked her arm through Annabelle's, and Annabelle now felt beyond even Allen's protection.

She remembered that she had a bottle of aspirin in her purse. During the hymns she took two of the white tablets, swallowing them dry, the chalky sour taste laying thick on her tongue.

"I like to hear them preach," her mother had said. "You take the measure of a minister by the way he preaches."

As Finch stepped into the pulpit to deliver the sermon, Annabelle could feel her mother straightening up in anticipation. She pinched Annabelle's arm and smiled. Finch, meanwhile, surveyed the congregation once again: but this time his look was not the rapid sweep he had given a half hour ago; this was a slow and probing journey. His own eyes well hidden behind thick brows, he spent, as he sometimes liked to, whole minutes making the census of the two-hundred-odd faces that watched his own.

Nor did Finch, in these introductory silences, merely move from the back to the front of his audience; he had an uncanny way of skipping round, of locking eyes first with someone from the front, then suddenly jumping several rows back so that you had the feeling as Annabelle had once explained to Allen, that he was trying to catch you unaware, that he suspected you of trying to wriggle off the hook of his righteous scales.

When they had first come to Salem and attended the church, Finch's eyes would stop at her, staring brazenly right from the pulpit, but after their affair had begun they had always skipped. Today, however, they went right to her: not to shock but to search for reassurance, telling her, Annabelle wanted to believe, that he was as baffled as she at this sudden turn of events. Then his eyes pulled away and Annabelle knew that in the same way he had sought her out, he was now measuring Nellie Tillson.

"Look at him," her mother whispered, as though Annabelle, along with every other member of the congregation, were not riveted on this, even for Finch, extraordinarily long silence. And then, shrugging his shoulders, he laid his hands out so that his long fingers could be seen overlapping the edge of the oak pulpit, and he looked for a moment down the centre aisle to the stained glass image of Jesus above the front door of the old church.

He was today, Annabelle thought, almost larger than life, like a movie of himself: his wide shoulders and big arms fairly strained at his suit. The black fringe of beard, disappearing into the black hair, and the dark shadowed eyes made him look drawn so deep into himself that even the probing stares of two hundred people could elicit nothing but an image of strength and silence. Even his wife in her wheelchair, and the two young daughters in matching pinafore frocks behind her, appeared, against the massive presence of the man, like mere extras; and not for the first time Annabelle wondered what success Finch might have found had he made his life in the city.

Finally Finch started, his speaking voice low and casual, a tone so natural and distinct that it seemed to be emanating not from Finch but from the oak-panelled walls of the old stone church.

"Today," Finch said, "I have no sermon to deliver, no special message to give from God to you, and for that I apologize." Once more Finch let his eyes sweep across the congregation but this time, Annabelle felt, it was not a look of curiosity but a caressing gaze, a silent soothing touch to prepare for whatever was to come.

"I have been minister of this church for sixteen years now, and had God willed it, perhaps I would have been for sixteen more; and yet today I find myself at a turning point." As always, Finch in the pulpit spoke with an absolute assurance, an ease of speech, almost a prettiness, that Annabelle could never find in his ordinary conversation. And now the hand that Annabelle had so often seen crash down on the oak pulpit, had felt searching out the sensuous nooks of her body, had felt pressing into the small of her back until it was holding her suspended above the wet ground, lifted in an automatic gesture; and then floated back down towards the lectern, the sound of skin hitting the wood only a light, defeated slap.

"Today," Finch said, his voice beginning to warm, "today I stand before you in shame, a shame I have been feeling for many months, and that I now must confess to you."

God, Annabelle thought, and then almost laughed at herself because all she could think was: Please not in front of my mother. Then she looked across her mother to Allen, wanting to ask him if they could leave, but Allen was leaning back in the pew, his legs crossed, his gaze stoically settled on Finch.

"This past winter," Finch went on, "this past winter," and if he wasn't giving a sermon it was beginning to sound like one because he was repeating himself and saying each word slowly, with emphasis, rolling them off his tongue the way he did when he was driving towards some elaborate sin, "this past winter something happened; it was a twist of fate that pulled the ground from under my feet; and since that time, friends, since that time I have been cowering in a dark corner of my soul; I have been cowering in the dark hell of my own guilt and damnation because I did not have the courage to face God and ask Him His forgiveness.

"And a man without God's forgiveness," Finch intoned gravely, "a man without God's forgiveness . . ." His voice trailed off and he looked directly at Annabelle. Her heart jumped and for a moment she thought the whole congregation would follow the funnel of his stare; and then, just as heads began to turn, he looked away and began speaking again, his voice suddenly louder and sharper.

"Now you might ask," he almost barked, "you might ask what your own minister is doing up here talking about his shame before God." With his long arm Finch pointed an accusing finger at the church in front of him. Beside her Annabelle heard the farm woman's breathing, a laboured panting that was like an echo of the cow giving birth, and then what she saw was not Finch's arm but the picture she had long ago constructed of Finch in Allen's office, Finch asking Allen his forgiveness and the two of them kneeling on the carpet looking piously upwards.

"Am I not supposed to be righteous?" Finch roared. "Am I

not supposed to set an example?" His fist crashed down on the oak pulpit and the crack of his muscle against the hard wood echoed through the church like a gunshot, a gunshot mixed for Annabelle with the sudden gasp of her mother beside her.

"Annabelle," she whispered, and clutched at her arm, and suddenly Annabelle wondered if her mother knew everything.

"For months I tortured myself, thinking that I, who was supposed to lead, had failed, had fallen like any man out of the eye of God. For what, my friends, is the knowledge of sin but the knowledge that you have broken God's rules? And what has every man since Adam tried to do then? Hide from God. Hide his shame and his soul from God's eye."

Now Finch leaned forward. "I hid from God," he whispered. "I hid from myself and I hid from you."

"What did I hide?" he suddenly roared. "I'll tell you!" This time the crashing of his fist into the pulpit shook the whole church. And then suddenly his arm shot out again, and this time the finger was pointing towards Nellie Tillson. "I'll tell you what I did," he shouted. And the fist came down again. "I'll tell you." Again.

"And when I tell you—" Finch was shouting at the top of his lungs and Annabelle felt suddenly trapped in a tunnel with a train roaring towards her. "And when I tell you, you will forgive me. Because *God* has forgiven me, and I have forgiven myself, and because I *need your compassion.*"

Though she remembered them later, Annabelle didn't exactly hear the words that followed. Instead what she remembered were moments that might have come out of a dream: the sudden smell released by the whole congregation, a scent of blood that burst through the church as though they were all hunters now, intent on the same prey; Maureen Finch's face jerking back, as it never did, to face the congregation for one second only, before her husband started talking, a look of mixed fear and contempt twisting her white skin, dragging down the corners of her heavily lipsticked mouth and making her look like the horror queen in the midst of her own worst nightmare; her mother's grip intense on her arm, her breath coming high and fast, so excited by Finch that Annabelle could hear small bedroom sounds starting in the back of her throat; the Finch girls making their own startled sound, like house-mice caught helplessly in a fire, and reaching for each other's hands.

That whole afternoon after Finch's sermon Annabelle longed for night to come so that she could be away from the curious eye of her mother and safe again in the lee of Allen's embrace.

Finch, as it turned out, had not once mentioned Annabelle's name.

He had spoken instead of his transgressions with Nellie Tillson. For what was only half an hour by Annabelle's watch, but for what had seemed a lot longer, Gordon Finch stood in the pulpit and praised his "golden angel of the Sunday school," the delights of her embrace. And not simply of her embrace, her "warm and human touch," but "that whole garden of golden pears that ache for the hand's touch, honeyed lips begging to be kissed," and on and on through the assorted parts of the body until Annabelle thought that the young yellow-haired Nellie Tillson must have been no mere woman but a tropical super-market, a dewy, biblical oasis spread out for Finch's delectation. In the end, when he had advertised Nellie's pears, her lips, her peaches and cream, her melons that "would have seared even Adam's lustful tongue," he said that he realized that God had been testing him, and that he had failed.

By this time Finch, along with most of the rest of the congregation, had been in tears. Annabelle, dry-eyed, had heard her mother hoarsely weeping beside her as Finch told of "those terrible times in the gathering shadows of the afternoon, those long nights I spent down on my knees, trying to open my heart to God"; and as her mother choked and snuffled, Annabelle wondered if Finch, confessing his sins with such a terrible sincerity, counted the afternoons when he had gathered shadows in her own, less illustrious, company as part of the sin or part of the penance. Because if Nellie Tillson had breasts like pears, lips like honey, other parts that the Bible was too discreet to name, perhaps her own smaller body had been a reproof to Finch, and the moans and the groans of his sexual comedy had only been noises of dismay.

"Will you forgive me?" he had finally shouted. "Will you forgive me?" And his strong right arm had shot into the air, a pose that was supposed to be pleading, but in fact was so threatening that even those who had been crying became silent.

"Answer me," Finch demanded. "Answer me." Annabelle felt the fat freckled arm of the woman beside her shift as she struggled with Finch's challenge.

"I forgive you," came a dramatic whisper, hoarse with tears. "I forgive you." Annabelle, shocked, looked to her right, to her mother who had been the first to break the silence.

"You are forgiven," bellowed the woman to Annabelle's left. "You are forgiven." And with that the voices began to chime in, one after another, first mostly women and then, reluctantly, their men, until the whole church rumbled with cries and shouts of forgiveness. And all the while Finch stood tall with his arms outstretched to permit these arrows of forgiveness an unobstructed path straight through to his heart, to the very soul that God Himself had forgiven first.

"Fantastic," Annabelle's mother said, "absolutely fantastic." The whole way home from the church she couldn't stop talking about the Reverend. After everything was done, Finch had stood on the steps of the church, Maureen in her chair beside him, and shaken every hand that passed. Annabelle's he had enclosed with such force that she had felt her knuckles begin to rearrange themselves; but when he had come to Annabelle's mother he had leaned over and kissed her on the cheek. "God bless you," he said, "you spoke first. I knew you would." Beside Finch and his wife stood their two children, chattering happily to their friends as though nothing had happened.

They ate lunch not at the pine table in the kitchen but at the almost never-used oak table in the dining room, and Mrs. MacLeod, with one of the pearl-handled fruit knives a relative had given as a wedding present, was carving slivers of pears and cheese onto her plate. "Did you notice how he said he knew I would? The man is so magnificent that I almost believed him. What a savage, what a magnificent savage."

Annabelle, trying to keep her face composed, poured tea for the three of them from their silver wedding set.

"You know," her mother said, "that man has something special. And there was more going on in that church than meets the eye, I'll bet. That man is shrewd."

Annabelle added milk and sugar to her mother's liking and pushed the cup towards her. It was tempting to tell her mother exactly what had been hidden.

"I'm a student of human nature, I like to think. It's the European way." She smiled at Allen. "We have to remember that we're only visitors here, after all."

Visitors where? Annabelle said, but only to herself because she knew her mother would like nothing better than to deliver a speech on the higher destiny of the human soul.

They took the tea into the living room. Church had run late and now it was well into the afternoon. Annabelle wondered what exactly Finch might be doing, whether he was sitting in his own home, drinking tea with his wife and the children; and then suddenly, as she was trying to picture this, all the distance and detachment she had built up over these two weeks, and even sustained during the worst moments in the church, collapsed. First she was struck by the pure audacity of what he had done. And then her eyes closed and she was wrenched back to that stormy afternoon by the lake when she had wrapped her arms so tightly around him and craved every thrust, begged Finch to drive her deeper into the wet ground. *Finch,* she thought, his presence and his name so strong that she was sure she had said it aloud. She sat up quickly, knocking over her tea.

"Damn."

"She always does that when she's nervous," Mrs. MacLeod said. "Have you noticed that? I've never seen anyone spill so many cups of tea and coffee."

"It's all right," Annabelle said. She pushed herself to her feet and, without looking at her mother, walked quickly into the kitchen. There she leaned over the sink and turned the cold water on full blast, hoping the noise and the spray would somehow distract her. *Finch.* He had peered down at her from the pulpit and gathered her up in his eyes like a second crop hardly worth the harvesting. *Finch.* Now, of all times, her need for him had blossomed.

"Annabelle." Allen's voice. His hand on her shoulder.

She turned to face him. He was calm, as always. Why was it that she alone lost control, while others like Allen and Finch broke the rules with impunity?

"Are you feeling sick?"

"I'm just looking for a rag." She followed his eyes and saw that she was already holding a cloth in her hands.

"Well," Annabelle said, "since you're here, maybe you should put on water for more tea." Control. She walked past Allen to the living room where she knelt and wiped the tea from the hardwood floor. "You see?" she said to her mother. "I've got a special place to sit here, away from the rug."

"I don't understand how you could be nervous," Mrs. MacLeod persisted, "not living in a peaceful town like this. Though they say that small towns are the worst."

"My life here is very relaxed," Annabelle said firmly. The tea had left an irregular white stain on the floor where it had melted the wax. Sometimes the clock would beat louder, loud as thunder, even threaten to take down the house. But like thunder, those times would pass; the house would still be standing and the clock would be background once more. "It's very peaceful here," Annabelle said, "but I've been working late."

She lifted her face up to look at her mother and her throat was so tight with choked up tears and words she could hardly breathe.

"I'm sorry," Mrs. MacLeod said. For a brief second something close to recognition passed across her face. But then her mother was staring distractedly out the window, as if whatever was being pursued had now disappeared from sight and mind.

When her mother left the next day, they kissed goodbye in that same dry, distracted way. Annabelle, standing at the window and watching her mother pull out of the drive, felt oddly deserted. It was just after lunch — her mother had left early, pleading the need to wash her hair and get organized before a new work week began.

She and Allen washed up the dishes and then, when Allen said he had some papers he wanted to look at, Annabelle retreated to her studio.

In the bright, glassed-in porch, a cup of steaming coffee in her hand, Annabelle sat down in her wicker chair and let the relief of finally being alone wash over her.

There was, in the centre of the floor, a thick shag remnant from their bedroom; and after a few minutes, when she had started to soak in the heat of the sun coming through the glass, she pushed the rug so that it was surrounded by light and lay down on top of it.

She closed her eyes and let the heat blanket her. Images of the service floated by: Nellie Tillson's bridal walk down the aisle and then the amazing moment when she had stood up in her blue child's dress and piped out, "I forgive you," the tropical paradise of her body suddenly represented by a tiny penny-whistle voice; Maureen's white face outside the church, sitting beside Finch as he shook the hands of the faithful; Maureen's white face like one more stone of the church, absolutely immobile, tinged a slight yellow by the sun that made Annabelle want someone to run up to this carved figure and rub her skin with buttercups until she laughed; Finch's hands around hers, but his eyes making their communion with Allen.

The sun was so warm she dozed off, woke up briefly and pushed the rug to the new centre of the light, then curled up and went to sleep again.

When she woke up the sky was a deep and darkening blue, and the reflections of the pink barred clouds were held in the windows. Annabelle got to her feet. She opened the door and stepped outside, where she was suddenly enveloped in the smell of fresh-cut grass and cooking meat. At the end of the yard Allen, wearing his old jeans and standing in his bare feet in front of the barbecue, was tending the fire and sipping a drink. It was all so beautiful: the changing colours of the sky; the deep growing green of the lawn; even the angles on top of the picket fence were etched into the air with perfect sharpness, little white steeples, little wooden prayers being offered up to the god of fences. This was how things should be, calm and perfect;

every person, every blade of grass, every little bit of wood living out its life in solitary perfection.

She went back into her studio.

The figures of the village were barely visible, bits of their awkward and grotesque colours shining madly out of the shadows. She stepped forward and picked one of them up: Paul Tadworth, the owner of the Salem Garage and General Repair. He was wearing white overalls, because he owned the shop, and an orange peaked cap with CASE on the front. It had taken her three tries to get the narrow-brimmed cap to survive the heat of the kiln. Now she wanted to throw it against the wall the way she had wanted to throw Isaac's watch.

She held it in the air.

The door opened and Allen walked into the studio.

"What are you doing?"

"Nothing."

"You looked like you were going to throw something."

"I was." The calm Annabelle had felt just a few moments before had been broken, like a layer of ice shrugged off by a suddenly swelling river. She was angry at her mother for having invaded her privacy, at Allen for having played her as a card in his elaborate poker game; at herself for having been sucked into the centre of other people's lives, for having a heart with boundaries so weak that it soaked up other people like blotting paper, letting them spread out inside her the way these ungainly clay pieces spread their awkward colours through the room. She stepped towards Allen, wondering if this was it finally, if she would break apart now and explode the way she had with Isaac, break apart and start hitting him until finally he bled real blood, shouted with real pain.

"You can't break those," Allen suddenly said. "You've made them, now you have to leave them alone. It would be like killing your own children."

"They're dead."

"But they're beautiful," Allen insisted, his voice dogged. "They're art. Even your mother says they're wonderfully real. And they are alive, alive to her and to me."

Annabelle tried to imagine Allen and her mother solemnly

discussing the artistic merit of her ridiculous little creations. When would this famous and brilliant discussion have taken place? In the middle of the night, when she was asleep? Or yesterday afternoon, when she was in the kitchen remembering the taste of Finch's beard?

"Well?" Allen demanded aggressively.

Now he leaned towards her, daring her to lose control, daring her, it seemed to Annabelle, as he had the day he gave her the envelope to take to Finch. But his face was as bland as ever. In her hand Annabelle was still holding the figure of Paul Tadworth, his orange cap digging into her palm. She squeezed it, needing the clay to bite into her skin, needing to throw it into Allen's face and break his little mask once and for all. She raised her arm.

"Don't," Allen said.

"*Don't!*" Annabelle screamed. She drew her arm back and threw with all her strength. Paul Tadworth whizzed by Allen's head and shattered against the wall. She was so dizzy with rage she could hardly see. She stumbled to her work table and picked up Jacob Beam. She held him momentarily then hurled him to the floor. Mandowski was next: his back split in two and his head fell off when she smashed him into the table.

Then Annabelle felt the hands descend to her shoulders: they came like blows, almost knocking her over. Allen's face, red with fury, his mouth open but silent as he jerked her towards him, shook her back and forth.

She could feel her head flopping like a doll's head, but she kept her eyes open, kept her eyes on Allen's face as he now finally spoke.

"Finch," he breathed. "Finch, Finch, Finch." Each time he shook her, he spoke Finch's name.

Then, as suddenly as they had reached for her, the hands released their hold. She spun dizzily across the floor, dancing crazily to keep her balance, then crashed into the wall.

Finch.

There was a roaring in her skull and then Annabelle realized that she was starting to swoon — the way she had when Allen surprised her and Donna. Not this time, Annabelle thought.

She heard a rhythmic panting, and above it the brittle music of breaking clay.

Looking up she saw Allen, his scarlet face working as he silently mouthed Finch's name, methodically throwing figures from her mosaic into the wall.

Fifteen

*W*hen the alarm went off Maureen Finch sat up, pushed back her hair and shook her head to clear the dreams she could feel crowding together but couldn't actually grasp. Manoeuvring carefully, she lowered her feet to the floor, then reached for her wicker wheelchair. On its back were her undergarments, a wrap-around skirt and a sweater.

Her nightgown was made of a white satin that slid easily between her skin and the sheets, and when she had wriggled it off she sat for a moment looking down at her body. There had been a time when she had delighted in taking forbidden glimpses of herself in the full-length mirror at her mother's house. Then her body, seen whole, appeared like an image out of a book: lean and white, the curves of hips, shoulders and breasts so beautiful to her eye that she would turn away, unable to believe that this creature in a unified skin could have anything to do with the young woman who was usually cut in half by skirts and blouses, sweaters and jeans, clothes that not only covered her up but sectioned her into pieces so that she looked like a jigsaw puzzle waiting for someone to put her together.

Now her breasts, softened by the children, hung lower; but her skin was still smooth and creamy down to her hips. There it suddenly changed; poisoned by the arthritis beneath, it turned a coarse red and wrinkled loosely over the places where the muscles had fled. Her thighs too had bagged, and from the waist down she looked exactly the way her mother had looked when

Maureen used to have to bathe her. For a moment Maureen wondered if she could accept Valerie and Clare witnessing her own slow slide into paralysis, the way she had witnessed that of her mother.

Reminded of them she put on her brassiere and a sweater. Then she opened the skirt onto the seat of the chair and, grasping the arms tightly, swung herself from the bed to the chair. There she tied the skirt around herself and covered it, in turn, with a shawl.

It was the day after Labour Day, the first day of school. She could hear Finch in the kitchen already up. As she wheeled across the room and turned the big steel skeleton key that unlocked her bedroom door she was sure that Finch, equally, would be listening for her. For a moment, with the cold metal imprint of the key still fresh in her hand, she thought about this, about the way they had divided up this house and farm so that windows, walls and even floors were membranes through which she and Finch passed their various messages. And then she wheeled across the hall to the bathroom where again she closed and locked the door behind her: as she splashed her face with soap and water, she thought of it still, of the thick oak that stood between her and the hall.

When she was finished, Maureen wheeled to the girls' room and woke them up. Once she was sure that they knew which clothes they were supposed to wear, she returned to her own room to sit at her desk. Inside was the first real letter she had written since her marriage. She had spent the whole of Labour Day composing it.

Labour Day, September. This was the razor blade that cut through the gauzy end of summer and separated holiday from work, warm careless mornings from the days that began with frost.

But today there was no sign of freezing: only grass bright green with the heavy dew and a yellow-red trim of light on the jagged oak horizon.

As always it was Valerie who was ready first, hastily dressed and stumbling into the room while still rubbing her eyes, wanting to have her hair brushed and pinned back.

"Where's Clare."

"She's still getting dressed."

The skin on Valerie's forehead was so wonderfully thin, so translucent and new that the blue veins were visible beneath, and pushing her daughter's hair, sliding her fingers along the girl's temples so it wouldn't fall across her ears, Maureen's hands trembled with pleasure.

Clare was different, more like Finch. Valerie's hair, like her own, was lustrous and thick. It was Valerie, the eldest, on whom all the burdens of the mother would fall — the caretaking and the genes too — so that one day, the doctor had said, there was a good chance that she would end up, like Maureen and Maureen's mother, in a chair. There was also, the doctor had emphasized, a good chance that she wouldn't.

"You go get Clare now."

But it wasn't necessary: Clare was already at the door, a gamin-faced girl with coarse black hair and bright almond eyes, Finch's brilliant eyes shining unexpectedly out of the face of this tiny and delicate girl. She hesitated for a moment, than ran into the room, still, Maureen thought, as transparent as a minnow, her arms opening wide for the first kiss of the day.

Finch, finishing the milking, washed the plastic milkers and hung them up in their place above the tubs. Then, as he always finally did, he drew a pail of cold water from the tap and washed off the stainless steel tank where the milk was kept.

There were times when he wondered if it was worth farming on a scale this small, unable to afford help and with a wife who had to be carried to the barn. But when he stepped from the room at the end of the barn where the milking apparatus and the bulk tank were kept into the barn itself and walked up and down the aisle of cows, the whole low, long space fragrant with the fresh, savoury smell of hay and warm milk, he was filled with such a pure and drowsy contentment that he stood at the beamed door and looked back with total satisfaction, ready to light the pipe that would mark the end of another morning's milking.

It was two days since he had preached, and he had felt, the

whole time since, a wonderful relief, an exhausted conviction that he had stood up in the pulpit and had managed to pass through the knot at the centre of his own life, throw off and break the curse that had been handed down from his father. And though he knew that nothing he himself said could restore his virtue, he had for once turned his oratory to good purpose, had for once struck back at the demon that grasped his soul.

Of course he had sinned with Annabelle Jamieson, with Nellie Tillson, with others too, but at least he had stood up and defied the worst that other men could offer and then shaken every one of their hands as they walked out of the church.

Finch sucked at his pipe and strolled down the aisle once more, checking the cows before leaving. In the church he felt himself confronted by mere men and women. But God Himself had not been there to strike him down. God, if He had an opinion on such a tiny matter, had yet to make it known.

Finch stepped outside and began making his way back to the house.

Even while he was still walking along the outside of the barn he heard the familiar motor of the schoolbus, a new purring sound that indicated the first muffler of the year; and he quickened his step so that he got to the drive in time to kiss his daughters goodbye as they scrambled out of the house and down to the road.

Maureen, he knew, would be in her room and waiting for her tea. The girls were allowed to make breakfast for her, but he was still nervous of their using the stove; and without looking up at her window he crossed the lawn.

At the door he knocked clean his pipe and put it into the top pocket of his coveralls. Then, once inside the kitchen, he stripped them off and went to the sink where he filled the kettle with water.

Since the sermon things had changed inside himself, and he had felt, if not cleansed, at least as if he had crossed a dividing line and was capable of starting to clear a new place in his life. And he felt, too, that with the sermon had been released all the fatigue of the past few years. These days it was easy to sleep, and his body sometimes protested as he dragged it through the chores. But with Maureen and the girls there had been no change. Just a strained silence from Maureen, which gradually dissolved into their normal routine.

"Gordon."

"I'm just getting your tea."

"Could you come upstairs a moment. I think the plumbing has burst under the sink."

He turned off the kettle and then climbed the stairs. There had been a time when he could read her moods by the tone of her voice, the exact measure of warmth injected into its dry base, but these days it was so precisely uniform that he had lost all sense of her.

At the top of her stairs he looked into her room. She was sitting near the door, in her wheelchair, with the blanket over her lap.

"It's right under the sink," she said. "I think one of the taps must be leaking."

He walked to the bathroom, seeing the water on the floor gradually pooling out from the base of the sink cabinet. Whatever it was didn't seem to be running very fast. He heard Maureen behind him.

"I think it must be right inside the vanity," she said.

He opened the cabinet door and then knelt down to look. With his head under the sink he felt suddenly naked. The sound of Maureen's breathing was eerily magnified.

"Right there," she said.

But aside from the water on the floor, he could see no sign of trouble. The explosion came as he was bending to take a closer look.

The bullet ripped into his back, forcing him forward and driving his head against the copper pipe. As the pain began to rise, the second bullet came. He was turning round to find a way through the darkness to her face when it hit: he felt it all — the metal slicing into his cheek, the explosion starting in the bone beneath his eye, the eye itself twisting suddenly with the force of the impact, twisting and tearing in the socket, then breaking free. It was with that eye that he saw her last: Maureen, in the doorway, her mouth wide open and her green Irish eyes burning like the Last Judgement as he tried to crawl towards her. Feeling nothing now, only the red, heavy curtain settling over him, drawing him down.

When she was finished in the bathroom, Maureen closed the door, then wheeled back to the secretary in the bedroom where she reached for the telephone.

"Is this Mandowski's grocery?"

"Yes it is."

"This is Mrs. Finch speaking. I'd like to place an order."

"Yes, Mrs. Finch."

Maureen, now completely calm, took a pencil and paper and made notes as she dictated her list over the telephone. She did not forget to include, because it was the first week in September, new lunch boxes for the girls, nor did she forget extra rolls of paper towelling to replace the ones she had used mopping up Finch's blood. When she was done, she asked the girl to read it back, which she did.

"Will that be all, Mrs. Finch?"

"No," Maureen said, "there's one more thing."

"Yes?"

"The Reverend is feeling ill, so he won't be able to pick the groceries up for me. I'd like Mr. Mandowski to deliver them, himself. Perhaps he could bring them at lunchtime."

"I'll tell him, Mrs. Finch."

"And would you ask him very kindly to stop at the drug store and pick up my prescription?"

"All right, Mrs. Finch."

And finally, before she hung up, Maureen said, "I'm sorry, but I don't recognize your voice. Could you tell me who's speaking please."

"It's Nellie Tillson, Mrs. Finch."

"All right, Nellie, it's been nice talking to you. Goodbye now."

"Goodbye."

Maureen replaced the telephone in its cradle and took out the letter she had written on Labour Day. It filled a bulging envelope and was addressed to Lorna McConnell. Then she opened the drawer where she had put the letters that had passed between herself and Finch. Someday her children would see these; perhaps they too would ask what had happened to the innocence and love.

She took a letter from the pile and opened it

Dearest Maureen,

I have arranged it with my father that he is to marry us in the church, when the time is right. He had objections because of the religious question, but I have convinced him that our love is strong, and that the faith we share in God and His works is larger than any differences.

Maureen dearest, I pray for the health of yourself and your mother, and I pray too for the day when the agony of this waiting will be over and we will be man and wife.

Your husband in his thought,
Gordon

She wondered sometimes if Finch would have been different had she married him right away. When she had found out about the first of them, long before Nellie Tillson, she had blamed herself for being cold, for making him wait. Though when it was a year, almost to the day, between their marriage and Valerie's birth, she had been triumphant, had counted the months over and over to herself: a full twelve months it had been and there was no one who could say she had been like the others in the village, married because they couldn't stop the boys from filling up their pants. Even Gordon Finch who, they said, was turning into the very image of his father, even Gordon Finch hadn't been able to bring her down. Maybe that had been pride, the kind of pride that was sinful.

Maureen wheeled over to her dressing table, where she looked at herself in the mirror. Then she took her silverbacked brushes and began pulling them through her hair, a hundred strokes from the roots, like her mother, her grandmother, her great-grandmother had before her. When she was gone Valerie would get these brushes. Valerie was already showing signs of having the family beauty, the fair skin and the copper hair, and she already had to brush her hair with Maureen every evening, a hundred strokes until her arm was tired.

Finch: she had loved him, he never knew that. When she found out about the first of them she swallowed her anger. When Mrs. McConnell told her, Maureen had said that she never wanted to hear about the subject again — this after she had the whole story. "Not one word," she told Mrs. McConnell. They were drinking tea out of the rose service Finch's aunt had given for their wedding. But the moment Mrs. McConnell left, Maureen had taken the tea tray — she could walk then — and carefully dumped the whole service on the floor: pot, milk pitcher, sugar bowl two matching cups and saucers. They all broke together; they made such a crash that Valerie, who was still an infant, woke up crying and Maureen had gone to comfort her.

"This sometimes happens," Mrs. McConnell told her, "when a woman has been pregnant and then had a hard birth, sometimes it takes a long time to come back—"

She had stopped but Maureen had almost giggled, despite herself, because she had been sure Mrs. McConnell, whose husband was a breeder of prize Holsteins, had been about to say "back into service."

"Come back," she had finally repeated. "You know what I mean."

"Of course," Maureen had agreed. "I guess you can let these things go."

Mrs. McConnell had nodded vigorously, gratefully.

"Well, Lorna," Maureen had said — because Lorna McConnell had been a friend of her mother's she had grown up calling her Mrs., but now if ever was the time to change — "you've told me everything now, and let's never talk about it again. Not to each other or to anyone else."

Lorna McConnell had nodded.

"I have to ask your promise on that," Maureen insisted.

"I swear, Maureen, I swear. I just thought you should know."

"I should. And now it's over." She had taken the white china teapot with the beautiful pink roses and poured them one final cup of tea. When the pot broke it was empty, but the roses seemed to stay whole, and she had saved one of them, a pink rose set in a field of white porcelain; she kept it with the letters from Finch.

Those were the days when she had been innocent, so innocent: she had saved the rose shard and she had swallowed her anger. Instead of chastising Finch she had mentioned the girl's name, once only, to tell him she knew, and then she had been so burdened with guilt at even that small revenge that she had, instead of punishing Finch, tried to make herself more desirable.

When she had finished with her hair Maureen changed her clothes, and then she wheeled herself to the top of her stairs. She didn't look at the closed bathroom door. At the bottom of the stairs, in the front hall was her portable wheelchair.

Maureen took the blanket off her lap and threw it down the stairs. Then she lifted herself out of the wheelchair, holding onto the banister, and lowered herself again so she was sitting on the top step. She pushed the wicker wheelchair into her room, out of sight, and then she lowered herself down the stairs, sliding from one step to the next. In her hand was the gun. For some nervous reason she was afraid that it would go off while she was descending the stairs.

By the time Mandowski arrived Maureen was sitting in the kitchen, in the portable chair. She was wearing her best blouse, one that buttoned right up to her neck, and over that she had her church suit jacket. Draped over her lap and legs was a thick wool blanket, the blue one with tasseled fringes that she liked to wear in the fall.

As always, Mandowski came to the door carrying the two cartons of groceries; but this time, because she had said Finch was home, he knocked and waited for Maureen to wave at him through the kitchen window.

"I can't stay," Mandowski said.

"Won't you have a cup of tea?"

"Well," Mandowski said, "all right. I wouldn't want to wake the Reverend."

What he meant, Maureen knew, was that he wouldn't want

Finch to discover him in his own kitchen, but Maureen only smiled and poured his tea. "Don't you worry," she said. "He's a sound sleeper."

She poured Mandowski's tea and added milk and sugar, as he liked it.

"A beautiful day," Mandowski said. "September is my favourite month."

"There are some cookies in the cupboard."

"I should be getting home for lunch."

Maureen sipped at her own tea. As always, she took it clear, more for the look of the liquid than the taste.

"I think it's been very brave of you to keep Nellie working at the store."

"She's the brave one," Mandowski said. "She knows she can't stay in hiding all her life."

"Got to face the music," Maureen said in a drawl, imitating Mandowski. "Best get these things over with."

"That's right," Mandowski said. "Best get these things over with."

He looked carefully at Maureen, that calculated and appraising look she remembered from when he had given her the gun.

For a moment she submitted to him. Then her eyes dropped to her lap. "It's not easy," she said.

"I'm sorry," Mandowski murmured. Voice like an undertaker. "I don't suppose it has been easy for you." The news of the sermon would have spread all over the county but this was the first time someone had mentioned it to her face.

"A person's got to do what a person's got to do," Maureen said. Her own voice sounded far away, as if she was starting to doze.

"I hope you're not angry with me."

"A little." The urge to sleep intensified and she looked up at Mandowski again; he was leaning forward, suspicious, and she snapped to alertness, a charge of fear surging through her.

"I guess I played my part in this."

"I guess you did," Maureen said. She tightened her hand around the revolver and the pain of the arthritis shot up her arm and into her shoulder.

"Well" Mandowski said. He pushed back his chair and drained the tea. "I'd best be going or I'll be late for lunch."

Maureen pulled the revolver out from under her blanket and aimed it at the centre of Mandowski's throat. He was halfway out of the chair, his hands on the arms, and as he saw the gun his eyes narrowed and his broad nostrils flared. A new wave of fatigue battered over her and Maureen squeezed the grip to wake herself up.

"No," Mandowski said. More like a grunt than a word. "No." He suddenly dropped to his knees, his hands clasped together in prayer.

Maureen backed away, suddenly irresolute.

"For Christ's sake, Maureen."

"I'm sorry, George."

"Maureen." He was crying. She could change her mind, she knew. She could tell him about Finch and make him carry Finch outside, hide him.

"Maureen."

Make him bury Finch so that he would be gone.

"Please."

His face was working and then all at once his body shook and Maureen was aware of his smell filling the room.

He lunged towards her but the shot caught him in the chest and he fell, screaming, at her feet. There was no spray of skin and bone, no fine rain of blood. Just Mandowski, twisted onto his back, a red slick growing on his chest. He opened his mouth, trying to breathe, and the blood fountained out. Maureen, gagging from the smell, took the blanket from her lap and dropped it over his face.

Then she picked up the telephone and dialled the store again.

"I'd like to speak to Nellie Tillson."

"Yes, speaking."

"This is Mrs. Finch, Nellie. Mandowski has had an accident. You'd better send for the police."

She wheeled herself to the front hall and picked up her crutches. Then, somehow, she got herself out the door and down the one step, built specially wide for her, onto the lawn.

In the old days, she had walked easily on crutches from the house to the barn, but it was years since she had made that trip; all she had done was her secret practising in the house.

By the time she had crossed the front lawn to the barnyard gate, her arms ached and her church suit was soaked in sweat. She had the pistol in her jacket pocket. With each swing forward it bumped against her thigh, threatening to knock her off balance. Her plan, her promise to herself, had been that somehow she would make it out to the stable, drag herself onto Sean's back and take a final ride — the way she had always dreamed. But even to work the gate open seemed to take whole minutes and soon she had changed her plan: as she dragged herself across the clumps of grass and manure surrounding the barn, she settled on the goal of simply seeing Sean, of putting her hand on his massive neck and feeling the familiar warmth of his body against hers.

And then, when she was at the corner of the barn, pouring sweat now and leaning against the post for support, the police car came up the drive, red light flashing and siren wailing. She hesitated for a moment, hoping they would go straight into the house. But they spotted her right away and came running towards her.

She took the pistol from her pocket, pressed it to her temple and squeezed the trigger one last time.

Sixteen

*T*he October sun burned through the clear sky, heating up the sidewalks and the storefronts and bringing the trees of Salem to a state of perfection. Each branch, each twig, each waxy leaf was magnified by the light: and every tiny detail was etched so finely into the crisp air that even the oldest residents of the town found themselves stopping in the course of whatever small journey they were taking and staring upwards at the trees that their ancestors had planted while the streets were still paved with mud and the store windows were filled with merchandise that sold for pennies, not dollars.

At noon exactly, on the exact midday of the month, Annabelle Jamieson stepped out the door of her house, closed it carefully, listening for the latch as she always did, and began the short walk to her husband's office. At the end of her sidewalk she paused to wave at Donna Wilson, who was raking leaves off her lawn across the street, and said to herself for the tenth or perhaps twentieth time that she must have a talk with Donna soon, one of the intimate talks that they used to have.

On the surface she felt as nervous as ever, her old quick and edgy self, ready to jump spastically or drop a cup of coffee at the slightest disturbance, but beneath that was running a calmer and more settled current, a relieved and fatalistic feeling that her life had finally passed out of her own hands.

"Good afternoon, Mrs. Jamieson."

"Good afternoon, Mr. Beam." She stopped as Jacob Beam

removed his hat and looked at her across the small space that separated the door to his print shop from the nearby door to Allen's office.

"It's a fine day, Mrs. Jamieson."

"Indeed, Mr. Beam."

He smiled at her; and there was something so sweet in his smile, so compassionate, that she felt for a moment as if he already forgave her secret. About the night they had met in front of the church, they had never spoken; nor had their conversation again expanded beyond these brief praises of the weather.

"Have a good day, Mrs. Jamieson."

"Mr. Beam."

Allen was waiting in his office. His papers, as always, were stacked neatly on his desk; and as she came in he got up quickly, putting on his jacket in the same motion.

"Where shall we go?"

"How about the hotel?"

"Did you make a reservation?"

"Sure," Allen said. "They put a brick on our table."

Soon they were outside again, in the magic weave of sun and golden trees. It had been an October day like this, a year ago, when they had first discovered Salem, and Annabelle, remembering, found herself taking Allen's arm and holding his sleeve the way she used to when she wanted to feel close to him, to feel safe.

They sauntered slowly from Allen's office towards the hotel, walking north, following the crowd as Finch used to say, making the long, common stagger towards the devil.

Now that the tourist season had passed the restaurant was hardly used, and the expanse of clean white linen gave the dining room an unexpectedly elegant air. But as they sat down Annabelle heard sounds of coughing from the kitchen, and as had become her habit she ordered a gin and tonic in the hope that the alcohol would kill anything fatal.

They were sitting beside a window and the heat pressed like a blush against her face. She looked up at Allen, who was about to speak, then plunged ahead, afraid if she stopped now it would never get said.

"I went to the doctor yesterday."

"And?"

"And I'm pregnant," Annabelle hurried on. "He said it could be two months."

His face stayed impassive for so long that Annabelle's arm jumped and a trickle of gin ran down her glass to her wrist. By the time she looked up Allen was smiling, his hands reaching out for hers.

"Allen," she whispered, "you know I don't know—"

"*I* know," Allen cut her off, but the unsaid word, *Finch,* still hung between them. "I don't care," he added.

She dosed her eyes, relieved, squeezing his hands. *Finch. I don't care.* Where was Allen behind the stony face, the perfect lines? Who lived there? Not a stranger, Annabelle thought, and not a friend. But he would have to stand by her during the birth, be a father to the child. For that she could trust him. And she could even hope that the child was a girl and not a boy.

Suddenly Allen withdrew his hands from hers and walked away from the table.

When he came back it was with a bottle of champagne and two clean glasses. The cork popped and it sounded so much like a gun that Annabelle had to bite her tongue to keep from saying it.

After lunch she drove the white MG to the cliffs that overlooked the lake. Here the wind was quicker, and colder too, blowing down the narrow lake from the north, and even standing in the sun, leaning against her car, Annabelle had to wrap her arms around herself to keep warm.

Finch.

The doctor had told her the news and she had looked down at the floor. If she hadn't had the miscarriage before, perhaps she would have asked for an abortion.

"Are you pleased?" the doctor asked.

"I don't know."

They were silent a long time. The doctor was an old man who had worked in Salem almost half a century.

"Well," the doctor finally said, "you can't give blood tests to a dead man."

Annabelle had jerked to her feet.

"You have to live with the truth," the doctor said, "even if you don't like it. For the baby's sake." He had a voice like Jacob Beam's but his shaved face was much older, the once-clean line of jawbone collapsed into a series of jowls and wrinkled skin.

"In a month or two," the doctor added, "we'll be able to hear the heart."

Hearts are good for pumping blood, Annabelle thought. She remembered once, at an all-night pyjama party in high school, that she had told a girl friend she wanted to know the human heart.

"Know what?" the girl friend had asked.

"Know its ways," Annabelle had replied, sublimely confident, "know its different countries."

Now, standing on the cliff looking out over the water, it didn't seem that she had learned very much. Not enough to keep her out of trouble. Not enough to draw a map of a continent, a country, or even a town.

Finch danced here, Annabelle thought. He danced on this cliff and the thunder rumbled down at him, and he was alive and dancing like a devil in the rain. For a long time she stayed like that, standing beside her car with her arms wrapped around herself, trying to define to herself what Finch had been. She closed her eyes and could see again his wonderful strut through the storm, feel his weight as he pushed himself into her; and she heard the voice he had spoken in — not the quick, greedy voice he had used when he first met her, or the desperate, maniacally persuasive voice he used that last time in church, but the quiet, true voice he had spoken with during their final meeting here: the sound of his shoes in the wet morning grass as he walked up behind her; the sound of his breathing as he shuddered and was released inside her; the sound of his silence as she had turned and walked away.

Finch.

The police had found Maureen first. They had seen her limping towards the barn, twisting on her crutches, and had run towards her. When they saw her raise the gun they thought she was going to shoot at them, and they had dropped into the long grass. Then there was the one shot, followed by silence. They had lifted themselves off their stomachs, old Sammy Warren cursing the grass stains on his uniform and his nephew, young Gerry, so nervous that he couldn't talk about it later without stuttering. Sammy had gone first, thinking she had hidden.

"Maureen. It's Sam Warren. Where are you?"

He was the one to find her. She was lying with her arms flung out and the gun beside her hand, as if the shock of the bullet had knocked her right over. "I've never seen a woman shoot herself," old Sammy Warren had said at the inquest. "A beautiful woman like Maureen Finch, too." He had shaken his head, stayed silent for a long time. Everyone knew what the message was: if she had just given herself up, if she had just left it to old Sammy Warren, there would have been no charges. "She had a hard life," old Sammy Warren had added, just so everyone got the point.

Then they had gone into the house. In the kitchen the smell was so thick that it overwhelmed them as soon as they opened the door. At least it overwhelmed Gerry, because even before seeing the mounded blue blanket in the centre of the floor, the blanket Maureen Finch wore to church every Sunday, he backed up and retreated to the front lawn, on his knees, retching.

So again it was Sammy Warren who went first, lifting the blanket to reveal Mandowski, his throat a maze of tendons and torn flesh, his mouth a tiny pond of blood. "He bled a lot," Sammy Warren said. "The blanket was heavy to lift."

They had telephoned for help and then sat and waited in the kitchen. It was only Gerry's curiosity that made him go upstairs. First he went into the bedroom, where he saw the letter to Lorna McConnell placed on the pillow of the bed. The letter had asked her to take care of the girls and to let them marry young if they wanted. But he hadn't opened the letter then. Instead he had gone into the room with the closed door. There he found Finch. A fist-sized hole was punched into his back and the side of his face was blown away.

"The boy called and I went upstairs," old Sammy said. "He was lying on his face, like he'd been crawling towards her. All over him and on the floor was paper towels. You'd have thought she was trying to clean him up." Then he had gazed out at the spectators. A triple murder-suicide. Salem had never known anything like it.

"He was a hard man," Sammy Warren said. "Though some might think he only got what was coming."

Finch.

The last detail was left for Gerry to discover. After the body had been cleaned up and removed, and the children met and taken to Mrs. McConnell's, Gerry had been checking through the house one last time. And in the upstairs bathroom, where they had found Finch's body, lying in the corner like a forgotten marble was Finch's eye. Bloodless, clean, a perfect eye with just a few shreds of grey muscle hanging from it.

Annabelle looked over the lake. It was long and narrow, like a crooked pointing finger, and she wondered what it would be like to be on the water, in a canoe, heading north into the sharp colours of the leaves and the white ice where the cold wind started.

Finch.

The lake hissed and shimmered with light. In the story the lover had leapt and proved his love. Now the girl was looking regretfully at the mouth that had swallowed him up.

The air was exploding around her and the trees and sky were bending with the pure force of it: for one moment Finch was inside her, making her see the world through his eyes, see the air as he had seen it when the first bullet jammed into his spine.

Finch.

He had been God's gift to the ladies of the parish, but they had survived it; now he was buried in the Protestant cemetery outside of town. Maureen had been buried beside him, both their coffins closed for the funeral; no undertaker in this small town could put together what Mandowski's gun had undone.

Annabelle tried to imagine once more what Finch had looked like, exactly how his skin had felt to her lips. But the memory had been mercifully obliterated. Now his persuasive voice, his hammering fist, his looming and muscular body belonged only to the past.

Finch.

She had loved him, or perhaps she had not. She had followed one more road on the map of her own heart, burned away one more year of her life.

She took a deep breath, pushing her stomach out the way Finch had taught her. The child would be a girl, she was sure of that. If she was dark they would say she looked like Annabelle. And if she was fair they would say she looked like Allen. *Finch.* Her blood would be coded with the sight of the church spire and the smell of wet ground.

Annabelle's mother came to stay again, near the end of the month, happy with the news and eager to help prepare the guest room for the baby.

"After all," she declared to Annabelle "it isn't every day that I get to be a grandmother. You know, there's a special understanding between children and their grandparents, a bond that skips a generation."

"They say," Annabelle said.

"In Europe, a grandparent is often closer to the child than her real parents."

Annabelle nodded. Like herself, her daughter would be an only child, a daughter born to parents who were afraid of her.

During her mother's visit there was an afternoon late in the month, when the sky had already darkened, and Mrs. MacLeod was sitting in the living room with the lamp on, reading in the circle of its light. Annabelle, looking at her as she passed, saw a meek and grey-haired woman, moving her lips and whispering as she read, holding the book a bit away from her because she was too vain to wear glasses. Protected by the shadows of the hallway Annabelle stood and watched her mother whisper her way down the page. As a child she had sometimes gotten out of bed to find her parents in the living room, reading, her mother whispering in exactly the same way. She had felt then that she was spying on her mother, spying with the same dedication that she hid anything her mother might want to know.

Annabelle continued on to her studio, the image of her mother still before her eyes: once more she had hidden without being caught, her afternoons with Finch a secret woven in so deep now that it could never be unravelled.

These days she was producing dishes again, working late into the evening on a new outburst of dinnerware to stock the stores for the Christmas season. In the corner were a few figures that had survived the night Allen had finally lost his temper. They were clustered together on a shelf, so gaunt and delicate they might have been made of iron, not clay. Occasionally, when her mind wandered from the task of making dishes, her fingers found themselves taking small bits of the moist clay to roll into limbs, and before she knew it one of the townspeople would be taking shape in her hands, tugging at that sleepy place in her mind that had burned so intensely during the summer.

She was sitting on her stool in front of her work table, preparing the glaze that she needed, when her mother came in and told her that Allen was home and dinner was ready.

Annabelle turned. With the same concentrated whispering look she'd had when she was reading, her mother was now staring at her.

That night Annabelle woke up. The moon was almost full and it made the church spire an eerie and dazzling white.

It was almost a year now since they had moved to Salem: only a year, but a whole second life had been lived.

She stood at the window, listening to Allen's smooth breathing and looking out at the spire. The cold wind outside suddenly made her shiver, and she could feel her skin bunch up beneath her nightgown, her nipples spring erect.

Finch.

She turned around.

Allen was sitting up in bed.

"What's wrong?"

"I couldn't sleep," Annabelle said. "Did I wake you up?"

She went to sit beside him on the bed. Her skin was on fire and Allen's hands only made it burn hotter, made her whole body want to break apart in the night. *Finch.* His presence was like a clock ticking in the background, and then Allen was above her, his shadow swinging back and forth across the window, swinging with the grim executioner's rhythm, going back and forth across the window until his face melted into a row of grinning masks: for a moment they danced like the toy angels in her own elaborate but useless mosaic, like the flowers she had saved from the lightning storm, like the ghostly white face of Maureen Finch — and then for the last time they dissolved as her body got its moment of reprieve, its own release, which was absolutely private and removed, carrying her into darkness.